The Secret Burial

by Adrian Frost

First published by Scott and Pine Publishing in 2023.
ISBN 978-1-7395385-1-4

Find out more at www.authorfrost.com

For Carol

Part One

1

21 March 2020

He'd been hearing distant noises all night: a fox yelping in the wood, an owl, a train that must have been a mile away. Quiet sounds that made him worry that the noise of his digging, or his breathing even, would carry beyond the confines of the walled cottage garden and perhaps, as far as the neighbour's house across the road, the only other house within a half-mile radius. So when the torch failed, and he swore, he made sure it was under his breath. These chunky torches were indispensable in any rural home where power cuts are all too frequent, but this one was an old, filament bulb type, and after just two hours of digging, the battery gave up the ghost. He struggled on with a few inferior pocket torches that had been provided as back-up, before he remembered his phone had a powerful light, and by balancing it on the bird table, he found he could see well enough to get the job done. That lasted another three hours before it too extinguished without warning. The old lady must have been watching him from the house, because within minutes she brought out a tray with four tea-light lanterns. They offered only a feeble light, but still fearful of making too much noise, he accepted them, rather than protesting. He positioned them at the four corners of the asparagus bed, where at least they gave him a sense of the boundaries of his work.

'Where do you want me to put the spare soil?' he whispered.

'There's an empty bay in the compost heap,' the old lady replied at her normal volume. 'Put it there and I'll cover it with matting later. It will come in useful for pots. I don't suppose you'd be able to riddle it for stones, would you?'

'There's not really time,' he said, not sure if she was serious. He knew he only had an hour or so before dawn, and he had to finish refilling the hole and replacing the asparagus crowns.

The old lady went back inside, and he continued with his work.

The night's digging had kept him warm, but now, as a faint glow appeared in the eastern sky, and he finished raking over the raised bed and sweeping the surrounding path, the sweat he had worked up cooled on his skin and he shivered. The four lanterns flickered as a light breeze finally broke the stillness that had threatened to betray him all night.

'This is insane,' he thought, for the hundredth time. 'Why am I doing this?' And once again, the only answer he could come up with was 'For her'. Anything to protect *her*.

He bent down to extinguish the lights and then stood up straight and stretched his arms. He noticed the knotted feeling in his stomach was still with him. It had arisen when he first realised what he was doing would lead to a lengthy prison sentence if anyone ever found out about it. But digging a six-foot trench had been quite a workout and the exercise temporarily relieved his stress. For a while, he felt perversely proud of himself. There was no way that he'd have been able to manage it a few months ago. Working out with a personal trainer via a video link had definitely been worth it then, although he'd never imagined that his toned muscles would have been put to such a macabre task. He took a last look at the raised bed before going back into the house. The soil was heaped up much higher than when he'd started digging. The asparagus 'crowns' — just clumps of matted roots as far as he was concerned — probably needed to be watered in if they were going to survive the upheaval. If she ran a sprinkler over them later this morning, it would also hide that freshly dug look. But the thought of the water seeping down through the earth and eventually reaching the corpse below made him shiver again.

'I'd imagine it would be safe, wouldn't you?' said Mrs McCracken as he came inside.

'Safe?' he asked, puzzled. Did she mean it would be safe for him to leave the house? He'd rather like to get warm again first. Or perhaps she was worried that the man he had just buried could still be a threat? He was well past that.

'Safe to eat,' said Mrs McCracken. '... the asparagus, I mean ... later in the year. But look at you! You're shivering. Your clothes are all damp. Get upstairs and have a hot shower. I'll warm your clothes through in front of the fire.'

Jason did as he was told.

Across the road, Julia was getting frantic. She'd noticed that her neighbour, Gillian McCracken, had had her lights on several times throughout the night. That wasn't like her at all. She was worried. Gillian must be poorly, and all on her own, poor thing. What if it was this virus that was in the news? It wouldn't surprise her, the amount of to-ing and fro-ing that had been going on at that house lately. Coronavirus was particularly bad for the elderly, she'd heard. She should check on her neighbour. But if it was that virus, she didn't want to risk catching it. It might not be that though, it could just as easily be indigestion. Or perhaps she'd had some bad news. What could it be? At 6 a.m., she couldn't bear it any longer. On the news, she'd seen doctors and nurses wearing masks and visors, which were in very short supply. But Julia knew how to improvise.

With a headscarf tied round her nose and mouth and wearing a pair of dark sunglasses even though the sun hadn't properly risen yet, Julia crossed the road and knocked on her neighbour's door. She looked like a terrorist. She heard footsteps, and the door opened.

'Julia!' exclaimed Mrs McCracken, recognising her neighbour instantly. 'Whatever is the matter? Come inside, quickly, you'll let the cold air in.'

Julia complied, and her sunglasses misted up instantly.

'You've not got the virus, have you?' she asked.

'No,' answered Mrs McCracken with a chuckle. 'Have you?'

Julia took off her sunglasses just as footsteps could be heard coming down the stairs. The door opened and a tall, young, red-haired man, wearing just a towel around his waist and with shoulders still pink from a hot shower, entered the room.

'Julia,' said Mrs McCracken, 'This is Jason. We're lovers.'

2

6 Months Earlier — September 2019.

It was a Friday night, and The Pig was in full swing, which for a pub in Hambourne, South Staffordshire, meant a dozen local 'regulars' and two couples who'd driven out from

Wolverhampton for a chicken pie and a change of scenery. Four of the regulars sat in their usual corner, talking their usual rubbish.

'Fish and chips, every time,' said Jason. 'From the Hambourne chippy, but served on a warmed plate. Don't give me that "they taste better from the paper" nonsense. They don't, and the chips go soggy. Salt and vinegar, no ketchup.'

'Yeah, but if you were on death row,' said Stuart, thoughtfully, 'you wouldn't be able to order them from a chip shop, they'd have to be prepared in the prison canteen.'

'No way!' Jason protested. 'It's my last meal. I'll have them brought in from wherever I want.'

'Yes,' said Sultan, 'Because as a convicted murderer, you'd be calling all the shots, wouldn't you, Jason? Come off it, mate. Or perhaps you're thinking that your millions will still make all things possible, is that it?'

Jason Tranter was used to being teased by his friends for his wealth, especially by Sultan. It was a small price to pay. He'd won a fortune on the lottery five months ago, and like many winners before him, pledged that money wouldn't change him and that he'd still want to hang out with his mates in the local pub. And here he was. He could put up with little jibes about his money. They'd get bored with it eventually, wouldn't they?

'Your turn, Sarah,' said Jason, eager to move the conversation on. 'What would your death row dinner be?'

'Hmm, well,' pondered Sarah. 'Do you remember our first night on board the *Rara Avis*? Our very first meal there, the grilled fish? Honestly? I've never tasted anything like it. So going by Jason's rules, where money and physical distance are no object, I'd have that grilled fish.'

Although Jason didn't like to be flashy about his fortune, that hadn't stopped him from joining Rara Avis, a secret society of millionaires, with its own super-yacht, also called *Rara Avis*, and a private island in the Mediterranean. He'd gone there with Sarah during the summer. In fact, Sultan and Stuart had been there, as well — they'd somehow got temporary jobs as crew members.

'You're joking, right?' said Sultan. 'Fish? From that place? Would you want salt and vinegar with that, madam? A little Novichok, perhaps?'

They all laughed, perhaps a little inappropriately considering that the incident that Sultan was referring to had been the attempted murder of a member of Rara Avis, when someone had laced his breakfast with a nerve agent. It had been an eventful summer.

'Mind you,' said Sarah, as the laughter subsided. 'It's well known that how good a meal tastes depends on where and how you're eating it. I mean, that night I was an escort to a millionaire on board a superyacht in the Mediterranean in the company of rock stars. Of course it tasted bloody great! The effect might not be the same for a social worker banged up in jail.'

Jason winced, though no-one saw him. He was uncomfortable when Sarah lied.

'Mine would be sausage, beans and chips,' said Stuart, 'And it would be fine if they came from the prison canteen, better in fact.'

'Explain,' demanded Sultan.

'Reckon I'd be looking for comfort food if I was about to face the chair,' replied Stuart. 'There's something really comforting about canteen sausages, you know, the ones with hardly any meat in, and canteen chips and beans. When I was little, I sometimes visited my dad at his office during his lunch hour. He'd take us to the canteen, and I'd have sausage, beans, and chips. It felt really special.'

'Ah! Food from our childhood is always very special,' said Sarah. 'What about you, Sultan? What sort of food memories do you have from when you were growing up?'

Jason bristled. He was conscious of the tips of his ears burning red.

'My round, I think,' he said. 'Same again, everyone? Give us a hand, will you, Sarah?'

The two of them stood by the bar waiting for Jeff, the barman, to finish his conversation with another customer.

'Sarah, can you at least try to be subtle in your questioning?' Jason spoke quietly, but there was a hint of anger in his words.

'Say what?' said Sarah.

'Asking Sultan about his childhood food memories? Are you ever off duty, DS Towers?'

'Shh!' hissed Sarah.

Sarah's big secret was that she was not Sarah Headly, social worker and occasional barfly. She was Detective Sergeant Robin Towers, working on an undercover surveillance operation, investigating a suspected terrorist cell. Early in 2018, the West Midlands Counter Terrorism Unit had received a report that a group of bearded young men — possibly foreign nationals — were meeting at The Pig regularly and talking about remote controlled drones and stuff. It was a ludicrous, paranoid suggestion, as Robin, or Sarah, had quickly found out when she started frequenting the pub. But instead of reporting that there was no threat to investigate, she had let things ride, and filed ambiguous reports to her seniors, suggesting there may be some substance to the rumours, and that she needed more time. If she'd been found out, it would have led to her dismissal, of course, but that was fine by her. Her previous deployment had been very stressful, and she was using this opportunity to recover and maybe rethink her career plans.

Then one of the 'suspects', Jason, had suddenly won a heap of money and invited her to join him on a jaunt to the South of France, an offer she found hard to resist. It hadn't quite turned out to be the relaxing holiday she'd hoped for, but it was pretty useful being a trained policewoman when there was a murder to investigate. She pulled in the resources needed to solve the case and yet remained undercover.

'It was just chat, Jason,' she said as they waited to be served. 'Unclench.'

'Easier said than done,' he said. 'You know how tense all this secrecy makes me. And there's no need for it.'

Jason might not have found out about Sarah's alter ego if they hadn't developed a bit of 'a thing' whilst on their short luxury cruise of the Med. But Sarah knew she'd face instant dismissal for having a relationship with a suspect whilst undercover and had called a halt to the romance. The incidents with Rara Avis had put her police career back on track. She'd helped to clear up an important murder case, and she felt motivated again. She'd been on the point of admitting that there wasn't any terrorist cell operating from The Pig so she could get reassigned to a fresh case when suddenly, weirdly, her superior officer had asked her to stick with her undercover work. Some new information had emerged. All she'd been able to tell Jason was that 'it's not what you think' and she'd sworn him to secrecy.

'No need for it?'

'You could give up the job and we could pick things up where we left off.'

'Aww, that's not fair, rich boy. I'm a career girl these days, not a playboy's floozy.'

She smiled and her eyes flashed. It was all that was needed to melt Jason's tension.

He sighed.

'So, anyway, what are you having, then?'

'Surprise me.'

'Well, okay, confession time. I've joined a single malts mail order society that sends out tester bottles. There's this one brand... Auchentosh... I can't pronounce it properly... it's superb. It's expensive, but I ordered a case as an investment. Well, it will be an investment if I don't drink it all. Anyway, Jeff's agreed to hold a bottle here, for my... our... exclusive use. So do you want to try a dram?'

'Ooh! "Dram". Get you, Jason McTranter,' laughed Sarah. 'Go on then. Can you ask Jeff to put a ginger beer in mine?'

'Sure, and a cocktail cherry if you like,' said Jason, now smiling broadly.

A few minutes later, Jason and Sarah returned from the bar with a tray, holding four whiskies and a small jug of water. No ginger beer and no cherries. One glass had a tulip shape, wider at the base of the glass than at the rim. The other three were standard tumblers.

'Okay,' admitted Jason. 'It's my own special glass that Jeff keeps for me. It came with the bottle, and it's specially designed for this whisky. The shape lets the ethanol vapours disperse whilst keeping the other aromas swirling in the bowl.'

The smirks from his three friends were enough; they didn't have to say anything.

'And tonight, of course, I'm more than happy to take a regular tumbler,' continued Jason. 'Sarah can have the Glencairn glass.'

'Anyway, Sarah Headly,' said Sultan. 'You're busted! We know your secret identity.' Straightaway, Jason tensed up again. He gulped down his whisky without tasting it.

Sarah took it all in her stride. 'Go on, then?' she said.

'Saw you on *Question Time*, last week,' explained Sultan, 'comparing immigrants to locusts or something. I must admit, I felt a little hurt. And now you've had your Twitter account suspended, I gather.'

'Oh, not you as well!' said Sarah. 'You're not the first, Sultan. Yes, I look a bit like her. I've been getting some strange looks from people all week. I'm trying to work out a way of suing her for defamation of character or issuing a cease-and-desist order on her use of my face!'

Jason exhaled again. False alarm: they were referring to Rebecca Leyden-Fuller, an alt-right journalist who'd upset many people on a political TV panel show this week and subsequently got herself barred from social media platforms. She did look remarkably like Sarah. He felt his eyes stinging. He couldn't keep this up. Something had to change.

3

The girl in reception at the clubhouse was new, and unfamiliar with the clientele of the Castle Park Golf Club. When she asked for a name of the party that arrived for the two o'clock slot, she didn't get a straight answer. The man who seemed to be the host of the trio gave her some banter that she didn't understand and wasn't interested in, anyway. She wrote three names in the register: Red Slacks, Tartan and Joggers, referring to the trousers that the three men were wearing. That would do until the duty manager got back and she could ask him if he knew their proper names. He was out with some site security company, playing with surveillance drones or something.

Red Slacks was the leader of the golfers, a large man with short, dark, curly hair and a round, knobbly face that seemed to alternate between two expressions, one of which was a puzzled sort of wince that left permanent wrinkle lines around his eyes and the other was an easy and genial smile that reinforced those same wrinkles. He winced as he led the party out, sniffing the air, checking the temperature, looking around at who else was on the course. Then he turned to his companions and smiled.

'I'll kick off, shall I?'

It was the same in every situation; he started with the puzzled wince, as if he were thinking 'What's this? What's happening here? Am I in control of this?'. And then, as soon as he realised that yes, he was indeed in control, the wince gave way to the smile.

They played the first two holes without conversation. On the third, Red Slacks took a powerful swing and drove his ball down the fairway, about a hundred metres from the green. He turned to Tartan, smiling.

'So, how's business then, Henry?' he said, addressing Tartan while he was teeing up.

'Och, business is fine, thank you,' said Tartan. 'Not many new clients these days...'

Tartan, or Henry, as he was more commonly known, was the eldest and the shortest of the three. He was a quiet, tidy man with a ruddy face and slightly bulging eyes. He practised his swing a few times in a half-hearted sort of way, distracted by Red Slacks' question.

'... but that means I can look after old, loyal customers like yourselves all the better,' he added, and took his shot. 'At my time of life, it suits me not to be chasing new business. It disnae seem worth it, getting to know new clients, y'know.'

Red Slacks winced.

'No,' he said. 'I meant "how's our business". I'm not really bothered about anyone else's business.'

'The money from Venice — how is that working out?' chipped in Joggers.

Joggers was the youngster of the group, a man in his early thirties. Jogging bottoms were not strictly allowed on the Castle Park green, but he had no appreciation of the etiquette of golf and being tall, broad and sullen-looking, he found that here, as in other walks of life, people rarely challenged him.

'Yes,' replied Henry. 'Well, it's coming in from the usual channels. I understand most of the merchandise has found new homes now. Of course, processing the receipts takes some time. It really needs to trickle in, you know. But your portfolio continues to grow satisfactorily.'

'I hope it does, Henry. I hope it does,' said Red Slacks. 'Tell me what commission you are working on again?'

'Half a percent.'

Joggers took his tee shot, driving the ball much further than his companions, further actually than the edge of the fairway. He swore and returned his club to the bag.

'Half a percent,' pondered Red Slacks as they walked on. 'Is that enough, Henry? Are you sure you don't need more? Your clubs are a bit old, aren't they? Can't you afford a better set than that? Your car ain't much, either. Same one as last year, isn't it? Same one for the last five years, if I'm not mistaken.'

'It is the same one, aye,' admitted Henry. 'It's running well. I don't change it if I don't need to. Look, I'm an accountant. I look after money. It's kind of what I do.'

'But perhaps you aren't getting enough of a cut, Henry,' said Red Slacks. 'I'm just thinking that maybe if you had a higher stake in the game, you might feel more inclined to get a better return for us. It might be more of an incentive. Surely you want to treat the old lady to a nice holiday somewhere, don't you?'

Henry stopped in his tracks and looked as if he was making his mind up about how to reply.

'My wife passed away three years ago. I believe I did tell you,' he said.

Red Slacks stopped and turned to Henry, but didn't speak. Instead, he gave his trademark wince, staring into Henry's eyes.

'No,' said Henry, feeling uncomfortable, and looking down at his shoes. 'I'm charging you the going rate and I'm confident that we are making the most of your assets under the circumstances.'

'That's good, Henry,' said Red Slacks as they resumed walking.

They were close to the perimeter hedge of the golf course, and suddenly they were aware of something like a large toy helicopter, with red flashing lights, flying along the line of the hedge about one meter above it.

'Wassat?' asked Red Slacks, his face screwed up tight.

'Drone,' said Joggers.

'I don't like it. I don't like it at all. Find out what's going on,' said Red Slacks, tracking the device as it flew out of view.

Joggers exhaled loudly, rammed his club back into the trolley, and started to wheel it back to the clubhouse.

'Not now, you fool,' said Red Slacks. 'We're playing a game. Find out later. Now where were we? Ah yes, Henry was telling us how well our assets are doing. Which is good, because I think it's time we realised some of those assets. I'm looking to get myself a place in Spain. A sort of retirement home, I suppose you might say. So I'll be needing you to start hatching that little nest egg you've been sitting on for me all these years.'

Henry seemed to make heavy weather of dragging his old golf trolley up the slight incline that led to the spot where his ball lay. His face looked a deeper shade of red as he squared himself up to take his shot. His practice swing looked tight and awkward.

'Hah!' he shouted, as he made his shot, but the follow-through turned into a sort of pirouette and Henry collapsed face-down on the grass.

Red Slacks approached, knelt and turned the man over, wincing as he stared into a face which, apart from a bluish tinge to the lips, was rapidly getting paler.

'Run!' he shouted to Joggers, who loped off back to the clubhouse.

But Henry had died before his golfing opponent could get help.

4

It was early on a Sunday morning, too early to be calling his friend really, so Stuart spoke softly into his phone.

'Hey Jason, your old boss at PKR, Malcolm Dunnet — what's he like?'

'Huh?' answered Jason. 'Umm, a bit saft. Pretty easy, really. Talks in short, clipped phrases. Why?'

'Sultan and I are parked just outside PKR waiting to see him,' said Stuart.

'Wait, what?' said Jason. Without the benefit of his first skinny macchiato of the day, Jason's brain was struggling with the idea of his friend calling at this hour, on a Sunday, from the place they both used to work. 'What are you doing there? And why is Dunnett there? He was made redundant six months ago, same time as me. He was going to leave just after me - he's not still working out his notice, surely?'

'No idea,' said Stuart, 'Anyway, PKR has had a spate of burglaries, and they've called in Tranter Diall Electronic Surveillance Services to solve all their problems.'

'Sweet,' said Jason. 'What's Sultan there for?'

'Dunno,' said Stuart. 'Just thought he'd like to see the place... hang on, Dunnett's here. Cheers, mate. Bye.'

Malcolm Dunnett came through a security gate into the car park and then locked it immediately behind him. He tilted his head back and eyed Stuart and Sultan with suspicion as he walked over to Stuart's van, parked close by. The only other car on site was Dunnett's own, parked right at the far end of the car park.

'Found us alright, then?' said Dunnett.

'Yes, I used to work here, in the test department,' said Stuart. 'And my business partner, Jason Tranter, worked with you. Didn't I mention it on our phone call?'

'Jason? Oh yes. Okay, is he? Business partners — golly!'

Dunnett seemed to process this information, muttering to himself as he led them back through the security gate and made them sign a visitors' book.

'Familiar with the site, then?' said Dunnett as they walked along the inside of the four-metre high, barbed-wire-topped perimeter fence. 'Take you round anyway. Show you the problem. Got nearly a square mile of territory here. Once a RAF repair base. You probably know. Second World War. Still got a runway, buried beneath the undergrowth somewhere.'

The main building of the PKR Aerospace Engineering factory was a grand affair, built in the Fifties and architecturally listed. The factory originally produced agricultural machinery but had later diversified into parts for the aviation industry. A well-maintained lawn spread out in front, where employees would take their packed lunches in summer months. On either side of the lawn, new warehouses and offices had been erected in styles more in keeping with the high-tech nature of PKR's business. Behind all these buildings, however, where the three were now walking, the rest of the site was mostly left to wilderness, with the occasional vestiges of old brick sheds and garages, dating from the war.

'Lot of land,' said Sultan, mimicking Dunnett's phrasing. 'Wide perimeter. Difficult to monitor ingress.'

'Spot on!' said Malcolm Dunnett, clearly impressed that someone was on the right wavelength. 'Got cameras, obviously, but not enough. And if I do spot anything... if Security does spot anything... some intruder, say, it can take ten minutes, quarter of an hour before I... Security can get on the scene. By which time, intruder has disappeared into the undergrowth. Like the Viet Cong.'

'Got it,' said Sultan, and smirked at Stuart.

'Why does PKR keep all this land?' asked Stuart. 'It must be a security liability and presumably it could be developed — a housing estate, perhaps? Or other industrial units?'

'Still needed,' said Dunnett and tapped the side of his nose with his finger. He leaned in towards Sultan, who seemed to be the one with his head screwed on, and said, 'Great space for testing. You know the sort of thing.'

They looked at one of the camera turrets and then visited one of the camera blind spots where, two nights previously, 'person or persons unknown' had used ladders and an old mattress draped over the barbed wire to get into the grounds.

'Took some sheet metal, a few reels of cable. That's all,' said Dunnett.

'Okay,' said Stuart. 'Time for a demonstration, I think. Can we just pick up some equipment from the van?'

Twenty minutes later, Stuart was describing the benefits of the OmniChopper TD 9000 to Malcolm Dunnett. They stood looking up at it as Sultan, holding a remote control, guided it back and forth along the path of the perimeter fence.

'So, the beauty of this is that we can program it to make an automatic patrol of the entire perimeter as frequently as you like. You might want two drones in tandem to double the patrol frequency and offer resilience, should one drone fail... which it won't, of course. You can see the high-quality video feed on the screen of my colleague's remote control there. At night, that will switch to infrared cameras, of course. But you don't need to spend your time glued to the monitors. If the drone's artificial intelligence decides that someone's attempting to access the target site, it will trigger the alarm and lock on to the intruder while the security team mobilises. The TD9000 can also link into your existing camera system, so that if the fixed cameras spot suspicious activity, the drone can be directed immediately to the trouble spot. That may be enough to deter anyone from trying to enter.'

'Yes, yes,' said Dunnett, his eyes fixed on the hovering drone. 'Very good.'

'The shame of it is,' said Sultan, improvising, 'UK regulations currently prevent us from taking the protection a stage further. In some territories, we can fix the drone with a small paint gun that can shoot permanent dye. Makes it easy to get a conviction when perps are arrested.'

Dunnett's eyes widened.

'Excellent. Yes. Pity. Don't suppose...'

A loud bang coming from the direction of the main offices interrupted him. Malcolm looked at Stuart and Sultan, as if they might explain the noise, but their faces were equally blank.

'Better go back,' he said.

They started walking back towards the site entrance, Sultan guiding the drone just ahead of them. As they reached the car park, there was another, even louder, bang and the drone fell out of the sky, shattering to pieces on the pavement in front of them.

'Down!' shouted Dunnett, and was instantly lying flat on the tarmac, with his arms covering his head.

Stuart and Sultan followed suit, but more hesitantly.

'What's going on?' whispered Sultan after a few seconds. All was quiet.

'Someone's shot our drone!' said Stuart. 'I don't bloody believe it!'

They got up, dusted themselves down, picked up the pieces of drone and made their way back to the car park.

'So that explains the first shot then,' said Stuart as they reached the van. Where the logo of Tranter Diall Electronic Surveillance Services had been was a roundish, pock-marked indentation about the size of a fist.

'Close range shotgun damage,' said Dunnett.

5

Until he received the alert on his phone, Jason had no idea how his Thursday was going to turn out. His days were often like that and, on the whole, he was comfortable with that feeling of randomness and spontaneity. Surely, this was what freedom tasted like? How many days had he sat behind a desk at PKR Aerospace Engineering, wishing he could be somewhere else, doing something else? That wish had been granted courtesy of the EuroMillions Lottery Rollover and now he had free range to do whatever he liked.

What he liked seemed to change from day to day. The smallest thing could set him off on a quest that might occupy him for hours or days, before something else diverted him. Often this started with the morning TV he watched whilst taking his breakfast of sourdough toast with Dundee marmalade, and whichever single origin variety of coffee was his current choice. One day, he had watched a documentary about the film director, David Lean. He'd decided he wanted to watch all Lean's films and spent the first part of the morning sourcing high quality downloads or Blu-ray discs. Then he decided that his home cinema equipment needed an upgrade before he watched them. This had involved a trip to Birmingham in the afternoon, and he'd settled down to watch Lawrence of Arabia in the evening.

Not all his distractions were so self-centred. Another time, he'd watched a local news report about a couple raising money for a sensory room for their child, who had severe learning disabilities. A sense of shame came over him as he thought of all the expensive audio and video equipment in his living room just for his idle pleasure. He spent three days making contact with the couple, and also with a group of design students from Aston University, who were interested in using the latest research to build a state-of-the-art sensory room for their final year project. He provided the money and let them get on with it. About six weeks later, when the room was finished, the parents rang Jason to thank him again. They told him that the local news reporter wanted to do a follow-up story, but Jason insisted his name wasn't to be mentioned.

This wasn't really modesty. He wanted to remain anonymous for several reasons, the most immediate of which was that he didn't want to be deluged with begging letters.

He'd never gone public with his lottery win. Even his parents didn't know about it. As far as they were concerned, he'd left PKR and set up a company that did electronic security and surveillance work, which was the truth, but not the whole truth. His company was, in reality, a modest affair run by his friend Stuart, who had found that there was a market for CCTV and aerial surveillance drones. Jason's parents had assumed from Jason's new clothes and car that the company was doing well, but that was as far as their interest went. They didn't realise or didn't care that he was hardly involved in the day to day running of the company.

Sometimes, Jason wondered whether he ought to get more involved in the business he was partly responsible for. It might keep his mind occupied. At other times, like at the weekend when Stuart had reported that someone had shot at a drone and the company van, he was pleased to let it all be someone else's problem.

And Jason didn't mind that his parents weren't interested in his business activities. In fact, it suited him to have as few people as possible scrutinising his life choices at this time. He instinctively felt an urge to put some of his money towards good causes, but couldn't work out how much philanthropy was enough. Where should he draw the line? He wanted to be free to enjoy his good fortune and be secure for the rest of his life, but how much money should he hold back, and how much was spare to give away? He hoped that his Rara Avis membership would help him answer these questions. The organiser, a man called Richards, and his assistant, Mr Smethwick, had some experience of helping millionaires manage their fortunes wisely, and Jason hoped he would get to meet some other people in a similar situation to himself. He hadn't actually got round to asking for help, though. It was something he kept putting off to tomorrow. And by about Thursday or Friday, 'tomorrow' had a habit of becoming 'next week'.

This particular Thursday morning, a phone alert arrived during his personal fitness workout.

'Sorry, Tré,' Jason said to the video screen fixed to the front of his exercise bike. 'I'm going to have to cut it short this morning. Something important's just come up. Same time tomorrow?'

Seven hundred miles away, in a studio gym on a private island in the Mediterranean, Tré raised an eyebrow, but agreed. Jason unfastened the bindings on the bike's pedals and the strap that monitored his heart rate and closed the video session down. Having a personal trainer, albeit a remote one, was one benefit Jason was getting from his Rara Avis membership. Maybe the advice he was getting was the same as he would have got from the Hambourne Fitness Centre, but somehow the combination of fancy gadgetry, and the encouraging words from attractive instructors, Simone and Tré, overcame Jason's natural laziness, and he had to admit he was starting to feel the benefit of his regular workouts.

The alert on his phone read: '7.11.19 9:45 AM hambourne heath crisis.plots.chimp waxwing JonWayne72' It was cryptic, but it told Jason all he needed to know. There wasn't time for his morning shower. He set the controls of his coffee maker to make himself a flask of coffee, then pulled on some warm clothes over his t-shirt and shorts. He put on his coat, grabbed the coffee, a pack of chocolate digestive biscuits and an expensive pair of digitally assisted binoculars, and left his home for Hambourne Heath.

Fifteen minutes later, he was picking his way across the uneven terrain of a wooded area of the heath, guided by his phone. He almost tripped over a man in camouflaged jacket and trousers, sat against the base of a tree with his legs stretched out.

'Watch it, mate!' said the man in an angry whisper.

'Howdy, partner?' said Jason, holding his phone to show the man the alert on his phone.

'Oh, right, yeah,' said the man. 'Hilarious. I haven't heard that one before. Well, I'm about done here, actually. I haven't seen him for the last twenty minutes. I'm heading off. Stick around if you want. You may get lucky.'

JonWayne72 got up from the ground, brushed himself down and left Jason alone at a three-metre square of woodland identified by the three word sequence crisis.plots.chimp. The combination of those three words when typed into the What3Words app on Jason's phone pulled up a map of the precise location that Jon had specified in his message. The spot from where, at 9:45 this morning, he had spotted a waxwing.

Jason had been turned on to birdwatching by Richards, the man behind Rara Avis. Richards maintained that of all the activities or pursuits that a man of means could take up, the most rewarding, the most satisfying, was sitting still in a secluded spot and watching birds. At first, this had seemed to Jason to be rather a bleak pronouncement on what life had to offer. After a while though, Jason had come to see the beauty of the thing; a simple pleasure which was available to anyone, of any means, was surely a path to supreme happiness. Of course, having money meant that you could get better equipment, travel to more remote locations, and see the most exotic birds.

A waxwing was likely to be the most exotic bird Jason was likely to see near Hambourne. He'd only recently been reading about them: pinkish-beige, crested birds, about the size of starlings, they are more often found in mainland Europe, especially Scandinavia, but occasionally, when berries are in short supply on the Continent, they cross the North Sea to Britain.

Jason settled down in the same spot that JonWayne72 had used and focussed his digitally assisted binoculars on a group of rowan trees about twenty-five metres away. These top of the range glasses, as well as having an impressive magnification, had built-in image stabilisers, and the images seen through the lenses could also be recorded in videos or still digital pictures.

Jason was glad that JonWayne72 had left the scene. Part of the attraction of birdwatching for Jason was the solitude and the chance to think in peace. Jason's thoughts soon turned, as they often did, to Sarah. What would she think, he wondered, about birdwatching? She'd probably tease him a bit, although she wasn't as quick to mock his nerdy habits as his other friends were. Besides, they had a lot in common, really. Lying low and observing the behaviour of the local fauna, without being seen; wasn't that exactly what she was doing herself? But the difference was that all Jason was going to do to the birds was take photographs of them. Who knew what D.C. Robin Towers', or indeed the West Midlands Counter Terrorism Unit's, intentions were?

Who, or what, was she investigating, exactly? There were several possibilities. It was easy to rule himself out as a suspect. She had confided her identity to him, after all. And besides, he had no criminal activity to hide. So it was either Stuart or Sultan. He'd be surprised if she were investigating Stuart. He had a similar background to his own, and had worked at PKR, where they had met. True, he was rather handy with computers, electronics, and gadgets. He'd be a useful asset to any terrorist or criminal organisation. But Jason knew his friend pretty well; he just wasn't the type to get involved in anything dodgy.

The same was true of Sultan, maths teacher at the local comprehensive, whose real name was Jamil Ahmed. Jason couldn't remember where the nickname Sultan had come from. Perhaps his pupils had invented it. Jason had to admit that he didn't know much about Sultan, who seemed to like to keep details about his personal life vague. If pressed, he claimed to come from North Alberta in Canada, which to Jason, seemed so unlikely and so specific that it must be true. He'd once tried asking how he came to end up in the Midlands.

'Growing up in North Alberta was tough,' Sultan had replied. 'Every morning, knocking the ice off my bed clothes... and then there were the bears. You have to keep a watch out for the bears, Jason. Actually, I liked the bears. I seemed to share a natural affinity with them. I got myself a job with the Canadian State Circus, not with the bears, though... it turned out they didn't have any bears. Anyway, did I tell you that my dad was the State Yo-Yo champion? I must have told you that? No? Well, anyway, when the circus came to town, Dad said he could pull a few strings for me. Never mind. I ended up setting up the ropes for the trapeze artists and high wire acts. It's a very important role... immense responsibility and actually very technical. You've got to calculate correct lengths and tensions and predict trajectories. As the stunts got more intricate, the calculations became more complex, and I had to study the mathematics behind it more and more. By the time the circus toured Europe and came to the UK, I had fallen completely in love with mathematics and decided that my purpose in life was to share the love. I enrolled at Dudley Teacher Training college and the rest, as they say, is history. Well, not History, actually; Mathematics. I thought about History, briefly, but decided on Maths.'

It was a good yarn, and Jason didn't mind that a brief trawl around the internet couldn't verify the existence of any 'Canadian State Circus'. All of Sultan's stories held the same scant regard for truth, but that was just Sultan's shtick; Jason didn't feel he was hiding anything. He just wanted to provide some laughs as they sat around their table at The Pig. Their conversations were never very serious, but once or twice Sultan had talked about the school where he worked. It was obvious that he was passionate about teaching and Jason had the sense that Sultan was actually a very good maths teacher indeed. It was a curious thing; Sultan was one of his best friends, but when he thought about it, Jason knew very little about him. Jason would have liked to ask Sultan more about his past, his family and so on, but those sorts of things had never been topics for discussion around the pub table. And now, he had another reason for not asking questions: he didn't ever want to be accused of assisting Sarah's investigations.

Anyway, just because he didn't know much about Sultan's background, it didn't mean that he had anything to hide. And Jason certainly didn't want to fall into the lazy trap of assuming that just because he was of Asian heritage, Sultan would be the most likely suspect regarding some perceived terrorist threat.

There was, however, another possible explanation for Sarah's continued undercover work. Back in the summer, when things had started getting weird on board the *Rara Avis*, Jason had met Sarah's boss, Detective Inspector Jeremy Wren, who had flown out to investigate what was going on. Jason had liked Wren. He was a very personable Black Country police officer, who was clearly not averse to being called out to a private Mediterranean island to hang out with millionaires. Jason wondered if when Wren had found out that Sarah had been running a bogus operation investigating a non-existent terrorist cell, he'd decided that rather than expose this behaviour to his seniors and perhaps discredit himself for not keeping a closer watch on a team member, he would play along with it instead. Perhaps it would bring further opportunities to enjoy the lifestyle of the rich and famous in the future. But surely, a Detective Inspector of Her Majesty's police force couldn't be that much of a chancer, could he?

There was no sign of the waxwing, yet. Jason's coffee and digestives, the autumn sunshine and the rural peace and quiet were all welcome treats, but he was starting to feel cold. He practised with his digital binoculars, captured some footage of a blackbird, and deleted it straight away. A blackbird was unlikely to get him any likes or followers on the Twitchers' Facebook group. Scanning the bushes in the mid-distance, he noticed movement and focused in on a young couple engaged in their own ritual courtship — shouldn't they be at school? Now that might well make a popular post, he thought, but quickly decided to look elsewhere.

A wave of frustration and self-doubt washed over him. What was he doing here? What had he become? This birdwatching lark was okay, but surely there'd be time for pottering about Hambourne Heath in his old age. Richards might be right about the simple pleasures of ornithology being as satisfying as anything else, but Jason felt that right now, at the age of thirty, he wanted something more exciting.

And that was the worst thing about Sarah's investigations. Jason thought he'd found someone he'd like to have a serious relationship with, but it was all on hold, because she couldn't be seen to be involved with him. He was fed up with it. He needed to get away from it all. He needed to meet someone else.

His fingers had found the contact for Rara Avis almost before he knew what he was doing.

'Hello, Mr Tranter, sir.' Smethwick's voice was reassuringly calm, almost as if he had been expecting Jason to call.

'Hi, Mr Smethwick, look, I want to get away,' said Jason. 'Meet some people, live a little bit. Do you know what I mean?'

'I think so, yes sir,' said Smethwick. 'We've got a few things coming up. There's a cruise around the Greek islands, our ski lodge in Switzerland opens at the beginning of December, but, and it's a funny thing, sir, just this morning, Richards popped his head round my door and asked me to let you know about a Safari trip that's happening around Christmas time. There's a new member who's going, and he'd rather like you to meet her.'

Jason was intrigued. Richards had a reputation for being a bit of a social engineer; arranging situations so that members would meet others he thought they ought to meet.

'South Africa, sir' said Smethwick, while Jason was still pondering what sort of opportunity Richards had in mind for him. 'Rara Avis are taking on a lodge in the Molatedi Game reserve. Very comfortable, I've heard, sir.'

'It sounds perfect, Smethwick, thank you,' said Jason. 'Can you send me the details?'

'Of course, sir. And will you be accompanied on this trip...?'

'I'll be travelling alone this time,' said Jason, and the thought of leaving Sarah, Sultan and Stuart behind suddenly thrilled him. It felt good to be taking control of his life. It was a small step, perhaps, but what did they say about the longest journeys? The entire universe was out there, with exciting technology, art, culture, and interesting people — people who were enjoying the best of the world and who weren't afraid to be noticed. He was rich enough to become one of these people and maybe he'd taken a first step.

Besides, he thought to himself; he had plenty of time to make his decisions. It was 2019. He was young, and the world wasn't going to suddenly come to a standstill.

6

Malcolm Dunnett was tired as he walked to his car at 6:40 a.m. and his vision was a little hazy. He'd just finished his handover with Dillip and now his mammoth shift was over. There were three of them in the security team for PKR Wolverhampton; Dillip, Sonia and himself. He was the most senior, but even though they had a complicated rotating shift pattern that was supposed to be fair to all of them, somehow he still seemed to end up working more than his share of double shifts.

It was demeaning. Only nine months ago he'd been a department head at PKR Digital Media Division, a well-paid job that had seemed to fall into his lap when the manufacturing company had briefly dallied with the idea that it needed an in-house team to run its website. He had a smart office and a small team of one — Jason Tranter — who did all the work, so

Malcolm could spend his day surfing the web and learning management theory. It had all come crashing down when a corporate restructuring exercise had inevitably determined that PKR didn't need a Digital Media Division after all, and they offered both him and Tranter rather meagre severance packages. Malcolm had applied for thirty jobs elsewhere while working his notice, but didn't even get an offer of interview. In the end, he applied for the security job at PKR out of desperation, and they'd given it to him, he reckoned, out of pity.

He still tried to make something of the job. He'd shown initiative in getting a demo of drone security to help improve the team's rather shabby record. But that idea had soon got shot down, so to speak.

It was still dark, and he rubbed his eyes; there appeared to be someone leaning against his car, on the other side of the empty car park. That was odd, and he didn't like it. There was some sort of confrontation about to happen, and he really wasn't prepared for it. Malcolm tried to summon up his courage, tried to remember what it was like to be someone with a bit more self-esteem. He thought about his wife, and his little girl (they'd still be sleeping), and told himself that whatever was about to happen, he wanted to feel proud when he told them about it. He briefly thought about turning round and going back to the security office, but no, he could do this. By the time he reached the car, he felt about an inch taller.

'Alright mate?' said the young man, in quite a friendly voice.

A wave of relief washed over Malcolm Dunnett. This should be okay.

'Yes. Alright. Just finished. Late shift. Umm... help you?' he said.

'Just finished? That's late, mate. Worked all night, haven't you?' said the young man. He was wearing a hoodie with a sleeveless puffer jacket over the top, jogging trousers and trainers. Perhaps he'd been out running and stopped to catch his breath.

'Yes, part of the security team.' Damn. Malcolm shouldn't have said that. They'd told him not to talk about his job to strangers; it could make him a target. But perhaps it sent out a message that he could handle himself, if necessary.

'Yeah, I know, mate.'

Okay, so this wasn't good.

'Tough gig,' the young man continued, quite pleasantly. 'Looking after security on an enormous site like this.'

'Yes. But a good team. Ten of us. And dogs. So, we get the job done. Anyway, be getting back home now.'

'Nah,' said the man, taking a couple of steps towards Malcolm. 'Just you and a couple of others, I reckon. No dogs anymore. Last one got poisoned, didn't he? Couple of months back?'

'What? How do you know that?'

The young man was now standing between Malcolm and the driver's door of his car. Malcolm decided he was going to make a run for the passenger door and hope that he could unlock it, get in and lock it again, quicker than his assailant could catch up with him. But he didn't move yet.

'It's alright, Malcolm,' said the young man, stroking his chin. 'It's all going to be alright. I'm just taking an interest, that's all.'

'We've got drones,' blurted out Malcolm. 'Jason Tranter's company. Jason used to work here. Jason's drones are coming. They'll see you.' He knew he was burbling, but he just wanted to distract the man, confuse him perhaps, so he could make his surprise rush for the passenger door.

Perhaps it was working. The young man laughed.

Malcolm dashed for the other side of the car.

It was just a couple of steps for the young man to catch up though, and then a sharp kick behind the knees and Malcolm buckled, falling face first onto the wet tarmac.

'Oh Malcolm,' the young man said, standing over him. 'Mate. I told you it was going to be alright, didn't I? You didn't have to run. That was daft. Oh, and drones? That's shit, and you know it. Who the fuck is Jason Tranter? Not Ginger Tranter, I hope? Listen, Malcolm, you need to get those sorts of ideas out of your head. This place hasn't got drones, it doesn't need drones, and it doesn't need any more dogs. It doesn't need any extra security. That's not why you were hired, Malcolm. Just do the job as you've always done. That's what PKR want.'

Malcolm Dunnett couldn't tell whether his nose was bleeding, or it was just the wet of the tarmac on his face. Anger welled up inside him, but it surfaced as a whimper.

'PKR don't want a security man with clever ideas, Malcy. What they want is someone who just does the basics, the things that keep their insurance company sweet. That's all. Then if they do lose some stuff from time to time, the insurance will cover it. See? Nice and simple. That works nicely for everyone, and no one gets hurt, get it?'

Malcolm Dunnett didn't really understand what the young man was talking about, but as he lay in a puddle on the car park floor, and the young man's boot collided with his stomach, it started to become a bit clearer.

7

Beverley Cresswell stared at her phone, hoping it wouldn't ring. Her boss had said he'd call at five and it was nearly twenty past. She finished at five-thirty, and if he didn't call in the next few minutes, she would switch the phone off and put off an awkward call until after the weekend. Procrastination wasn't usually her style, but she had an idea he was going to lose his temper, big time. She couldn't face it tonight, not with the news she had to tell him. It had been bad enough on Monday; it was going to be six times worse today.

What a wally she had been to take this job in the first place. It was just some short term, casual work she'd taken on, hoping to earn some money before Christmas. 'Secretarial Work — six weeks only. Experience of legal and accounting req'd' it had said on the advert. Strange that the interview was at Costa. This guy, Terry Flint, had turned up with a ring binder full of bank statements for various business accounts, and just said 'I'm winding down some businesses. I need you to close these accounts and transfer the balances to my personal account. Reckon you can do that?'

She'd looked at them and asked why all the statements were addressed to a Henry McCracken.

It was a reasonable question, but he'd screwed his eyes up and looked at her as if she was stupid. 'He was my accountant. He's died. So you'll need to deal with banks, report the death, close the accounts. It won't be a problem. I'm the registered business owner. Can you do it or not?'

Of course she could do it. There wasn't anything difficult about it. Whether she wanted to do it was another matter. This bloke looked like a right bastard. It wasn't going to be worth the hassle.

'Yes, I can do it,' she'd said.

A few weeks later and the first of the accounts, worth £81,232 according to the statement, had been closed, and the balance transferred to Flint's personal account. She let her boss know, and he'd seemed very pleased. 'Sweet,' he'd said.

But five days later, on Monday, he'd rung back and indicated that he was not happy.

'Beverley, I'm not happy. Please don't tell me I've made a mistake in hiring you. I went to withdraw some money from my account today. You know, the account that you told me had just had eighty grand paid into it. Well, it fucking hasn't — excuse my French — and I was left... embarrassed. Now, are you stupid, or are you screwing me over? Which is it?'

Beverley had apologised and said she'd find out what had gone wrong. She got onto the bank quickly. The bank confirmed all the details, the account numbers, sort codes and so on. 'So where is the eighty-thousand pounds?' she asked.

'The balance of the account was fifteen pounds and thirty-two pence,' she was told. They couldn't explain why her copy of the statement gave a different balance. They would send her a full statement with a list of transactions for the last year.

And then, during the week, the same pattern had emerged for three more business accounts. Flint Trading Associates, T Flint Exports, Flintex - the statements in the ring binder all showed that there were hundreds of thousands of pounds to be transferred. The total amount transferred had been just over a hundred quid.

Five-thirty. Beverly switched her phone off and went to the fridge to pour herself an early glass of wine. As she pulled her living room curtains to, she saw the heavily built figure of Terry Flint walking up the path to her door.

8

'Mothers are strange people, aren't they?'

Rebecca Leyden-Fuller sat in the make-up room, staring at her reflection in the lit mirror while Francesca, the make-up artist, worked on getting her camera-ready. Francesca found it difficult sometimes, working on people that she personally loathed, but that was one of the hazards of working on a lunchtime TV discussion show. They regularly booked in controversial guests to keep the programme interesting. This one had caused quite a stir on BBC's Question Time a month ago, and since had her Twitter account suspended. Now she was doing the rounds, championing free speech, and moaning about cancel culture. Perfect for 'Lunchtime with Lucy'. Mostly, the guests were silent in the make-up chair, not interested in making conversation with the behind-the-scenes staff. This one wanted to talk; nerves, probably.

'Mmm...,' replied Francesca, not wanting to either agree or disagree with Leyden-Fuller.

'Well, mine is, anyway. So, I get a call from Ma,' continued Rebecca Leyden-Fuller, happy to talk to her reflection, 'and it's only then that I find out what it's really like to be cancelled. "What are your plans for Christmas this year?" she asks me, and, "would you mind if they didn't involve coming home?" Bloody cheek! Apparently, it's because brother Joseph is bringing his new boyfriend this year, which is frankly astonishing. We've never brought partners to stay at the familial home, mostly to save the embarrassment of the other halves. Ma and Pa are a tad on the eccentric and outspoken side... don't smirk... and whilst they'll have no problem with Joe bringing a chap home, they'll still find every opportunity they can to cause mayhem.'

Francesca tried not to listen. Rebecca Leyden-Fuller carried on.

'Case in point: she puts Pa on the line, and he says, "What do you think about that then, eh? Never thought we'd have one in the house, yet alone two! Remainers! Both of them!" Then he roars with laughter before saying, "Dear God, I'm going to have some sport... hang on... here's your mother again." Then Ma's back on and she's explaining that Joe and Stefan are going through a "difficult time in their relationship" and they "need a bit of quiet". I mean, seriously? She's worried that me being there as well will be just "too much" at the moment.'

Rebecca Leyden-Fuller was satisfyingly forced into silence while Francesca did her lips, but soon resumed her monologue.

'I suppose she's just trying to protect her sensitive little darling, which is sweet and everything, but there's not a thought about whether I might need a bit of quiet. I mean, I have had quite a year. Well, good luck to them all. In fact, it suits me down to the ground. I don't need a bit of quiet. I need a bit of fun. And for once, this Christmas, I may get it. I started ringing around to see whose holiday I could hijack. I called my stepbrother, but he's jetting off somewhere exotic, as per usual. Africa this time. It's the same every year. He'd do anything to avoid being with the rest of us. He calls Ma, occasionally, but he has no time for Pa or Jo, never has had. It's difficult with him. He doesn't like what I do... all this... who I am, really. Guess I'm too much like Pa. I'm surprised he bothers with me at all, but he does, and he's lent me a bit of cash from time to time. I half wonder about asking if I can tag along with him on his jaunt, but he's not at all keen on that. Then, weirdly, he mentions an old friend of mine, asks if we keep in touch. That's a joke, given what happened in Cambridge, lately.'

'Oh, when you pulled out of that talk at the university, you mean?' Francesca said.

'When I was deplatformed. Almost certainly by my old chum, I should add. Anyway, I phone her mum and within minutes she's telling me about her little darling's Christmas plans. And then it all falls into place. My step-bro, the sly bastard, is off to Africa with my old roommate! I shouldn't have thought she was his type, and there's a hell of an age difference. Anyway, I persuade the mother to give me all the details so that I can plan a little Christmas surprise for them both. And don't worry, she won't spill the beans; "Mum's the word," she jokes. Poor woman, she has no idea whether I'm planning a nice surprise or a nasty one. To tell the truth, neither have I.'

Francesca started working on Leyden-Fuller's eyes. It was within her gift now to make her subject look extra-severe, the pantomime villain, but of course she didn't. She trusted that Rebecca Leyden-Fuller could express her true personality without any help from her.

9

Sam Flint was having a bad time. Wolverhampton Wanderers had lost two-one to Spurs on the Sunday afternoon. When he'd got home from the pub later that night, his girlfriend, Letta, had refused to allow him in her flat, saying that she knew what he was like after the Wolves lost. He'd shouted through the door, and she'd threatened to call the police. He'd ended up spending the night in his BMW X5. When he woke up, he found all his stuff in plastic bags arranged around the car. Her brother was staring down at him through the flat window. That was that, then. At four months, it had been one of his longest relationships. As he packed the bags into his car, he pondered over how he would get revenge on Letta, once her brother was out of the way, but it wasn't at the top of his priority list. That honour belonged to Tranter Diall Electronic Surveillance Services. For various reasons, they were starting to annoy him.

He'd first heard of the company in September when he'd been on the golf course, the day Henry McCracken had suddenly died. While he waited around for the ambulance to take the body away, he'd asked about the aerial drones they'd seen flying round the place when they'd been out playing. Turned out that Tranter Diall had been demonstrating their kit to the golf club manager; aerial drones that would patrol the golf course perimeter, streaming pictures back to the clubhouse and using artificial intelligence to report anything suspicious. All very clever, but quite a few of the golfers had complained, not liking the idea of being on camera when out on the course or being put off their stroke by 'some robotic whirligig'. It was explained that they would only use the drones out of hours, when the course was empty, and would be helpful in the fight against trespassing teenagers taking drugs and having sex in the bunkers.

Sam's objection was different. He already had an arrangement concerning the security of the golf club and its grounds, and he didn't appreciate any new arrangements being made without first being consulted himself.

Then, in October, the same outfit tried showing off their equipment at PKR in Wolverhampton. Luckily, he'd been tipped off about it in time to get round there with a shotgun, and with a single barrel, he'd provided a compelling counter-demonstration of the inherent weaknesses of a robotic system. He'd discharged the other barrel in a very satisfying way into the side of the Tranter Diall van.

He hadn't realised that the 'Tranter' part of Tranter Diall was actually Jason Tranter. That piece of information came from a discussion that he'd had with Malcolm Dunnett in the PKR car park. Little Ginger Tranter. Memories of his primary school came back to him.

Sam was stronger and tougher than the rest of his class. Tranter was one of the weedy kids, and Sam enjoyed taunting him. One day, he nicked all the stuff from Tranter's bag and hid it around the classroom. Tranter, red-faced and looking like he was about to cry, went to the teacher, who instantly knew the culprit, and told Sam to return all the objects to Jason while the rest of the class sat and watched. The teacher asked Jason if he'd got everything back.

'Everything except the protractor, Miss,' Jason said.

'Give him back his protractor, Sam,' said the teacher.

'What's a protractor?' said Sam with a cheeky look on his face.

The class all laughed, and for a moment, Sam thought they were laughing along with him. But quickly he saw they were laughing at him, and for days afterwards, 'What's a protractor?'

became a playground taunt. It was the end of his reign over Class 6.

Well, that was all ages ago, and Sam wasn't someone to be messed with. He had important business concerns and, he liked to think, prospects for even greater things. The golf club was small beer, but the PKR operation was important to him, and to his uncle. The gear that they regularly lifted from that site fetched good money, even after the kickback to the PKR managers. He couldn't let that arrangement get disrupted. 'Security', as they called it, was the one part of the business that his uncle let him take care of by himself. His uncle was a bit of a wuss when it came to the 'wet work', but that was okay, because Sam found that side the most rewarding. He saw it as the cornerstone that everything his family had built was founded on. Without violence, or the threat of violence, the whole empire would come crashing down around their ears.

It was getting more and more difficult, however. In the old days, people looked to the police to protect their property and businesses, and persuading a few bent coppers to turn a blind eye was a relatively straightforward affair. Now, with police cutbacks, there were more private security firms popping up, like Tranter Diall Electronic Surveillance Services, for instance. These newcomers didn't understand the business landscape and were making everything more difficult. Tranter Diall had paid no attention to the warning shot fired into the side of the van. He'd seen the van driving round, good as new, the following week and lately, in the run-up to Christmas, he'd seen their flyers lying around provocatively on some of the premises that he visited on his rounds.

Just who did Tranter think he was? A Johnny-come-lately, bursting onto the scene with a load of high-tech gear and shiny new vans. Who was bank-rolling him? he wondered. Diall, probably. Time for a visit. And for once, he would play it subtle.

He drove to his old flat. He'd been letting it to a Syrian guy while he stayed at Letta's.

'Sorry, Hassan, mate. I need to move back in. Piss off, will you? I'm going to have a shower.'

By the time Sam had finished in the shower, Hassan was gone, having had only one rucksack of belongings, anyway.

Sam pulled on a hoodie and drove over to the small industrial estate unit in Sedgley at eleven in the morning. Two Tranter Diall vans were parked outside, looking smart and clean, and above the unit door was a sign bearing the Tranter Diall logo. Sam felt his anger rising. He swallowed hard and entered the door.

It was a pretty basic affair. A young woman sat behind a reception desk, busy on a computer. There was a picture of a hot-air balloon on one wall. A bearded guy sat tinkering with some cameras at the back of the unit.

'Hi,' said Sam. 'I'm looking for work. Wondered if you were taking anyone on at the moment?'

'Hello,' said the woman. 'You'll need to speak to Mr Diall. He's the boss. Stuart?'

The bearded guy put down his tools and came over.

'Sorry mate,' said Stuart. 'We're not taking anyone just now. Deepa's only just joined us. We might look again in a few months.'

'Oh. You're Diall, right?' said Sam. 'I'm an old schoolfriend of Mr Tranter's. He said it would be a good idea for me to call. Is he around?' It was worth a try.

'Er, no. That's funny.' Stuart looked confused and suspicious. 'Jason... Mr Tranter... doesn't usually get involved with the business on a day-to-day basis. He's a non-executive director.'

'What? The man with the money?' said Sam, picking up a Tranter-Diall coffee mug off the desk.

'Well, that's a private matter. Look, if you'd like to leave a CV, or email it to us, we can contact you, if anything comes up. Do you have any experience in...'

'Business good, is it?' Sam interrupted. 'I've seen your flyers.'

'It's fine thanks,' said Stuart, and walked towards the door, and held it open. 'We're quite busy at the moment actually, but thanks for dropping by.'

Sam's face betrayed he didn't like being shown the door by some puny-looking beard-o. He looked at the mug for a moment, weighing it in his hand, but then put it back down on the desk.

'Where's Tranter?' he said angrily. 'I want a word with him.'

'He's not available at the moment,' said Stuart, a slight waver in his voice.

Sam grabbed the front of Stuart's sweatshirt and pulled him closer.

'I'll ask one more time. Where is he?' said Sam.

'He's on Safari!'

On a cold wet, December morning in Sedgley, it seemed such an unlikely reply that Sam felt obliged to punch Stuart in the face.

Later, when he had gone home and had calmed down a bit, Sam called his uncle.

'Do we have anyone we know in South Africa? I might have a job for them.'

10

'Tell me he's got a Safari Suit,' said Sultan. 'Please, tell me it's true.'

Stuart had just let Sultan know Jason wouldn't be joining them at the pub that night, and the reason why not.

'I don't know what a safari suit is,' Stuart said. He had a black eye and a plaster over a cut on his cheek, but, characteristically, Sultan had not mentioned or asked him about that.

'Khaki cotton jacket with pockets on the outside and a belt at the front. Epaulettes. Think Roger Moore,' explained Sultan.

'Cool,' said Stuart. 'Yeah, come to think of it, Jason does have a kind of Roger Moore vibe going on.'

'Jesus! What happened to you?' Sarah had just arrived at The Pig and clocked Stuart's face straight away.

So Stuart explained his injuries, and told the story of the weird bloke who'd visited Tranter Diall, looking for work, that morning.

'Oh Stu! That's dreadful. Must have been really painful,' said Sarah. 'Did you report it to the Police?'

'No,' said Stuart. 'The Feds just love it when there's trouble at a security firm. I didn't want to give them the satisfaction. Besides, Deepa... the new girl... she was in total shock. It was a hell of a job to calm her down. I kept telling her that this sort of thing hadn't happened before. See, I didn't want her to think the job was dangerous. I mean, there was the thing with the van getting shot back in October, but that was before her time. I haven't told her about that.'

'What?' asked Sarah.

'Ah! Haven't told you either, then,' said Stuart, and then recounted that story.

'You need to tell all this to the Police,' said Sarah, authoritatively. 'Do you know if there's any CCTV cameras nearby?'

'Remind me where Stuart works again?' said Sultan gleefully. 'It's an electronic surveillance company, isn't it? Hmm, yes, I believe there may be CCTV cameras. Covering every bloody angle, I should think! And for that blunder, Ms Headly, it's your round.'

11

Jason was just changing for dinner, and putting on his favourite shirt, when he thought he saw a face at the window, peering in. It couldn't be, could it? Sarah? Not possible. The face was already gone. He went over to the window, which looked out onto an open veranda, but all he could see was the rain splashing onto the decking. He must have been mistaken. There was no-one out there, and she was thousands of miles away. It must have been some strange reflection. But even though he knew it was nonsense, just the thought of Sarah spying on him irked him. That showed how messed up his mind was. He'd done the right thing, putting some distance between himself and all that subterfuge. And yet, he realised, his pulse had quickened at the thought of her following him all the way to Africa.

Donning a sharp new Italian jacket, and leaving his lodge, Jason walked from his suite towards the dining hall along a covered wooden walkway. Curtains of rain on either side prevented him from getting any view of the local scenery, but he was already becoming resigned to not seeing anything of Africa. The car from the airport had had its wipers on for the entire journey. It hadn't dampened his spirits, though. He was excited to be on a different continent, for the first time in his life, meeting new people and spending a Christmas in a very different style to his usual celebrations.

'Bless the rain,' he thought to himself.

The thatched covering over the walkway was doing a great job. Rain was clearly a sufficiently regular feature around here to warrant it. Yet Smethwick had told him that this was the dry season. Jason made a mental note to pull him up about that, in a friendly way, of course.

As he approached the dining hall, even over the rain, he could hear the sound of polite conversation and laughter, and he caught a scent that he hadn't smelled since the summer; the smell of rich people. 'I'm going to meet new people, broaden my horizons. Business ventures, investments, philanthropic work — it's time to make the most of Rara Avis, and all it has to offer. This could be a whole new chapter in my life,' he thought.

But as Jason entered the dining hall, he realised that as he scanned the room, as well as looking for any familiar faces, he was really checking whether there were any young attractive women. It was understandable; there was someone here that Richards wanted him to meet, and Jason was curious.

It was the smile that caught his attention. It seemed to shine across the hall like a guiding light. Jason was barely conscious of being handed a glass of champagne by someone standing by the doorway. He mumbled some thanks, but he kept his eyes locked on that smile, and walked towards it.

The owner of the smile was a tall woman with shiny black hair and a glowing amber complexion. She'd offered the smile as a genuine welcoming gesture to the stranger who had just entered the room but now, as the stranger drew nearer, although the width of the smile didn't diminish, its welcoming aspect faded and turned to something that if it wasn't quite alarm, was certainly apprehension.

As Jason crossed the floor, he noticed the subtle change, and he too realised the potential for awkwardness. He figured that as an opening gambit, 'Hi, I'm Jason' was probably as good as anything, but he didn't know how he would follow it up if she just responded with her own name. He became conscious of the man she was talking to, a lithe figure with jet black hair, wearing a light grey tuxedo, and standing with his back to Jason. Presumably sensing the uneasiness, the man turned, and Jason recognised him as Jack Tang, the TV celebrity chef.

Jack Tang was one of the reasons that Jason had come to join Rara Avis. Earlier in the year, when Jason had visited Jack's exclusive Birmingham restaurant to celebrate winning his fortune, someone had slipped him a discreet Rara Avis business card, along with the complimentary wafer-thin chocolates.

'Hey, Jack,' said Jason, grateful for an 'in'. 'Remember me? Jason Tranter. You're kind of the reason I'm here! With Rara Avis,

I mean. You passed me one of those business cards when me and my mates visited your restaurant, back in May. Do you remember?'

'Oh, wow!' replied Jack with a wide smile. 'Sorry, I don't remember that at all. We hand out lots of cards, man. I'm sorry.'

It would have been a different reaction if Sarah were with him, Jason felt. He remembered Jack Tang paying a great deal of attention to her that night.

'Hello Jason, I'm Paige,' said Tang's companion and held out her hand. Jason wasn't sure whether to shake it or kiss it, but went with the former. Until recently, Jason would have considered a woman this beautiful and this self-assured to have been out of his league, but he had a growing confidence. All thanks to his money, no doubt, but hey, you had to play the hand you were dealt, right? The woman standing before him was, as his father would have said, 'a real stunner', but Jason was determined not to act stunned.

'Tippin' it down, out there, ay it?' he said in his most relaxed Black Country twang.

Paige looked puzzled.

'He's saying that it's raining hard,' said Jack Tang. 'It's okay. After seven years in Birmingham, I'm only just getting the hang of the Brummie accent.'

Jason decided not to bother explaining that his Black Country accent, faint though it usually was, came from an area west of Birmingham, and was very different to how they spoke in Brum.

'Where are you from, Paige?' he said, instead.

'Ah, I never know how to answer that question,' she said, placing the tips of her fingers on Jason's arm, as if taking him into a confidence. 'I have a place in London. My main home is in Paris, but I was brought up in Gibraltar. My dad was born in India and my mum was French-Canadian.'

'I bet you were good at Geography at school,' said Jason. He was rewarded with another of Paige's smiles.

'Paige was great at all her subjects, weren't you, hun?' said Jack, feeling that if anyone were complimenting her, it should be him. 'Especially Art. She's probably one of London's top design consultants now.'

'Oh, I wouldn't say that,' she replied, and then added, 'Not the probably part, anyway.'

'Ah, Jason, you've made it!' Richards' voice boomed across the dining hall, and the sound of chatter subsided a little. Tall and distinguished looking, probably in his sixties, he still looked like he had stepped out of a shampoo advert. Anyone could have guessed that he was the man in charge. He crossed over the hall, all eyes following him as he made his way towards Jason.

'That's excellent. I think we're about ready to sit down then,' he said. 'Was it a tough journey, Jason? A real shame about the rain, but I think it will clear up tomorrow. I see you've met Jack and Paige. Sorry, but I'm going to have to break you up. I want Jason to meet someone on my table.'

Jason was bemused by all this attention from Richards, who had always seemed rather aloof. Perhaps this was what it felt like when you became one of Richards' projects. He was getting more and more intrigued to find out who it was that Richards was so keen for him to meet. Disappointing that it wasn't the fabulous Paige, but she was already with Jack Tang, so perhaps that was for the best.

Just outside the perimeter of the Molatedi Reserve, a Jeep was pulled up alongside a black Land Rover Discovery, and the two drivers were conducting a heated conversation through their windows.

'No way! You cannot ask me to do that!'

'I thought we had an understanding, Dodge?'

'Our "understanding" was about bushmeat. This is on another level, man!'

'Is it? Seems to me, it's the same thing. Anyway, I can't sit here talking. The rain is spoiling my interiors. Just see to it, Dodge.'

The Land Rover window glided to a close, and the car pulled away.

'Shit!' shouted Ranger "Dodge" Mhlongo.

Today had been a bad day. Earlier, a couple of poachers had evaded him near down by Jacob's Bend and he would have dearly liked to at least wing one of them. Thieving bastards! They should just try getting themselves proper jobs, instead of stealing his animals, the lazy dickheads.

He drove through the reserve to the gates of the Molatedi compound, where all the lodges were. Where all the tourists were. If there was one thing Dodge hated more than poachers, it was tourists. And what was this now? Some jerk had left the pedestrian gate open. Now that meant he'd have to do a patrol of the compound as well. Or else someone might find a lion in their hot tub in the morning.

He wasn't Head Ranger for nothing; he knew exactly where to look. If either an animal or a thief had got in, they would take cover until the guests had gone to bed and the compound was quiet. And the best place to take cover would be under the wooden decking by the lodge verandas. He took his torch with him, but left it switched off. For this to work, he needed to keep the element of surprise. He moved swiftly and silently from lodge to lodge, crouched down and gave a quick sweep with his torch beam, listening intently for any sign of movement.

Before he even reached the fourth lodge, he had a sense that this was going to be the one. It was as if he could smell it. In fact, yes, he could...

'Eish! Hello stukkie, like to explain what you're doing here?'

'Take your seats, gentlemen and ladies,' called out Richards, and then in a lower voice, to Jason he added, 'I can't quite get used to being master of ceremonies. It was useful to have Ms Fortune to do all that. Never mind, come with me, Jason. I'd like you to meet Mrs Gillian McCracken.'

Jason tried not to let any disappointment show as Richards introduced a short lady with wavy grey hair, sharp blue eyes, and a smile that was polite, rather than warm.

'Mrs McCracken has recently taken your title, Jason. She is now Rara Avis's newest member,' explained Richards. 'I thought you'd be able to help her find her feet. Coincidentally, she is also practically your next-door neighbour. Shropshire, isn't it, Gillian?'

'That's right,' said Mrs McCracken, 'Are you a fellow Salopian, Jason? How lovely!'

From somewhere in the back of his mind, Jason remembered Salop was an old term for Shropshire. 'Well, I'm from Hambourne actually, which is South Staffordshire. We look on Shropshire as being our country park, for walks at the weekends,' he said.

'Wonderful,' Mrs McCracken replied, 'We rather look on South Staffs as a sort of no-man's-land between us and the West Midlands, where one goes to buy fridges or washing machines, or to get a new used car, that sort of thing.'

'That just about describes it perfectly,' agreed Jason.

A starter of cold meats and relishes arrived, during which they established that despite living in separate counties, they were probably only twenty minutes' drive away from each other. Jason found that Mrs McCracken was easy to talk to. She listened closely to what Jason said and was interested in the smallest details.

'Electronic Surveillance?' she said. 'How interesting! Yes, I can see that there would be money in that business.'

'Well, to tell the truth, the company is a recent thing. I owe my good fortune to Alan Dedicoat's lucky balls, actually.' It surprised Jason to hear himself admitting this, but there was something laser-like about Mrs McCracken's attention, and he didn't think he'd get away with his usual blag that he'd made his fortune in security technology.

'Ah, splendid! The National Lottery! I often have a little flutter myself. How lovely to find someone who's actually come up trumps. Well done, you, I say.' She leant in conspiratorially and said, 'Earned money is very overrated, if you ask me.'

'I must say, you've found me an excellent dining companion, Mr Richards,' she said, turning to him. 'I rather wish we'd travelled over together. It would have been very pleasant. There was nothing to see, with all the rain.'

'So, you've just arrived, too?' said Jason. 'You're looking very well on it, if you don't mind my saying so?' Blimey, he thought, complimenting old ladies now, is it? You're on fire, pal.

'Thank you, young man,' said Mrs McCracken. 'Do you know, I've never understood why people say that travel makes you tired. I haven't walked all the way to South Africa. I haven't swum. I've just sat on my bottom for twelve hours. Less tiring than gardening, I can tell you that.'

The conversation flowed easily, like the excellent wine, throughout three more courses, with Jason telling his new friend a little about his experience with Rara Avis so far. A glance from Richards was enough for him to understand that it wasn't wise to go into too much detail about some of the goings-on in the summer, though. No point in frightening a new customer.

'That's enough of me rabbiting on though, Mrs McCracken,' Jason said after he realised he'd been hogging the conversation. 'How do you come to be here?'

'My husband died suddenly in September, I'm afraid,' she said, suddenly very sober. 'I couldn't bear to be at home for Christmas, and especially New Year.'

'Oh. I'm sorry to hear that,' said Jason. 'Too many memories, I suppose?'

'No,' said Mrs McCracken perking up again, 'It's just that otherwise I'd have to stay at my sister's, which is very nice of her and everything but between you and me I just can't abide dry turkey, and I absolutely hate haggis.'

'I'm with you on the haggis front,' said Jason, 'But I must admit I'm rather partial to some dry turkey.'

After the meal and coffees were over, Mrs McCracken decided it would be best if she retired to her lodge to get some rest.

'Hopefully,' said Richards, 'the rain will stop soon, and we'll be able to get out in the jeeps tomorrow. Will you be up for that, Mrs McCracken?'

'I'm game...' she said, '... but don't shoot me!' She gave a short, restrained giggle. 'Now I know I've had too much wine, and it's past my bedtime. When I start making silly jokes, it's time to pack myself off to bed.'

Before Mrs McCracken could rise from her seat, she was distracted by a disturbance by the doorway. A woman was complaining about being forced into the dining room.

'Get your hands off me, you great big...'

'I'd watch what you say, lady. You really don't want to get me angry.'

Ranger 'Dodge' Mhlongo had the woman's left arm held tight up behind her back and he bustled her through the swing doors, into the dining room. The dozen or so diners that were still left fell silent. Dodge marched the woman up to Richards.

'I've just found this lurking under one of the verandas. Am I correct in thinking she's not expected, not one of your party?' asked Dodge.

Jason looked hard at the woman. She was still struggling to break free and her hair was partly falling over her face, but there was no doubt that this was the face that he had seen at his window earlier. He could see why he had mistaken her for Sarah. The hair colour and shape of face were similar, but this woman looked fierce and sullen. Her eyes scanned the room, as if she was looking for someone she knew.

'You are quite correct,' said Richards. 'She's certainly not one of our party. I think it's best if I deal with this somewhere else.' He turned to the guests at his table. 'Excuse me, everyone. Enjoy the rest of your evening.' He left with Dodge and his prisoner, who seemed more compliant now.

'Did you recognise her?' Mrs McCracken asked Jason.

'Er... For a moment, I thought I did, but no,' he replied.

'Rebecca Leyden-Fuller,' said Mrs McCracken, 'the journalist. Do you know the one? Rather unpleasant. She's a frequent guest on discussion panels, and I think they only invite her on to spice up the debate.'

'Ah!' said Jason. 'That explains it. She looks a bit like one of my friends in Hambourne. That's why I thought I'd recognised her. I wonder what she's doing here?'

'Yes, I'm wondering about that. I've met her before, actually, and it's strange to find her here. We'll have to grill Richards in the morning. But now I must be trotting along. Perhaps I'll see you at breakfast?'

Jason agreed that would be nice and wished her goodnight. He had hoped that tonight was going to be rather different. He thought he'd meet some people of his own age, and preferably an attractive single woman. But if that wasn't to be, then he had to admit that Mrs McCracken had been charming company, and he'd had a good night.

As she left, Mrs McCracken said, 'Thank you, Jason, I've really enjoyed this evening. I'm looking forward to introducing you to my niece, Bernie, tomorrow. She was too tired after travelling to join us this evening. A shame... I'm sure you two would get on like a house on fire.'

12

Richards followed Dodge Mhlongo as he frog-marched Rebecca Leyden-Fuller into the Lodge Office. She put up token resistance, but there was a hint of a smile on her lips.

'What are you doing here?' said Richards, once the office door was closed.

'Well, you know,' said Leyden-Fuller. 'I'm a journalist. I get around a bit.'

'And you trespass on private property a bit,' said Dodge. 'Perhaps we'd better call the police a bit, and get them to lock you up a bit?'

'That may not be a good idea,' replied Leyden-Fuller. She turned to Richards. 'It depends. Do you want my story about Rara Avis to be favourable? Or not?'

'I'd prefer there wasn't a story at all,' said Richards.

'So, that could be arranged,' said Leyden-Fuller. 'Look, brother-of-mine, don't act surprised to see me. You practically invited me when you mentioned Bernie's name the other day. Anyway, there's such a shitstorm going on in the UK at the moment and I needed to get away. I decided to surprise you both and join you and Bernie on your romantic getaway. But then snooping around I found it wasn't a romantic holiday after all, and that Gus Richards is hosting a party of high net-worth individuals for a Safari holiday. I mean, what the hell is going on, bro? You've always been a dark horse, but this time you've really got my journalist's juices flowing. I thought I'd snoop around to see if there was a story.'

'Well, there isn't,' said Richards.

'I'll reserve judgement on that, if you don't mind,' said Leyden-Fuller. 'I've learnt that in journalism, there's no such thing as "no story". It's always a question of "what's the story?" I guess there are two options. You can turn me over to the police, I suppose, and they'd probably keep me overnight, and I'd sit in my cell wondering how best to write my story about secretive millionaires hiding away in an exclusive game reserve, imagining what terrible things they might get up to. And, of course, there are some interesting names on the guest list. Interesting to me, anyway, and I'm sure I could find a way of making them interesting to my readers. I saw Jack Tang was here, for instance.

And who was the beauty on his arm, I wonder? On the other hand, you could let me stick around, perhaps? And maybe you could show me how innocent everything is, and we could all have a relaxing time, and I'd be so relaxed that I wouldn't even think about writing a story at all. How does that sound?'

'It sounds like you're attempting to practise blackmail, when there is nothing remotely underhand going on that would be the slightest bit interesting to even the most priggish of your readers,' said Richards, and he paused for a moment. 'But I'm quite prepared to believe in your ability to create a story where there is none. It's late. Perhaps I should sleep on the matter. Dodge, do we have anywhere we can let Ms Leyden-Fuller stay the night securely?'

'I can find somewhere, man,' said Dodge. 'Leave it with me. Okay, let's go, Lady.'

He took her arm and marched her to the staff accommodation. He knew there was a room there with no windows and with a lock on the door. The kitchen porter would have to sleep somewhere else that night, that was all.

'Hey, slow down, will you? You're hurting me,' said Rebecca Leyden-Fuller.

'Sorry, Lady. I've had a long day. I'm tired, and because of you, I'm soaking wet. I just need to get you to your room, okay?'

'Yes, well. Okay. But I've just got one thing to say to you...'

'Which is?'

'Which is...' She paused as if she wasn't sure whether to continue. 'Which is... I am incredibly turned on right now.'

Dodge let a smile creep across his mouth for the first time that day.

13

Jason awoke the next morning, feeling equally excited about the surprise appearance of Rebecca Leyden-Fuller last night, going on his first safari this morning, and the prospect of meeting Mrs McCracken's niece. The rain had other plans, however.

He stared over the wet decking outside his window to a watering hole. Someone last night had said that this unseasonal rainfall might mean that there'd be a chance of 'some decent wildlife' at the watering hole, but at present there were just a few large, long-necked birds, standing hunched, waiting for the rain to stop. He grabbed his digital binoculars and captured a picture of one of them. In seconds, he'd used an app to pull the photo off the binoculars and onto his phone, and then fed it into an image search engine. A spur-winged goose, *plectropterus gambensis*, his first African fauna, on his first African morning. It wasn't quite the opening scenes of *The Lion King*, but he still got a bit of a kick out of it. He'd slept well on a comfortable bed, with white cotton sheets. His lodge was well furnished in a style that somehow successfully combined modern chic with colonial tat, even down to some antique books arranged on sleek maple bookshelves. He'd browsed through a copy of some Boy's Own adventure of exploration and exploitation whilst lounging on a padded recliner and sipping a reasonable coffee. And outside was a whole new continent. He felt the urge to share.

He picked up his phone and messaged Sarah.

'Guess what? Your lookalike Leyden-Fuller turned up at safari lodge last night.'

'Ur joking! Glad to know she's out of the country. Enjoying urself?'

'Pretty good, yeah. Saw this from my window.'

He sent the picture of the spur-winged goose.

'I think they've got them in Dudley Zoo. You needn't have bothered. Have a great Xmas xxx.'

He'd forgotten that today was Christmas Eve. Hambourne felt a world away. Tonight would be the best night of the year in The Pig and he allowed himself a pang of regret at missing it. He pictured the crowded scene. The Pig was only ever crowded on Christmas Eve and New Year's Eve. It would be loud and boozy, and even the regulars, who tended to ignore or scowl at Jason and his friends on all other days of the year, would be warm and friendly. He remembered that last year, Sultan had gone from table to table with a big box of crackers that had been left over from his school's Christmas dinners and pulled them with strangers, getting everyone to wear party hats. He'd insisted on reading out the jokes from all the crackers, and somehow hearing that Good King Wenceslas liked his pizzas deep pan, crisp and even, had never been funnier. Sultan had gained many new, if temporary, friends that night and a fair few free drinks.

Jason remembered saying to Sultan, 'You're a big fan of Christmas, then?'

Sultan had suddenly looked sober. 'Never celebrated it as a kid, making up for it now.'

Looking back, that was the most Jason had ever heard Sultan say about religion. It just wasn't something they talked about. He'd lazily assumed that Sultan had probably been brought up as a Muslim, out in the unlikely frozen wastelands of Northern Alberta. Jason smiled to himself. Was that even a thing? Was Islam practised in Northern Alberta? What was Northern Alberta even like? And where was it, exactly? He felt rather ignorant.

Googling on his phone while the African rain dripped off the eaves of his lodge provided some answers. It turned out that Northern Alberta was an informally defined region of the Canadian province of Alberta, sparsely populated, with mining and forestry industries, and yes, with quite a long-established minority Muslim community from as far back as the beginning of the twentieth century. So Sultan's claim to come from those parts wasn't as far-fetched as it might have originally seemed. He tried searching for 'Jamil Ahmed, Northern Alberta' but the results came back with lots of Facebook and LinkedIn profiles of people that looked nothing like Sultan. Evidently, that was a common enough name. He tried 'Jamil Ahmed Northern Alberta Circus' but unsurprisingly, there were still no useful results. That circus story had to be rubbish anyway, didn't it?

Expecting a similar set of results, he tried 'Jamil Ahmed Northern Alberta yo-yo champion' - and bingo! A result from the Canadian Yo-Yo Association. 'Mohammed Khan, pictured here with sons Reza and Jamil'. Jason clicked on the link and there it was, a picture of a man, proudly holding up his yo-yo and grinning from ear to ear. In front of him stood two boys, one aged somewhere between eight and ten years old and beaming, the other a more circumspect teenager. It was confusing that the name was given as 'Khan' rather than 'Ahmed', but Jason recognised the smile on the face of the younger boy. That was Sultan's smile. There was no doubt about it.

Jason felt his heart beating faster and felt slightly dizzy. It was such a strange experience finding details of his friend from Hambourne's past life in Canada, while he himself was in South Africa. He shared the link to the webpage in a message to Sarah and then instantly regretted it. What on earth was he doing? The last thing he wanted to do was assist Sarah in her snooping on his friends. And worse, he couldn't imagine himself delving into Stuart's family history like this — was he showing some racist bias here?

14

A knock at the door. Richards was there.

'This rain will clear up in the next hour,' he said, making it sound more like an instruction than a forecast. 'It's too late for the full safari trip that we had originally planned, but I'm suggesting a trip to a nearby hide. It will mostly be birds, I expect. Interested?'

'Sure, I'm all about the birds.'

'Good, the McCrackens are coming too.'

'What happened to the woman... the gatecrasher... last night? Turned over to the police?' asked Jason.

'No,' said Richards, and gazed out into the distance. 'Just a mix-up. She'll be staying with us for a while.'

'Rebecca Leyden-Fuller, isn't she?' said Jason. 'Mrs McCracken recognised her. Said she'd met her before.'

'Hmm,' said Richards. 'Has she now? Well, it's a small world, Jason. See you in about an hour.'

The weather obeyed its instructions and, an hour later, Jason was climbing aboard a covered jeep, wearing his sunglasses and clutching his binoculars.

'Ah Jason,' Mrs McCracken's voice came from the dark interior of the Jeep. 'Bernie, this is Jason. The man I was telling you about.'

'Hello,' said Jason, not sure who he was speaking to, as his eyes adjusted to the change in light.

'Hi,' said a young woman, turning to look at him but then turning away again. Presumably, this was Bernie, Mrs McCracken's niece. He could make out two other people in the car, a couple from Yorkshire that he'd briefly met last night. Richards joined them and sat next to Jason. Last to join the party were Dodge, the Ranger, taking the driving seat and Rebecca Leyden-Fuller, who sat in the front passenger seat.

It was a twenty-minute journey to the Lagoon Hide. Jason tried to engage Mrs McCracken and her niece in conversation, asking how well they had slept, and whether they had a good view from their lodge. Mrs McCracken answered him and provided her own small talk about the excellent breakfast, but Bernie kept silent. As they climbed out of the jeep, having reached the hide, Jason noticed she had ear buds inserted, so presumably hadn't even heard his questions.

The short walk between the vehicle and the hide was Jason's first chance to catch a glimpse of what Bernie looked like. She was tall and wore a green sleeveless vest and khaki shorts. She had short, wavy blond hair and a sullen expression, but people often have a vacant look when they are listening to music, thought Jason. He wondered what sort of music she was listening to. That would tell him a lot about her.

Dodge led the party along a short dusty track that soon transformed into a trench with wooden sides. Eventually, they arrived at a set of steps leading down into the hide. Everyone instinctively lowered their voices. The room was cool, dark and narrow, with a long low window stretching over one side. Comfortable-looking swivel chairs were arranged behind a row of tripods for cameras or binoculars. Behind the chairs, there was just enough room for one person to stand behind each chair.

The view was impressive. They were sitting almost at a level with the water, and just a couple of metres away, a black heron stood motionless, unaware of its observers behind the glass. Beyond the bird, about fifty metres away across the lagoon, a rhinoceros stood by the shoreline with a range of grey mountains providing a distant backdrop.

As people found positions within the room, they all lifted their cameras and binoculars and trained them on the rhino.

'Okay, everybody, listen up,' said Dodge in a calm, authoritative voice. 'You're in luck. That's Sally. The old girl has decided that she'll grace us with her presence. Sally is a white rhino, but the bright ones among you will have noticed that she isn't white at all. The name "white rhino" comes from a lazy translation by the English. The early Dutch settlers used the Afrikaans term "weit" meaning "wide" to describe the mouth of the rhino, distinguishing it from other species of rhino which have narrower mouths. So now you know. Sally is a bit of a sad specimen. Her mate died a couple of years ago, and she just mopes around the place, looking sad ever since. Anyway, take your pictures. The old lady loves it when she gets on Instagram.'

'Really?' Bernie asked from the left-hand corner of the room. 'I thought there were rules about not posting pictures of rhinos on social media? So that poachers can't work out where to find them.'

'Oh, hi!' said Dodge, 'Pleased to meet you. I was wondering which one of you it would be. There's always one, right? If you look closely, you'll see that old Sally has been de-horned. She's quite safe from poachers.'

'That's barbaric! Mutilating a poor animal is a lazy way of protecting it, don't you think?' said Bernie.

Jason caught her aunt smiling at her in admiration.

'You call it mutilating,' said Dodge. 'I call it saving it from extinction. It's done carefully, and we sedate the rhino. It's whipped off very quick, and it doesn't hurt a bit, so don't you worry about that, darling.' He stood at the other end of the room, with his legs apart, arms folded across his puffed-out chest.

'I wonder if you'd say that if someone whipped off your horn,' said Bernie, and sat down.

'Mr Richards' said Mrs McCracken. 'Have you seen Jason's binoculars? I've been admiring them. I wonder if we could persuade him to let us take a peek through them?'

She ushered Richards and Jason towards the seats next to her niece in a rather obvious attempt to diffuse the hostile atmosphere that was building up. Richards was visibly grateful.

Jason took the chair next to Bernie, but she had slumped down and now rested her feet up on the window ledge. She had pulled down her sunglasses over her eyes and was listening to her music. Jason, only slightly distracted by her long, tanned legs, focussed his digital binoculars onto the rhino, and then passed them on to Mrs McCracken.

'Oh, that's wonderful!' said Mrs McCracken. 'So clear, so steady! What's that on the rhino's bottom? It's a bird, isn't it?'

She passed them onto Richards.

'Remarkable,' he said. 'They're powerful, aren't they? Very good. Yes, that's a red-billed oxpecker. I've always wanted to see one.'

'Let's see then.' It was Rebecca Leyden-Fuller, who had sidled up to Richards. 'Hello everyone, by the way. I'm Rebecca.'

She leaned forward slightly to look at Bernie and added, 'Oh, hi, Bernice.'

Bernie turned and stared at the woman, but with her sunglasses on, it was impossible to detect any sign of recognition, and she said nothing.

Leyden-Fuller held out her hand for the glasses and clicked her fingers. Richards frowned but passed them to her, anyway.

'I've heard about the oxpecker,' she said while focussing the binoculars. 'Attenborough did a piece on them. You see them perching on wild animals, eating the ticks that have attached themselves to the animal's body. Scientists used to use the oxpecker as a lovely example of symbiosis, the little bird performing a service to the noble beast and getting a meal as a reward.'

She turned and addressed her speech to Bernie. 'But nowadays we know that once the host is free of ticks, the bird often remains, feasting on the blood from any open wounds, and pecking at them to prevent them from closing. It turns out that the red-billed oxpecker can be quite a nasty parasite.'

Bernie didn't react. Mrs McCracken looked at Jason and raised an eyebrow.

Rebecca Leyden-Fuller stood looking pleased with herself. Dodge stood behind her and started talking softly in her ear. But Dodge wasn't great at volume control, so most people could hear him anyway.

'Ox-pecker was my nickname at school. Just saying.'

Leyden-Fuller snorted, loud enough to startle the black heron, who leaned its long neck close to the water and threw itself into the air and flew lazily off to a quieter stretch of the lagoon.

After nearly two hours in the hide, most people had had enough, and Dodge led the company back out to the Jeeps.

Bernie and Rebecca were the last to leave the hide, and they hung back a little.

'So, Bernice,' said Leyden-Fuller, 'Surprised to see me?'

'For sure,' said Bernie, coolly 'I thought snakes and crocodiles were the only reptiles I was going to see this week.'

'Ouch! That's no way to greet an old friend.'

'Is that what you were?'

'Something like that.' Rebecca Leyden-Fuller smirked. 'I can't believe you've forgotten. Or perhaps it's something you're trying to forget? Funny, there's a lot of people nowadays who forget they ever knew me. I could get paranoid.'

'Well, perhaps you only have yourself to blame. Perhaps it's the offensive opinions you seem to have cultivated that are putting people off?'

'Hmm. I kind of see it the other way round, sweetie. I've always had strong opinions. People just seem to get offended more easily these days. I'm not complaining, though. It pays the bills.'

She paused, and the two stared at each other.

'Except when it doesn't,' she continued in a lower, more serious voice. 'It hurts a bit when suddenly I'm cancelled. That gets me pretty cross. That's why I decided to look up my old mate, Bernice, this Christmas. Let her know that I still remember her, if she doesn't remember me. I remember everything.'

On the way back in the jeep, Bernie looked more sullen than ever, and Jason tried to engage her in conversation again.

'What's the music?' he mouthed, pointing to her earbuds.

'Killers,' she said.

Later that night, in the bar, Richards pulled Jason to one side so that they could speak privately.

'That was an unfortunate business between Rebecca Leyden-Fuller and Bernie Tenant in the hide today.'

Jason waited for him to say more, to explain why he wanted to discuss this now, perhaps, but Richards just stared at him enquiringly. It made Jason feel that somehow Richards was holding him responsible for the 'unfortunate business'. That was Richards' way. Make people feel uneasy and see how they react.

'I get the feeling they may have history, yes,' said Jason. 'But don't ask me what. Bernie's hardly spoken to me.'

'Hmmm, she lacks the natural charm of her aunt, doesn't she?' suggested Richards.

'I'm sure she's fine,' Jason said. 'Perhaps safari holidays aren't her thing. Funny, how Leyden-Fuller turned up the way she did the other night. Do you think she was deliberately tracking down Bernie?'

'I'm afraid so, and it's my fault, I'm sorry to say. Rebecca is my half-sister. She knew Miss Tenant at college, I believe. Rebecca and I don't talk often, but she called last week, and I couldn't resist mentioning Bernie's name, just to say that our paths had crossed. I suppose I wanted to see if she twitched — childish of me, really. I fear I provoked her into tracking us down. Never mind, can't be helped. Let's see if we can't keep things running smoothly, eh? Anyway, early start tomorrow. I'll leave you to finish your drink.'

Jason felt he had just been told that it was his bedtime, much like his mother used to on Christmas Eve.

Dodge Mhlongo came in, walked up to the bar, and asked for a cold bottle of champagne and two glasses to take away. As he walked back with them, he passed by Jason's table and stopped.

'You're Tranter, right?'

'Yes, Jason Tranter. Hi.' Jason smiled, briefly amusing himself with the idea that the champagne might be for him, and that the two might enjoy a late-night tête-à-tête.

Dodge stared at him deadpan for an uncomfortable few seconds and then said, 'Yeah. Just like to put a face to the name,' and left.

15

Birmingham was winding down for Christmas. On New Street and Corporation Street, shoppers were busy searching for desperate last-minute bargains, while shop staff watched the clock, knowing that after closing time they'd need to dress the stores ready for the post-Christmas sales before they could go home. In other parts of the city, office workers had already clocked-off, some heading home eagerly to their families, others preferring to delay that treat for a few more hours and heading for the bars and pubs, for a last festive drink with colleagues.

As Christmas celebrations went, the West Midlands Counter Terrorism Unit's affair was a quiet one. The last few days had been busy ones for Detective Superintendent Liz Sharpe as she'd been fighting against budget cuts, and it was only on Christmas Eve morning that she realised she really ought to stand a round of drinks for the handful of detectives and clerical staff left in the office. Two tables pulled together in the bar of The Royal were enough to seat everyone.

'So, well done, everybody.' She knew to keep her toast short. 'Another year. No major incidents on our patch and some significant arrests recently. I hope you all enjoy a well-deserved break. Merry Christmas and happy holidays! Get another round in, Jenny.'

Detective Inspector Jeremy Wren, nicknamed Jenny, took orders and went up to the bar. Looking across the counter to an adjoining room, he saw a face he recognised. He turned to his colleagues and said, 'Won't be a minute,' and left the bar.

He met DS Robin Towers in the corridor.

'What are you doing here? Are you trying to blow your cover? Quick, let's step outside.'

There was a yard outside with a couple of benches, all unoccupied.

'Sorry boss, but I needed to talk to you before your holiday. A bit of a breakthrough. I came to the office but there was no-one there. I guessed this was where you'd be.'

Jenny relaxed, and his eyes twinkled. He was a roundish sort of man, with an open face, and a smile that made anyone it was directed at feel important. 'Go on then,' he said.

'Jason Tranter sent me this, this morning. He's found a picture of Jamil Ahmed when he was a boy, growing up in Canada. Only his name is Khan, not Ahmed. That's him on the left.'

'Interesting.' Wren looked at the Yo-Yo champion picture on Robin's phone. 'You sure it's him?'

'Deffo. And the change of name explains why we haven't been able to find anything about his past before. But here's the thing. Check out the taller, sulky looking one. That's Sultan's brother, Reza Khan. I've done a bit of digging on him today and look what I've turned up.'

She showed him a news story from the Edmonton Journal. 'Man charged with failed bomb attack at University of Alberta. Reza Khan is being held under the Anti-Terrorism Act.'

Wren sucked in air between his teeth. 'This is good. Well done, DS Towers.'

'You mean you didn't already know? When we spoke in September, you said you'd found something out, but you wouldn't tell me what it was. I thought this...'

'All I'd found out was that Jamil Ahmed's story didn't stack up. We checked his records at the school where he works, and all the correct documentation was there. They had details of his Canadian passport, visa, work permit and so on. But when we tried to match those details to Canadian birth certificates, we came unstuck. Your news probably explains why. At some point, he's changed his identity.'

'So what happens now?'

'That depends. I take it there's still no other suspicious activity from Jamil himself?'

'Nothing, boss.'

'Right, I'll get the team to look into the details of all this. It's no crime having a convicted terrorist for a brother. That's if Reza was even convicted. And the name change might just be Jamil starting a new life overseas, putting his family behind him. Perhaps that's why he calls himself Sultan, now. But it justifies keeping you as an OCU. Which is just as well, as I've just had Sharpie trying to tighten my belt.'

Robin Towers looked at Jenny Wren's portly figure.

'Not at Christmas, boss, surely?'

16

The world felt like a different place when the guests of the Rara Avis safari party awoke early on Christmas morning. No dripping rain. Bird calls sounded out across the plains. There was a bustle about the lodges as the staff packed the jeeps under cloudless blue skies. The morning air was still cold, but the promise of warmth was tangible. As instructed, the guests assembled for a light breakfast at six o'clock and were surprised and delighted to find that Santa had left presents for everyone.

Jason joined a table where Mrs McCracken, Bernie, Jack Tang and Paige were already seated. Paige was showing Bernie a silver bracelet from the parcel she'd already unwrapped.

'It's gorgeous,' said Bernie. 'It'll look great against your arm. My skin is far too pale for silver.'

'It'll have to be gold for you then,' said Paige with a smile. Then, turning to Jack, she said, 'Did you choose this, Jack? It's perfect. It's just my style, you clever man!'

'Nothing to do with me, sweetheart,' said Jack, 'But I do have great taste, you're right. Let's see what I've got.'

He unwrapped a gold-rimmed shaving mirror.

'Oh wow! This is great,' said Jack. 'I've wanted one of these for the longest time. I've just been using the regular bathroom mirror, but this magnifies the image. Just think, my face, but twice as big.'

'And twice as handsome,' said Paige, winking at the others.

Bernie unwrapped her parcel and stared at it open-mouthed. It was a clear plastic envelope that contained an antique-looking piece of paper.

'What have you got there, Bernie?' asked Paige.

'It's a...' Bernie cleared her throat. 'It's a letter written by Sir Walter Scott. With his signature. It's amazing.'

'Cool,' said Jason. 'Has it got a South Pole postmark?'

'Walter Scott....' Bernie started to say, but as she diverted her eyes from the letter, she saw Jason was grinning. 'Very funny.'

'What's funny?' asked Paige.

'They don't have post offices at the South Pole, babes,' said Jack Tang, 'Or they didn't then.'

'Bernie has a bit of a thing about Sir Walter Scott,' said Mrs McCracken, moving the conversation along. 'Don't you, my dear?'

'My thesis on his Waverley Novels kind of got me my job at Cambridge,' said Bernie, blushing slightly.

Jason hadn't seen her looking interested and animated before. Perhaps yesterday had just been a bad day. Perhaps she'd still been tired.

Richards arrived.

'I'm sorry to hurry you,' he said. 'Perhaps we can leave the rest of the presents until later. We need to set off now. You see the best of the wildlife early in the day. We'll return to the lodges around eleven, and there'll be a brunch. We're advised to rest up, maybe use the pools, until three, when we'll set off for a sunset safari and Christmas Dinner under the stars. It will be cold then and it's pretty nippy now, but there are shawls in the jeep for everyone, so you can all keep warm.'

Bernie's making full use of her shawl, anyway, thought Jason, as the open-sided jeeps rattled along the game reserve tracks. She had slouched down in her seat, so that her eyes just peeped over the edge of the shawl. Everyone else was looking around, pointing and shouting out about the animals and scenery that were on display, but she kept mostly still, only turning slowly to see the giraffe and the wildebeest when Dodge slowed the convoy so that people could take photos.

Jason was curious about Bernie. At breakfast she had seemed lively and pleasant, but now she had the same sulky aura as yesterday. It was probably a reaction to Rebecca Leyden-Fuller, who had taken the passenger seat at the front, next to Dodge again. Or was it a reaction to himself? He had the sense that he irritated her, but didn't understand why. Her aunt, on the other hand, looked like she was enjoying herself immensely.

'Is this your first safari, Mrs McCracken?' Jason asked.

'Oh goodness, yes!' she answered. 'I've always wanted to see elephants, lions and zebras, ever since I was a wee girl. But we never had the money for this sort of thing. Best we ever had was a trip to Edinburgh Zoo.'

'So where are your usual holiday haunts then?'

'When I lived in Scotland, I never had holidays at all. Just days by the sea, at Portobello. Then I got married, and we moved down to England, and after that we spent our holidays back in Scotland. Apart from one rather disastrous package holiday in Spain, about thirty years ago, this is the first time I've been abroad.'

'That's amazing!' said Jason, even though he was no globetrotter himself. 'Was your husband not interested in travelling then?'

'He was! He was as keen as I was, Jason,' Mrs McCracken insisted. 'But we just didn't have the money. Times were hard. It's only recently... since Henry died... that I've had enough to...'

'Yes, well, there's no need to go into that,' Bernie said, stirring. 'Look! More elephants.'

Five elephants, four adults and one youngster, were gathered by a tree, just twenty metres from the road. Dodge stopped the convoy and satisfied coos and sighs came from all three jeeps.

Rebecca Leyden-Fuller tutted.

'First time they've seen them, I guess,' she said to Dodge, but so that everyone could hear. 'They'll soon get used to them. Bloody hundreds of elephant around here. They are literally vermin. How much to shoot one, Dodge?'

'No shooting on this trip, honey. Strict orders,' said Dodge. 'Besides, you couldn't afford it. One of these beauties would set you back forty grand.'

'You're joking, right?' said Bernie, standing up. 'I was told this would be a photo safari. No hunting on this game reserve. That's what I was told.'

Dodge laughed.

'That's what I just said, lady,' he said. 'Don't get your panties in a bunch. There's no shooting on this trip, that's what Richards arranged. But sure, we have shooting parties, other times. It's a game reserve. The clue is in the name. It's not a nature park. Beccy's right, if we left the elephant population in this park unchecked, first they'd strip the place and then they'd starve to death. Hunting keeps the balance.'

He turned to Leyden-Fuller, grinned and added, 'Pays pretty well, too.'

'It seems to me, Mr Richards,' said Rebecca, 'that your friends could easily afford a bit of sport. What's with the no shoot policy?'

'I have no problem with game hunting, personally,' said Richards. 'My "friends" as you call them, or this set of them, anyway, are just not interested in that aspect of the safari. And rather than set up a trip where some are pro-hunting and others against, and risk arguments, we've arranged for this trip to be "bloodless", as it were. If I get any interest in a shooting party, I'll arrange that some other time.'

Jason didn't remember being asked his own opinion on blood sports before the trip. He'd never given it a lot of thought and the thought of killing animals repulsed him, but at the same time, there was something about the mechanics of shooting that fascinated him. All that explosive energy, directing a small ball of metal with deadly accuracy to a target. Like Bernie, however, he'd imagined that big game hunting was a thing of the past.

The party watched and photographed the elephants for about twenty minutes, while the sun rose higher and the air smelled warmer. The little calf was obligingly cute and stole the show. Mrs McCracken asked Jason if she could 'view the little fellow through your fancy field glasses', and soon seemed to be more interested in binoculars than the wildlife being watched through them. She pressed Jason into demonstrating their capabilities, and Jason was happy to oblige.

'I'd like a pair of these,' she said.

'They're quite expensive,' said Jason without thinking.

'Oh, I think I can afford them,' said Mrs McCracken, smiling.

'Of course, I didn't mean...' Jason blushed at his own *faux pas*.

'It's alright, Jason,' said Mrs McCracken. 'I know I don't look it, and I haven't got used to the idea myself yet, but I'm a lady of considerable means.'

At this, Bernie, who was the only one of the party still slumped in her car seat, buried in her shawl, rose and said, 'Okay, have we done with elephants now? Should we be moving on?'

'I think we'll stay a bit longer,' said Dodge. 'There are some giraffe coming in from the west there. Today, the big five are making it easy for us. They're tracking us down. If we sit here quietly, we'll get a superb view. Beccy, pass round the flasks of coffee while we wait a few minutes.'

They passed around flasks and mugs, and Jason poured out three for Mrs McCracken, Bernie, and himself.

'Thanks,' said Bernie. 'For future reference, I'm capable of pouring my own.'

'Don't be so ungracious, Bernie,' said her aunt, with fondness in her voice. 'It doesn't suit you.'

'Suits me fine,' said Bernie under her breath, and then to Jason 'Sorry, thank you. Cheers!'

'Cheers!' said Jason. 'It's fine. I didn't mean to be patronising. I get the feeling this safari isn't quite your thing, then?'

'You do, do you?' Bernie replied, turning towards Jason and looking at him with piercing green eyes. 'It's not what I expected, that's all. I was looking forward to being in the African landscape - romantic dreams of unspoiled wilderness, I suppose. Then yesterday they took us to an air-conditioned tank where we could watch a rhinoceros through a window. Then today we find that the animals in the park are basically bred for commercial slaughter. It's taken the edge off things for me, sorry.'

'I'm afraid my niece has an answer for everything, Jason,' said Mrs McCracken. 'I suppose it comes in handy for her job. She's a university professor at Cambridge. Has to keep one step ahead of the students.'

'So I gather. What do you teach?' asked Jason.

'English,' replied Bernie, and sensing that her aunt wouldn't let her get away with such a curt answer, added, 'I specialise in deconstructing notions of realism in the Victorian novel.'

'Sounds like a Dickens of a job,' said Jason.

Bernie's lips strained to resist a smirk. 'Nice try,' she conceded, and took a sip of her coffee.

'Cambridge University!' said Rebecca Leyden-Fuller, proving that no conversations were private on safari. 'What do they know about realism there? I was supposed to be speaking there in November, but they cancelled me with three hours' notice, wasn't I Bernie? Nothing very realistic about that.'

'Nobody cancelled you. You pulled out after learning about the format of the debate,' said Bernie. 'You wouldn't agree to being questioned by a panel.'

'Those were conditions you introduced at the last minute.' Leyden-Fuller's nostrils flared. 'It was a setup from start to finish. Like everywhere else these days, the University is run by bloody snowflakes! This country's gone haywire.'

'Not this country, Beccy,' said Dodge, standing behind her and putting his arm around her waist. 'This country's too hot for snowflakes.'

'Yo! How we doin', over here?' Jack Tang's perpetually cheerful voice broke through the tension. He and Paige had walked over from one of the other Jeeps. 'Someone said you guys have coffee over here. Any chance of a cup?'

Jack may have been oblivious to the atmosphere, but Paige quickly saw how uncomfortable Bernie was looking.

'Hey, Bernie, mind if I sit by you and share that shawl? My legs are still cold in these shorts,' she said.

Bernie looked grateful for the support and Paige climbed up onto the Jeep. Jason regarded them both sitting side by side. They were dressed similarly, in green t-shirt, linen jackets, shorts and bush hats, but every item Paige wore looked like it had been designed for her, and this was the first time she had worn it. Her face alternated between a tender kindness for her new friend and excitement at being out on safari. For the tenth time, Jason felt a surge of jealousy for Jack Tang and incomprehension that Paige had somehow hooked up with him.

But as he looked at the two women sitting together, he noticed how his eyes kept returning to Bernie. Despite her grumpiness and her temper, or perhaps because of those things, he found her fascinating. Those green eyes challenged him. Just to get a kind look from those eyes, or a smile from that stern mouth, felt like his primary ambition just now.

17

The pills that her doctor had prescribed were no longer enough and Beverley lay awake at nights wishing she had never answered Terry Flint's job ad, and wondering how on earth she could quit.

When Flint had found that the bank accounts that he'd hire Beverley to wind up were empty, he'd smashed his enormous fist so hard on the kitchen table that her mug of tea had bounced off and broken on the floor. She'd stared at him, shaking with fear, and he had stared back. She still remembered that stare, that face. Sitting motionless, his huge head nestling between hunched shoulders while the corners of his mouth, his eyes, and the wrinkles on his brow flickered with tiny twitches, signs of the boiling rage inside that he was fighting to suppress.

And then he'd apologised. He'd stooped down, picked up pieces of the mug, and looked for something to mop up the tea. Beverley had remained terrified and for the rest of Terry's visit she couldn't speak.

'You've closed the accounts, like we agreed, Beverly,' he'd said. 'But you haven't finished yet, I'm afraid. I need to find the money that was in those accounts. The money Henry said was in those accounts. Someone's moved it, haven't they? Don't worry, I know it's not you who's moved it...'

His facial features had reconfigured themselves into a broad smile, but even so, Beverly was still terrified.

'... It's Henry what's moved it. But you can look into it for me, can't you?'

Beverley had shaken her head, her throat too tight to give voice to the word 'no'.

'Yeah, you'll be able to do it. I only need some information, any information at all, about where Henry's put the money. I'm not saying he's stolen it, Beverley. Don't go thinking that. He's probably put it somewhere safe. Henry knew I like to keep my financial affairs private, away from the prying eyes of the taxman, as you might say. He might have put it somewhere safe for me, that's all. But then he died, really unexpectedly. I was with him when he died. And he never told me what he'd done with it, see? Of course, he might have stolen it...'

The face had reverted to a thunderous frown.

'Keep working at it, Beverley. Let me know what you find out.'

Now it was Christmas, but there were no glad tidings of comfort and joy for Beverley. She'd cancelled her plans to stay with her brother's family over the holiday. There was no way that she could have coped with kids running around. Her nerves were shot, and she knew her sister-in-law would have spent the whole time fussing about the weight Beverley had lost. It was better if she stayed at home, with her computer and her phone, and maybe she'd get somewhere with Terry Flint's accounts.

She looked at the accounts in a different light now. Before she had witnessed his rage, it was just about plausible that this man was a successful, legitimate business owner, with a set of companies whose financial affairs he'd entrusted to an elderly, sole trader accountant. There must be people like that. Now however, she saw the possibility that he was one of those business owners that the presenters of TV's 'Watchdog' consumer rights show chase down streets whilst on camera, shouting 'Have you anything to say to the people you've defrauded, Mr Flint? Why haven't you paid any tax in the last five years? Why won't you talk to us, Mr Flint?'

But she mustn't jump to conclusions, she told herself. Things aren't always as they first appear. She remembered the odd sight of him crouched down on her kitchen floor, trying to mop up tea. His genuine regret over losing his temper. He couldn't be all bad, could he? He'd admitted that he liked to keep details from the taxman, but Beverley had some sympathy with that. She wasn't declaring her earnings from this casual work herself, even though he was continuing to pay her well over what she'd normally get for bookkeeping work. Despite the decent money, however, she'd have traded a month's pay for a single, decent night's sleep just now.

She spent all her time studying the information she had. None of the banks would give her any details other than what was on their published statements. Some banks had offered to get the accounts checked by their fraud departments, but a gut feeling had told her that Terry wouldn't want that; something that a quick text message exchange with him had confirmed.

'DNT LET THM NO ANYTHNG SUSSPICOUS' he had replied, and she shuddered at the thought of his fat fingers stabbing at his phone.

The terror that Terry provoked wasn't the only thing that kept her chasing his money now, though. She was genuinely curious. The bank statements and statements of account that Terry had passed to her at the outset looked straightforward on the face of it. For example, 'Flint Fine Art' looked as one would expect for an international art dealer. There was income from sales, outgoings that were attributed to purchases, wages, premises rental (in Venice!), and other expenses. Other businesses looked similarly simple. There was 'Flint Floral' importing flowers and vegetables. 'Flint Finance' was slightly more complex. Some of the other companies appeared to borrow and pay back sums to and from Flint Finance, and they also seemed to do a trade in Bitcoins, something that Beverley knew nothing about but decided she would research.

When the banks sent the closing statements for the accounts, it was the discrepancy in the closing balance that she immediately focussed on and panicked about. It was only when she closely scrutinised them, she realised that the bank statements that Terry had passed to her at the outset were fakes. Close comparison with the closing statements had shown little telltale flaws in the page's layout. Someone had put these documents together using a desktop publishing package. Presumably, that person was Henry McCracken.

Okay, so he had been cooking the books. Terry had told her that Henry would have diverted money into hidden accounts to avoid paying tax. But why would he create false statements that made it look like these companies had more money than they really had? That was the opposite of a tax dodge, surely?

The only reason Beverley could think of was that Henry was defrauding Terry, siphoning off money from Terry's businesses into his own hidden accounts. She could well believe that Terry wouldn't have been able to spot this. He was a 'big picture' person. He didn't seem like a man who dealt in the details.

So where had the money gone? Where had Henry hidden it?

It was eleven o'clock on Christmas morning. Beverley was still in her dressing gown and sat in front of her computer. She logged in to the same website that she had visited repeatedly for the last fourteen days. It was the 'Find a Will' service on the Gov.uk website. It was possible to search for probate records for anyone who had died in England and Wales since 1857. Recent deaths took a long while to appear on the register. Some deaths from eighteen months ago were only just appearing now. But bizarrely, today, on Christmas Day of all days, there it was. She typed McCracken into the search box and up popped the record for Henry McCracken, Died October 1, 2019. For £1.50, she'd be able to download a copy of his will. Then she might find out who had benefited from Henry's death. Which would be interesting.

18

At three o'clock on Christmas afternoon, instead of tuning into the Queen's Speech, as he knew his parents would be doing, Jason was lying in a hot tub watching antelope. They didn't do much, just grazed on the savannah. The novelty of watching them from the hot tub soon wore off. Perhaps Christmas afternoon was boring no matter where you were. He found himself raising an imaginary rifle and taking aim at the gazelles. He wished he wasn't alone.

It wasn't long, though, before he was out on the second safari drive of the day. They'd taken the covers off the Jeep now, and Jason was enjoying the views with his companions; Jack Tang, Paige, Mrs McCracken and Bernie, who was still looking fed up. Dodge and Rebecca Leyden-Fuller sat up front.

After a couple of miles, the Jeep halted so they could all watch a pack of wild dogs feeding off an impala carcass.

'You're very lucky today, ladies and gentlemen,' said Dodge. 'These dogs are the pride of our reserve. They're a critically endangered species and we're one of the few reserves where you can see them. They don't look very glamorous, but they're an important member of our Molatedi family. We take a great deal of care of these animals, and no-one's allowed to shoot them.' Dodge had his eyes fixed on Bernie as he said this last part.

Then he turned to Leyden-Fuller and said, 'Besides, they bring in some great government grants and a lot of tourists.'

She laughed.

They drove on to a campsite where a table awaited them, laid out in the open air for Christmas dinner, complete with Christmas crackers. It was a stupendous setting; the table was standing on a rocky promontory overlooking the river and offered the best view Jason had seen of the wide open landscape, with the sun sinking over distant hills. The menu of ostrich kebabs, goat stew and rum cake, on the other hand, was one that he would have readily swapped for whatever his parents had left over back in Hambourne.

'Still,' said Mrs McCracken, sensing Jason's misgivings, 'not a Brussels sprout in sight, so it can't be all bad.'

A constant supply of good South African wine helped wash down the food, although Bernie and Paige stuck to a rather deadly punch.

Most of the guests agreed that rum-soaked cake was a reasonable substitute for Christmas Pudding, and they were invited to take their seats to a separate area where they could enjoy drinks and watch the sunset.

'Meanwhile, the guys will clear away all the food,' said Dodge. 'The smell of the food will attract all sorts of unwanted guests, but the campfire and the noise of you lot chattering will keep most of them away. If not, I have this.' He held up his rifle.

'But people, don't go wandering off. I can only keep you safe if I can see you,' he added.

'Mind if I take a look at your rifle, mate?' said Jason. He'd been thinking that it was time that he tried to engage with Dodge. The tension between Bernie and Dodge was affecting the entire party. Jason wanted to show, in a friendly, respectful way, that Dodge didn't intimidate him, and that there was an alternative where they could get along more equably. He was also quite interested in the rifle.

Dodge eyed him suspiciously.

'Know much about them?' he asked, cautiously holding out the rifle.

'Absolutely nothing,' said Jason.

Dodge drew back the rifle. 'Best not, then. A dangerous tool in untrained hands. I thought you didn't approve of shooting, anyway?'

'Don't know where you got that idea,' said Jason. 'I mean, if it's true what you were saying yesterday, about how the wild animals would starve if the population wasn't properly managed, well I guess that makes it kind of okay.'

'Well, there you go...' Dodge started to say, but Bernie chipped in.

'But it's not true, is it?' she said. 'The animal populations only need to be managed because these game reserves aren't natural environments at all. They're artificial. The big five aren't wild animals, they're farm animals! They're farmed like back in England we farm cows and sheep. It's a business, and someone somewhere is monitoring the animal populations and saying, "Oh yes, the buffalo are popular game at twenty-grand a pop, that's a great price-point. We need more of them. Take out the dingoes!"'

Bernie delivered the last part in her best attempt at a South African accent, and it was either this or the reference to a species of dog found in Australia which drove Dodge over the edge.

'Don't you just love it when a white girl comes over and tells an African how to run his country?' he said.

Bernie stood up.

'Are you serious?' she said. 'Do you really want to bring race into this? You might want to ask your new girlfriend about that.'

Bernie pointed to Rebecca Leyden-Fuller, who seemed to be enjoying the argument.

'She's usually got plenty to say about race,' continued Bernie. 'Ask her about it. Anyway, I looked up the owners and directors of Molatedi Game Reserve online. I didn't see many native African faces there, Dodge. Don't you realise you're just a token?'

There was a silence. Bernie knew she had gone too far. She was red in the face and her eyes were watery. She stomped off away from the gathering.

'Stupid little cow,' said Dodge.

'Bernice!' Mrs McCracken called after her.

'I'll go after her,' said Jason. He followed her down a narrow path from the rocky outcrop to the river's edge.

She spun round to him suddenly.

'What are you doing, following me?' she asked irritably. 'Not getting anywhere with Aunty Gill, then?'

'What?'

'Don't worry, she already thinks the sun shines out of your backside. You've primed her ready now. She'll invest in your business or give you your loan or whatever it is you're after.'

'What?' Jason exclaimed. 'Don't be daft! I'm not trying to get money from your aunt! Why would you think that?'

'Because I've been around long enough to know why young men hang around rich old ladies,' she shouted.

Jason laughed. 'Well, thanks for the "young" anyway. I don't hang around your aunt. You have no idea, have you? I've got bloody loads of money, thank you. A lot more than an accountant's life insurance payout, anyway. But that's not the point. I enjoy talking with your aunt because she's kind and fun, and because I feel sorry for her having such a stuck up sorry-arse for a niece.'

Bernie turned away from him. There was still enough light for him to see her face was glowing red, and she didn't want that. Jason turned and looked back up the hillside at the main group to see if they had witnessed the argument.

He could see Dodge and Leyden-Fuller had. But that wasn't important. What was important was that Dodge had raised his rifle and was pointing it in their direction.

Without thinking about it, Jason spun round and launched himself at Bernie, knocking her to the ground just as the shot rang out across the savannah.

The sound seemed to echo for ages. Jason realised he'd closed his eyes, and he opened them to find that he was sprawled across Bernie. He looked up the hill towards Dodge who was standing with rifle still raised.

'The maniac!' he said.

'Wild dog,' said Bernie, facing down towards the river and looking at the corpse of a dog about ten metres away. 'What the hell...?' she gasped. Jason had knocked the breath out of her.

'I thought he was aiming at you,' Jason said. 'I thought... I don't know...'

They got up and dusted themselves off.

'I'm sorry,' said Jason. 'Are you okay?'

'Yeah,' said Bernice. 'I think I'm fine. Umm. It's probably me who should apologise. I shouldn't have said... Oh Christ, here comes Dodge.'

They stood awkwardly while Dodge, still carrying his rifle and looking angry, and Rebecca, grinning from ear to ear, picked their way down the path to join them. As they approached, Bernie decided to speak first.

'Look, I'm sorry, okay?' she said. 'I must have drunk too much. It was wrong of me to say those things and get you angry. And it was stupid of me to flounce off down here. It's my fault that one of the famous wild dogs has got shot. Will there be trouble?'

'Yeah, well, I shouldn't have lost my temper with a guest,' said Dodge in a low voice. 'I've been told about it before. I'll get myself in trouble one of these days and lose my licence. You know I wasn't aiming at you, right? I judged you were in danger. That's why I took the shot. And don't worry, that wasn't a wild dog. That's a black-backed jackal, a female. There are bloody hundreds of them in this area. Don't worry about her. She's dog meat now. You've probably given the wild dogs an easy meal.'

'You have to feel sorry for the bitch though, don't you?' said Rebecca Leyden-Fuller, and turned and walked back up the hill, smiling to herself.

19

'... and I guess that was the start really, Bernie, wasn't it? I remember on the drive back to the lodge, in the Jeep, you fell asleep, and your head rested on my shoulder. I knew then things had changed, shall we say?' said Jason.

'I wasn't asleep,' said Bernie. 'Truth is, I was embarrassed and didn't want to look at anyone. And burying my face in the jacket of the man who'd just leapt in front of a bullet for me felt, well... okay.'

'Oh! How romantic!' said Sarah. 'Jason, you absolute hero!'

Jason flushed and looked down at the table. Bernie squeezed his hand and smiled proudly.

'He is a hero, isn't he?' she said.

It was a Friday night, ten weeks after the Christmas Safari, and they were sitting around a table at The Pig, Hambourne. There were six of them, Jason, Bernie, Sarah, Sultan, Stuart and Deepa. It was the first time since before Christmas that Jason had been with them at the pub, and it was Bernie's first introduction to the gang, who had insisted on a description of how they had met.

'So, wait... can we just roll back a second,' said Sultan. 'Did you really say, "Take out the dingoes"? Excellent! Do you mind if I get that on a t-shirt?'

Stuart and Sarah laughed. Bernie squeezed Jason's hand and looked at him quizzically.

'You can never tell what is going to appeal to Sultan's sense of humour. Don't worry about it,' said Jason.

'But that was all three months ago,' said Sarah. 'What's the rest of the story? You've been Missing In Action, Jason Tranter. We've only had Stuart's intel that you'd returned from your safari safely and hadn't been eaten by a lion.'

'There's different kinds of man-eater though, eh?' said Stuart.

No-one laughed. Bernie glared, and Deepa punched Stuart's leg under the table.

'Yeah,' said Jason, feeling the need to move things on. 'I'm sorry I've been off the radar. I've been in touch with Stu about the business, but even he didn't tell me his news... about you, I mean, Deepa. Are you sure you know what you're taking on?'

It was all change at The Pig. On the same night that Jason was introducing Bernie to his friends, Stuart was coming clean about the office romance that had blossomed between him and Deepa. There was some discussion about whether this had happened because of, or despite, them being the only two people regularly working in that office.

'Don't worry, Jason,' said Deepa. 'This is a purely professional arrangement. I told Stuart I'd only go out with him if it advanced my career. I'm getting a new comfortable swivel chair on Monday, aren't I, Boss?'

Stuart smiled proudly, and Sarah and Sultan exchanged appreciative glances. Deepa was a good thing.

'But go on,' said Deepa. 'You were telling us what happened with you two.'

'Okay, so Bernie and her aunt were booked up to go on from Molatedi to Sydney for the New Year celebrations,' said Jason. 'On Boxing Day, at the Lodge, I got a note from them asking if I fancied tagging along. Sod it! I thought. Why not? So it was all fixed up.'

'My Aunt and I had arranged to stay at the Glenmore Hotel,' said Bernie, 'Which has these fantastic views over the harbour and a rooftop party at midnight and all the rest of it. All quite swish, but then Jason gets involved and suddenly the entire experience gets an upgrade. He arranges a helicopter tour of the bay in the afternoon, dinner on this massive private yacht, and a party with Sydney's best DJ and the best view of the fireworks. I mean the best.'

'Our friend Mr Smethwick may have helped a little,' said Jason, to answer the enquiring eyes of his friends.

'But then, on New Year's Eve morning,' continued Bernie, 'my aunt says she's not feeling so good, and wants to just stay in the hotel, so then it's just me and Jason. Which... worked out pretty well. Except I can't tell you much about the midnight fireworks, because, well, Jason was kind of blocking my view throughout those.'

'Too much detail!' said Sarah, smiling.

Jason scrutinised her smile, trying to work out how sincere it was. He wanted her to like Bernie. Perhaps just a small part of him hoped she'd resent her also, just for a short while.

'So you guys have been together since then?' she asked.

'Yep,' said Jason. 'Bernie lives in Cambridge. I've been hanging out there. Well, we've been away for some weekends. Amsterdam, Venice, Paris.'

'Wow!' said Sarah. 'You've certainly woken a spirit of adventure in old Jason, Bernie. He's always treated a trip into Birmingham as a bit flash. Finally living the high-life, Jason? Weekends for two in the city of love. How sweet is that?'

'Three, actually,' said Bernie. 'My Aunt was with us.'

Jaws dropped. Stuart accidentally snorted some of his beer.

Jason raised his hand. 'Alright, don't start,' he said. 'It was my idea, actually, and yes, I did check with Bernie first. Mrs McC has always wanted to travel, and now she can. And I felt bad about Sydney at New Year. Bernie and I are together all week, so it's fine having her along. She lives close to Bridgnorth, so I pick her up on the Friday mornings — gives me a chance to check in at my house first, pick up the post, get clothes and stuff — and drop her back on the Monday. It works well. Anyway, she's top company. I'd have brought her along tonight, but she's going round to her neighbour's.'

Sultan and Sarah watched Bernie while Jason was speaking, trying to work out how she felt about this arrangement, but her face was expressionless.

'Anyway, we're planning some trips for just the two of us soon, aren't we?' said Jason.

'You want to be careful, mate,' said Sultan. 'You've got to watch out for this virus they've been talking about.... No, not that virus. Good grief! Bernie, honest, I swear I meant coronavirus.'

20

The whole country was a mess. Sam was beginning to wonder whether Brexit had been worth it. He'd voted Leave, and they'd won. The country had left the EU. Now there was all this talk about getting 'a deal'. Why was nothing ever as good as you thought it was going to be?

His uncle was a remainer. What was that all about? He said that imports and exports would be more difficult if we weren't in the EU, so now he was winding the operation down. Lame bastard! How was the country going to pull itself up to its former glory if people just gave up the ghost when it came to a bit of extra paperwork? Where was the entrepreneurial spirit? It made him wonder whether The Firm was all that it was cracked up to be in the first place.

Like last year, when he'd asked if they had anyone in South Africa who could do a job for him. 'No problem,' his uncle had said. They'd got contacts with a firm out there that owed the Flints a favour. But had it happened? Well, no, apparently.

In the old days, Terry had been involved in everything. Okay, he kept his distance from the violent stuff, but he kept an eye on what was going on and made sure they carried his instructions out. But not this time, obviously. He'd been going off the boil for the last couple of years, and it had got worse ever since Henry had died in October. Sam knew that Henry and Terry went back years, but life goes on, doesn't it?

When he asked his uncle if he was okay, Terry said, 'Nothing for you to worry about, son.' But something was wrong. Sam hated the way Terry didn't trust him with any information about The Firm. Fair enough, if Terry wanted to retire to Spain or somewhere, and leave the criminal world behind, that was understandable. But why not train up his nephew and let him take over the reins? Why wind the thing up?

Sam was sitting in his car across the street from Tranter's house in Hambourne, for maybe the twentieth time. Ever since he'd got Tranter's address from Companies House, he'd drive out there from time to time, just out of curiosity. He had little else to do lately. Since Letta, there hadn't really been any women in his life. He must be losing his touch. He was losing his figure, that was for sure. Too many pizzas and curries, ordered from the Just Eat website. Just Eat. It was pretty much Sam's life-motto now.

The first time he'd driven out to Hambourne, he was pleased to see Tranter's place wasn't a fancy house at all. He may be a company director, but he wasn't doing all that well, by the look of things. That had calmed Sam down considerably. He didn't like the idea that Ginger Tranter was getting on in life better than he was. A small, detached house on a quiet road, with a messy garden. No-one ever seemed to be there. He drove by at all times, but there was never a light on, or a car in the drive. Once, in January, there had been tyre tracks in the snow, but not a sign since.

Today was different. Today there was a white Aston Martin DB5 pulled up outside. And there was Tranter, getting out. Unmistakable. The ginger hair. He looked fit and well turned out. And there was a posh-looking woman getting out of the car, too. She looked fit, too. Sam drove home, seething with rage.

21

Terry Flint was parked up in his Jaguar, in a Blue Badge space in a Sainsbury's car park, pondering on the nature of evil. The way he saw it, there was naughtiness and there was wickedness. Naughtiness was acceptable; wickedness wasn't.

He'd been naughty all his life. Stealing was naughty. He'd robbed shops, offices and factories over the years. That was how he'd started out. Terry hadn't been handed life on a plate like some people. His parents weren't wealthy, and they'd never pushed him towards academic success. He'd left school with one O-level in maths and a well-honed disrespect for authority. Thieving was just his way of redressing the balance, making up for the injustice of a system that was built on privilege. Obviously, you didn't rob poor people; that would be wrong. But people with insurance were fair game. Where would insurance companies be without thieves? He'd seen the big offices of the insurance companies, stuffed full with people. He knew some people who worked in insurance, from the golf club. He was putting bread on their table, the way he saw it.

He didn't approve of violence, but saw that sometimes it was necessary. It was the same thing as sausages, when you looked at it. He didn't like the idea of killing dumb animals, but a hot dog was a hot dog, and the ends justified the means. You shouldn't hurt innocent people, but sometimes people needed persuasion, or encouragement, let's call it, to do the right thing. Here and there, a little slap was needed to keep things moving in the right direction, just as a jockey might apply a horsewhip. It was all perfectly acceptable in the name of business efficiency.

Wickedness was a different thing. Lying, cheating, double-crossing... these things couldn't be tolerated. All of Terry's business interests, although they didn't always pay heed to the relevant legal framework, were built on a solid foundation of trust. Betrayal of that trust was wicked, and wickedness should not go unpunished.

'Henry McCracken, the sly scotch bastard,' said Terry, voicing his thoughts as he sat alone, waiting in the car. 'Thought he could cross me. Thought he could make off with my money, my retirement, my villa, everything I'd worked for.'

The passenger door opened and a slim man in a black leather jacket over a hoodie got in, carrying a large pack of toilet roll.

'Okay,' he said.

'What's the toilet roll for?' asked Terry.

'I need toilet roll.' answered Gregory.

'Okay, Gregory, what did you find out?' Terry asked calmly. He switched on the ignition and the Jaguar purred patiently.

'Nothing, boss,' Gregory replied. 'The place was stripped back to the floorboards. No paperwork or anything. Even the whiteboard was cleaned.'

'Did you leave anything behind?'

'Two broken windows. And the toilet will now flood the shop downstairs by morning,' said Gregory.

'Good job, Gregory. Nice work.' said Terry, easing out of the parking bay. Using a parking space designed for people with disabilities, was neither naughty nor wicked, in Terry's philosophy. It didn't register on the scale.

22

'One door closes, another one opens,' Dodge reflected. He'd just had conversations in quick succession that proved the point.

The first happened at the edge of the Molatedi reserve, through the windows of his Jeep and a Land Rover Discovery.

'What happened, Mhlongo? You didn't deliver.'

'Look, I told you, man. I don't do that stuff. I never accepted that job.'

'Since when did you think you could choose to either accept or refuse? It was an instruction. You didn't follow an instruction.'

'I'm not owned by you. Why are we talking about this now, anyway? The Tranter job was months ago.'

'The client has only just realised that Tranter is still alive.'

'Jeez. It can't have been that important then...'

'Point is, Mhlongo, how are you going to make this alright again?'

'Hell, I don't know! I don't see how I can...'

'Think about it, Mhlongo. Get back to me — soon.' The Discovery pulled away.

Dodge gripped the steering wheel of his Jeep to stop his hands shaking. Until now, the occasional work he'd done for the Johnson Brothers, the local organised crime family, had been petty stuff, like supplying bushmeat, or waving through fake hunting permits. He'd gone along with it because you try to stay on the good side of influential families like that. But a hit job on a Molatedi customer was a step too far, even if Tranter had been an irritating little shit and had sorely tempted him. He'd figured that doing a job like that would only have given the Brothers an even tighter hold on him. So he'd just ignored it. But it was mad to think that just because he'd heard nothing more about it that the problem had gone away. The Brothers' reputation should have told him the danger of not following through on their 'requests'. Now he needed to get out of Molatedi, out of South Africa, as quickly as he could.

The second conversation came like an answer from heaven, delivered via the 3G network to his mobile phone.

'Hello, Dodge. It's Richards, from Rara Avis. You remember me?'

Yes, he remembered Richards. Dodge's opinion of the Rara Avis leader had improved since they'd first met at the Molatedi game reserve. His first impression had been that he was just another one of those snooty rich bastards that he saw all the time coming out for their lifestyle-defining, status-affirming, safari holidays. The kind that treat rangers like they are some sort of rep for a cheap package holiday. But Richards had shown him respect and Dodge was impressed by the way he managed his party of millionaires, and the way he'd dealt with Beccy when she'd turned up as the camp intruder. He knew about bird life, too.

'So, the thing is, Dodge, I'm looking for someone to take on a security role in Rara Avis. I wondered if I could lure you away from Molatedi?'

23

Jason nearly missed the sound of his doorbell; he was playing his music so loud. He'd just received a vinyl copy of Anna Calvi's *Hunted* album and it was a recording that cried out for playing at high volume. Bernie didn't like music to be played too loud and always asked him to turn the volume down, but she had gone shopping in Birmingham with her Aunt, so now was a perfect time to crank up his amplifier and let his thousand pound speakers do their work on those dirty killer guitar riffs and soaring vocals. It was only when a track faded that the sound of the doorbell cut through, and an instinctive pang of guilt made him grab the remote and turn the music back down as he dashed for the door.

He was surprised to see Sarah there.

'Toilet roll,' she said, holding out a large pack containing sixteen rolls. 'You said you couldn't get any. Well, I had to fight someone with my bare hands to get this, but here you are.'

'Thank you,' said Jason, laughing. 'You're amazing. I'm pretty sure all the panic buying is down to my mother. In fact, it might have been her you had to fight. Anyway, thank you, come in.'

He made her a coffee, remembering how she liked it. It had been a long time since she'd popped round. Not since they'd returned from last summer's trip to the South of France and the Isola Gallinara. And this was the first time they had been together alone since an evening in September last year when she'd told him that her undercover operation was still an active investigation.

'It was nice meeting Bernie the other night,' said Sarah, standing in the kitchen with him. 'She's very nice.'

'Yes, thanks,' said Jason. 'She's out at the moment. Gone shopping with her aunt in Birmingham.'

'Nice.'

'Sarah,' said Jason. 'Or Robin, really. Look, I'm just going to say this. What's going on with your operation? Why are you still undercover?'

'Jason, you know I can't talk about that.'

'But it's just bogus. You know it is!'

'Maybe. Maybe not. Look, all I can say is that I've been told to keep my cover intact. I agree, there's been nothing to report since...'

She looked down at her feet.

'... well, nothing ever really,' she continued. 'It's literally the cushiest operation there has ever been.'

'Cushy for you, perhaps. But not very fair to Sultan and Stuart, is it? Yet alone me, having to be your accessory. Every time I see them, I feel like I'm betraying them by not telling them who you really are.'

'Jason, I'm sorry. Cushy was the wrong word. Believe me, there is nothing I would have liked more than to stand the operation down and come clean with you all. It's messed up my life, too.'

'What does that mean?'

'It means... it means... nothing. Look, I'm glad you've found Bernie. You deserve to be having fun. I just wish...'

Her eyes brimmed with tears, and Jason couldn't bear to see her looking so upset.

'I'm sorry,' he said, and moved to give her a hug.

He was surprised by the force with which she returned his embrace. They stood locked in each other's arms, their heads hooked over each other's shoulders, and were silent for what seemed like minutes. Jason stared through his kitchen window at the rain falling steadily. Sarah had her eyes closed.

'We can still be friends, can't we?' she said softly.

'Of course, best friends,' he said, the words coming out without him consciously choosing them.

'Jason,' she whispered, and turned so she could kiss him.

The kiss continued while each tried to work out what it meant. And then it was already too long for it to be a 'Oh well, goodbye then' kiss. It was definitely an 'Are you thinking what I'm thinking?' kiss. Hands explored and tugged at clothing.

Jason broke away. 'We could go upstairs,' he mumbled. They kissed again. Not to be kissing would mean facing up to what they were doing. They didn't want to face up to anything, they wanted to be carried away. They continued kissing as they shuffled out of the kitchen and into the hall. Somehow Jason picked up the amplifier remote, and turned Anna Calvi back up to full volume, as they stumbled and fumbled towards the stairs.

Which is why neither of them heard a car pull up outside, or footsteps coming up the path, or a key turning in the lock.

Mrs McCracken stood in the open doorway.

'I've come back to pick up an umbrella. Bernie said you'd have one,' she said mechanically, as she looked at Sarah and Jason. 'She's outside in the car.'

There was no way that they could try to explain that what they were doing was anything other than what it seemed. Guilt radiated from them.

'Yes,' said Jason. 'I'll get it.' He ran up the stairs, leaving Sarah facing Mrs McCracken.

'It's my fault, I swear,' said Sarah after an embarrassing pause. 'I just kind of threw myself at him. I'm an old flame. He wasn't interested, though. Fought me off, actually. I promise.'

Jason returned with the umbrella, just catching what Sarah was saying.

'It's true,' he said. 'I'd never do that to Bernie. I'd hate it if she thought... if she heard...'

'You and I will speak later, Jason Tranter,' said Mrs McCracken. 'Thank you for the umbrella.'

24

Gregory's a good lad, thought Terry. He shows initiative, gets the job done. It was Gregory's idea to park up in the supermarket, get himself spotted on the CCTV entering the store and then slipping out via a blind spot to do the job on Henry McCracken's office. Then discreetly back into the shop, buying something, and then coming out on camera. A nice tidy way of getting an alibi.

There was never any fuss with Gregory. You could trust that he'd do the job without making a song and dance out of it. Some lads these days couldn't help but act like they were on a TV show. For example, if Terry had got his nephew to do this little job, it would have been completely different. He pictured the furtive glances Sam would have made when approaching the shop, arousing suspicion from anyone who saw him. Perhaps the store security would have followed him. Maybe, maybe not. Either way, when Sam arrived at the office, he would probably have made a big deal of breaking in, smashing glass, or setting off an alarm. That would have meant that someone might check out what was going on, in which case there wouldn't be much time to do a thorough search of the premises. Sure, Sam would have had no trouble dealing with anyone who disturbed him, but that would have meant unnecessary mess. Terry could see it all, including a breathless dash back to the car, with Sam barking, 'Go! Go! Go!' as he jumped in.

And then later on, drinking with his mates, Sam would brag about what a close call it had been and how he'd sorted the nosey bastard. Very untidy indeed.

Terry worried about his nephew. He knew Sam wanted to take on more responsibility in the firm, but he couldn't envisage that working well. Running an outfit like this wasn't just a question of being tough. You needed to understand people, anticipate how they would react in a certain situation... what they call 'emotional intelligence'. Sam had all the emotional intelligence of a pork chop.

If Terry was going to pass on the reins to anyone, it would be to someone like Gregory. That lad was keen to learn and prepared to use a bit of his own initiative. It was such a pity that Gregory wasn't family. He was just some lad that had come recommended from a local bent copper, no-one really. There was no way Terry was going to spend any effort passing on the empire to him. He'd decided long ago that when the time came, he'd just wind the whole thing down and retire to Spain. A nice villa, drinks by the pool, his mind resting easy that there was no ongoing business that could suddenly turn nasty and lead to someone rudely interrupting his siesta.

But now it was looking like there might not be an empire to pass on anymore. It all depended on finding out what Henry McCracken had done with the Firm's money, which was why he'd got Gregory to break into McCracken's old office to see if there were any clues that might shed light on McCracken's personal life. From Gregory's report, it sounded like whoever had closed down the premises had done a thorough job of cleaning the place out. Never mind, the key thing was to see what happened next.

Two days later, Gregory reported back to Terry.

'The windows and the flooding have all been taken care of by Bradmore Property Services,' Gregory told him.

'And?' Terry screwed his face up tightly.

'They're about to invoice Mrs Gillian McCracken, from Ottershead, near Bridgnorth.'

'Are they? Who's she then? His missus is dead. Perhaps she's his sister. I never heard of any sister.'

'I'll soon find out, boss,' said Gregory. 'I'm paying her a visit. I've told them I'll take the invoice directly to her. Told them she'd had trouble with the post lately. It should be easy to work out if she's got your money... and explain the urgency of getting it back to you, perhaps?'

'Oh! Very tidy, Gregory,' said Terry. 'That's excellent. Go easy though, son. I don't want anyone to get hurt.'

25

Her phone screen lit up, and the phone rattled on her coffee table. Beverley saw the name of the caller and her throat tightened in response. It was Terry.

'Beverley, does the name Gillian McCracken mean anything to you?'

'I've not seen anything about a Gillian in any of the papers you sent, or any of the bank statements,' she replied.

That was accurate. But Beverley had found Gillian's name via the probate search, something she'd omitted to tell Terry. That way, he couldn't accuse her of lying, she thought.

As if that mattered. As if someone like Terry would bother with the distinction between lying and avoiding the full truth.

26

20 March 2020

The drive out through Bridgnorth unsettled Gregory. His usual work was centred around industrial estates in Wolverhampton or betting shops in Dudley. His BMW was used to stop-start traffic and his clutch foot felt idle as he sped along the open roads. He reckoned he'd been caught on two speed cameras, but that didn't bother him. His car had reg plates cloned from a similar model car in Cardiff or somewhere.

As he negotiated the narrow streets of Bridgnorth and crossed the River Severn, he saw tourists. And that was the difference between Bridgnorth and Bilston. Some loyal Bilstonians might feel pride and affection for their town, but there weren't many tourists. People in Bilston were there because they were born there or had ended up there through circumstance. He thought about his own life, about the gang that he'd hung round with as a kid, nicking sweets from the corner shop, taking bottles of vodka into the park, and how that had slowly led him into a more serious gang altogether. There was never a conscious choice to get into the world of organised crime. He had just drifted into it. His dad always said that he was bright enough to get a job as a lawyer or a banker or something if he studied hard, but he couldn't see the point of that. He'd never heard anyone speak highly of lawyers or bankers. Besides, in those worlds, everyone was brainy. In his world, very few were. It gave him a competitive advantage. His bosses soon saw a quick thinker that they could trust to pull off a job, and he rose through the ranks easily. Now, at the age of twenty-five, he was working directly for the man at the top of the tree, trusted to handle the most sensitive of operations, the retrieval of several millions of pounds.

The roads west of Bridgnorth were even quieter, with houses now few and far between. Some of the houses looked pretty swanky, with gated drives and private swimming pools. Could he ever see himself getting a place like that? The thought that he could end up being neighbours with lawyers and bankers amused him. He wouldn't have much in common with them to talk about over the barbecue. Or perhaps he would; as he worked his way up the ladder, he noticed he was having more and more contact with so-called professional types.

Gregory reckoned that if he handled this job well, it would secure his position as the boss's right-hand man. And he knew Terry was thinking of stepping back anyway. It would be a short step from right-hand man to natural successor. And it might be possible to miss out the right-hand man bit and go straight to the top. It all depended on how things went with Gillian McCracken.

The road narrowed to become a country lane with high hedges on both sides. Ottershead appeared to be just two houses, one on either side of the road. Gregory parked the BMW on the verge outside one of the cottages. A car pulling up was obviously something of an event around here; Gregory noticed curtains twitching in both cottages. He took a moment to go over his strategy. Terry was right, there may be no need to get heavy. It was still possible that Henry McCracken had squirrelled away the money in private accounts, still intending it to reach its rightful owner. If it was now in the hands of Gillian McCracken, she was probably surprised to receive such an enormous windfall. He knew lots of people back in the Black Country, who, however surprised they might be, would hang on to unexpected cash like a pit bull terrier hanging on to a bit of rope. But Gregory knew that there were people... strange people... who couldn't sleep at night if they had something that didn't belong to them. This looked just like the sort of place you would find someone like that.

As he walked up the path, the door opened. A small elderly woman stood with a hammer in her hand.

27

Two hours earlier, Gillian McCracken had received a phone call. The voice was wavering and tearful, but the words came in a rush and didn't allow any interruption.

'Gillian, it's me. The one that sent you all those papers in January. I won't give you my name - it's better for us both if you don't know. Look, you're in great danger. I'd leave the house if I were you, I really would. Terry Flint knows about you. He's just called me to find out if I knew about you, but I said I'd never heard of you. He's dangerous, Gillian. He scares me. If he comes, don't tell him about this call. You mustn't tell him about this call or the papers... Oh, sugar! I should never have called... I should never have got involved at all. I'm hanging up... Get out!'

And then the phone went dead.

28

'Mrs Gillian McCracken?' asked Gregory with a broad smile.

'That's right, young man,' said Mrs McCracken. 'You've come at just the right time.'

'Sorry? Were you expecting me?' Gregory looked confused.

'No, my dear,' said Mrs McCracken. 'It's just a lucky coincidence. You see, I just heard something down in the cellar. I think it's a wee rat again. I was just working up the courage to go down and sort him out.' She brandished the hammer. 'Now, a strapping young fellow like yourself turns up. You wouldn't mind helping an old lady in distress, would you?'

'Well, I guess...,' said Gregory. 'I'm here with the invoice from Bradmore Property Services, for repairs to Henry McCracken's office.'

'Oh aye,' said Mrs McCracken, pausing while she thought about that, 'Well come on in, we can talk about it after we've sorted this rat.'

Gregory stooped as he entered the cottage. The door led straight into a living room, with old armchairs around a gas fire standing in a brick fireplace. Across the room, there was a staircase, beneath which was a wooden door. Mrs McCracken opened this door and showed Gregory a steep flight of steps leading down to a dark cellar.

He looked at the old woman, weighing up the situation.

'I'd better take the hammer then,' he said.

She handed him the hammer and followed him down the stairs. At the bottom, she pointed to the light switch.

A bare lightbulb illuminated the musty cellar, which had old furniture around the walls, a sack of potatoes in one corner, and some onions hanging from the ceiling. They looked around without speaking but could see or hear nothing moving.

'No sign of a rat,' said Gregory, checking over the sack in the corner.

'So it seems,' said the old lady. 'I'm sorry to have put you to trouble.'

'No trouble,' said Gregory, 'So, I guess you are a relative of Henry's. A sister perhaps?'

'Well, let's go back upstairs and we can talk. You're from Bradmore Property services, you say?' Mrs McCracken started climbing back up the steep, narrow stairs.

'Did Henry leave the office to you when he died?' asked Gregory, following her closely.

'Has Terry Flint sent you?' asked Mrs McCracken, halting and turning around.

Gregory was too close. He leaned back to keep his distance, but somehow lost his balance and tumbled backwards down the stairs.

29

Stuart and Deepa were sitting with Sultan at their usual Friday table in The Pig but unusually for them, it was mid-afternoon. The only other customer was Steady Reg, a quiet, elderly gentleman who could be relied upon to be at his post, standing next to the bar most lunchtimes. He'd stand alone, nursing his drink, smiling to himself from time to time, listening to the conversation, but hardly speaking to anyone. When he'd had slightly more than enough, his smile would become permanent. He'd say goodbye to Jeff, the barman, and head for the door. No-one really knew his name, but as he weaved his way back up the road from the pub, he could be heard to say to himself, 'Steady! Steady!'

'How come you could make it at this time in the afternoon?' Stuart asked Sultan. 'Shouldn't you still be peddling algebra or trig to vulnerable teenagers?'

'Poets day,' said Sultan.

Deepa looked puzzled.

'Piss Off Early. Tomorrow's Saturday,' explained Stuart.

'So, who are we meeting?' asked Sultan.

'Malcolm Dunnet. Jason's old boss at PKR. You remember we demoed a drone system to him a while back but...' Stuart looked nervously at Deepa. He still hadn't told her about the drone and the van being shot at. '...it didn't go well, and they decided not to buy after all. Anyway, he phoned me today and asked to meet up. He sounded very furtive.'

'He always sounds furtive,' said Sultan, who'd only met him that once. 'Misses words of sentences. Talks like spy.'

'Well, he's brave coming out to meet us,' said Deepa. 'Everyone's scared to come out at the moment. But I still haven't heard of anyone who's had this virus yet.'

'There's a lad in my class who says his mother reckons she's had it twice already,' said Sultan. 'Almost killed her both times, apparently, and now she's got it a third time. Not sure I believe him, but he says she's told him not to hand in any homework to any teachers, just in case it passes on any germs.'

Malcolm Dunnet walked into the pub on the stroke of two o'clock, as arranged. He bought himself a soft drink and came over towards their table and sat down a couple of metres away. He looked disconcerted to see that Stuart wasn't alone.

'Won't shake hands,' he said. 'Everyone well?'

Everyone confirmed they were. Stuart introduced Deepa as the Sales Manager at Tranter Diall, and reminded Malcolm that Sultan was an occasional employee, as well.

'But really, I'm just here because I never miss an opportunity to soak up the vibrant atmosphere here,' said Sultan. Over at the bar, Steady Reg smiled to himself.

'What is it you wanted to talk about, Mr Dunnet?' asked Stuart.

'Yes. Well. A bit on the QT, actually,' said Malcolm, but being two metres away, there was nothing quiet or intimate about Malcolm's tone of voice. It wasn't something he knew how to do, anyway. 'Thing is, saw in your brochure, you offer GPS tracking service, yes?'

Stuart confirmed it was true. Tranter Diall offered a service where discrete black boxes could be attached to valuable assets: cars, machinery, equipment. The black box devices used GPS to work out their location and sent out the information via intermittent radio signals that could be traced if these assets were later stolen. 'So, do PKR want us to track something, then?' he asked.

'Not PKR. Me. Want to track some PKR equipment, but for my own reasons. Don't want them involved. That okay?'

'It's a bit irregular, Mr Dunnet. It wouldn't really be ethical to allow you to track someone else's property without their knowing.'

'But if we supplied you with the devices,' said Sultan, 'for you to attach to whatever you liked, we wouldn't need to know what you'd attached them to, would we?'

'That's the ticket,' said Malcolm, remembering that Sultan was the guy who spoke his language. 'Umm. Thing is... doing this on my own... out of own pocket... so was wondering... mates' rates?'

30

Slumped forward in an armchair in front of the gas fire, Gregory stroked the back of his head. There was a lump growing, but he couldn't feel any blood and didn't think the skin was broken. He'd grazed his elbow, though, and it hurt like hell. He felt dizzy and nauseous, as if he was still tumbling.

Mrs McCracken entered the room carrying a tray with a teapot and cups and saucers.

'It's China tea, I hope you don't mind?' she said.

'That's fine,' said Gregory. He'd never had China tea, but expected that it would taste the same as any other.

'How are you feeling now?' she asked as he poured him a cup.

'My head's spinning a bit,' he admitted. 'Tea will help.'

No milk was offered with the tea, and it tasted smoky and strange. He tried to concentrate on the purpose of his visit.

'The thing is, if Henry McCracken has left you the money... Mr Flint's money... Mr Flint is going to want it back. Mr Flint can get very angry...' He needed to make the old lady see the danger of her situation, while at the same time convincing her he was someone she could trust. It would be a delicate negotiation at the best of times, but with his head in this condition, he was struggling to talk coherently.

'Don't worry about that now,' said Mrs McCracken. 'Drink your tea and try to rest. I'm wondering if I should call for an ambulance.'

'No,' said Gregory. He was pretty sure that was a bad idea. He drank more tea, trying not to think of the disgusting taste. 'You need to be careful with Terry Flint. He can be nasty. It might be better if you let me handle things... See if we can work out an arrangement. After all, if Henry... Henry left money to you... you're entitled to... oh. Shit. Oh!'

Gregory's legs shot forward, and his back straightened. For a few seconds, he was rigid, and then he slumped back into the chair.

Jason Tranter was watching the BBC News. Italy seemed to be getting it worst. He thought back to his recent trip to Venice with Bernie. They'd been lucky not to catch it. Now they were reporting more cases of the coronavirus in the UK and things were looking very serious. Then the call came.

'Hello, Jason?'

The sound of Mrs McCracken's voice always made Jason smile. She had an ancient landline phone, and the compression made her sound like she came from a bygone age. Tonight, she also sounded frail, and uncharacteristically panicky.

'I'm afraid I need you to do me a favour, Jason. A few favours probably. How soon can you get here? ... Can it be sooner? Good. Probably best to wear gardening clothes.'

Part Two

1

With a headscarf tied round her nose and mouth and wearing a pair of dark sunglasses even though the sun hadn't properly risen yet, Julia crossed the road and knocked on her neighbour's door. She looked like a terrorist. Footsteps approached, and the door opened.

'Julia!' exclaimed Mrs McCracken, recognising her neighbour at once. 'Whatever is the matter? Come inside, quickly, you'll let the cold air in.'

Julia complied, and her sunglasses misted up instantly.

'You've not got the virus, have you?' she asked.

'No,' answered Mrs McCracken with a chuckle. 'Have you?'

Julia took off her sunglasses just as she heard footsteps coming down the stairs. The door opened and a tall, young, red-haired man, wearing just a towel around his waist and with shoulders still pink from a hot shower, entered the room.

'Julia,' said Mrs McCracken, 'This is Jason. We're lovers.'

Jason looked as startled as Julia did.

'Oh, I'm sorry!' said Julia. 'I didn't mean to disturb. I hope you don't think I was being nosey, Gillian. I just wanted to check you were alright. We neighbours have to look out for one another,' she added, looking at Jason, or rather, at his bare feet.

Jason was still speechless. He smiled weakly, grabbed his clothes from the clothes horse in front of the fire and went back upstairs.

'Well, thank you, Julia,' said Mrs McCracken. 'That's very kind. I'm perfectly well, thank you. But I'd better be getting Jason his breakfast. He's got a lot to do today. We're not really lovers, Julia. I was only joking. Och! You should have seen your face! I'm sorry, my dear. My sense of humour will get me into trouble one of these days. Jason is a friend of Bernie's.'

'So you've not got a toy boy after all then,' said Julia, looking relieved. 'But I saw you had another gentleman caller yesterday afternoon, didn't you?'

'Oh, you saw him, did you?' said Mrs McCracken. The colour drained from her cheeks. 'Yes, well, he was dreadful. Trying to sell me double glazing, loft insulation and solar panels for my roof! I simply couldn't get rid of him. This is the trouble for us single ladies, Julia. They think we're easy prey. He must have been here for three hours! In the end I phoned Jason from the kitchen and he came round about half-past six.'

'That was good of him,' said Julia. 'You could have called me, you know?'

'You'd have been no better than me. He'd have tried to sell windows to you, as well. But anyway, Jason soon put him in his place. He left just before seven o'clock.'

'Yes, I heard the car leaving,' said Julia. 'I was watching the local news.'

'Aye, you never miss that, do you?' said Mrs McCracken. 'Anyway, Jason stayed for dinner, and we had a drop of wine, so he slept on the spare bed. Now I must get on with his breakfast.'

Julia left and Jason came back downstairs fully dressed and with a serious face. His shower had washed away the madness of last night. He needed to have a serious talk with Gillian McCracken. But first, he had a burning question.

'What were you thinking, Mrs McC?' he said. 'Telling your neighbour we were lovers? What on earth...?'

'Sorry Jason. When I saw she'd come snooping, I told myself I needed to act normally, be my usual cheerful self, but I may have over-compensated. Still, I've explained that I was only joking, so don't worry about that. Anyway, the good news is that she didn't see you driving away the poor man's car. I told you she wouldn't be looking out of the window between six and seven.'

'It makes no difference. Someone from the pub is bound to report that car when they find it still in their car park this morning,' said Jason.

'No, I've thought about that. People leave cars in pub car parks all the time, Jason. And knowing what line of business he was in, I expect it was a stolen car, anyway. You used gloves to drive it and there are no cameras anywhere around. You said you didn't think that anyone took any notice of you running back here. I can't see any way someone will trace that car back to here or to either of us.'

'But it's crazy,' said Jason, louder than necessary and with a noticeable crack in his voice.

'What are you trying to say, Jason?'

'Well, I know it's a bit late now, but I still think it would have been simpler to have just rung for an ambulance and tell them that someone had fallen down your stairs, and that you thought he was okay, but he died suddenly while you were making him a cup of tea. I mean, that's what happened, isn't it? No-one needs to know that he was threatening you.'

Mrs McCracken plated up the bacon and eggs and toast.

'Oh, Jason,' she said, 'I wish it were that simple. I've been agonising over this all night. You've got to realise who we're dealing with here. I told you, he wasn't just some opportunist, leaning on an isolated old lady. He knew about my inheritance from Henry. He intimated there were others involved, and if I didn't cooperate with him, then other, "more persuasive" people would follow. I've read about this sort of thing. Organised criminals that monitor the births and deaths columns, and check the probate records, looking for vulnerable-looking victims they can intimidate. I suppose on paper I must look like a prime target.'

'On paper, maybe,' said Jason.

'Anyway, if the gangsters who sent this man round found out that he died at my house, then a whole new world of trouble would open up. But I imagine his disappearance may go unnoticed for a few days. People who live outside the law lead very unpredictable lives.'

'Where did you learn all this cloak and dagger stuff, Mrs McC?' asked Jason.

'From the "Great Ems". Miss Marple, Morse, and Midsomer Murders,' said Mrs McCracken. 'Now, the next thing for me to do is go far away where no-one can find me. As it happens, I'm due to be showing Sannah House to Richards and co this week. I'll just go up there early.'

He sat down at the dining table. Somewhere in the back of his sleep-deprived brain, he knew that Mrs McCracken was wrong. Much more clearly, he knew that he had been wrong to go along with her plans. He knew that unlawful burial was a serious offence. All the anxious feelings that he'd staved off by physical labour last night rose in him again. He couldn't believe he'd let her talk him into burying a corpse. How had she done that? He knew she could be persuasive, but he didn't think he was such a pushover.

Her talk about the dead man being some member of an underworld gang sounded far-fetched, but even if it was true, he was still a human being, somebody's son, someone's brother, husband or father, perhaps.

On the other hand, maybe she had a point. He wasn't a big fan of Miss Marple, or Midsomer Murders, but he'd watched enough episodes of Peaky Blinders to realise that criminal families weren't averse to making bloodthirsty reprisals. Could he really trust the police to protect her from that? His instinct to 'do the right thing' and report an accidental death to the police was balanced by a strong survival instinct for himself and his girlfriend's aunt.

And she was in her seventies. He was sure that she'd done nothing wrong, but proving that might be quite a daunting prospect, especially if the dead man's family or friends could hire expensive lawyers. Mrs McCracken was fit both physically and mentally, but an ordeal like that would put a strain on anyone, yet alone someone of her advanced years.

As he ate his breakfast distractedly, there were two other thoughts that made Jason feel easier about not contacting the police. The first was that the old lady was possibly correct in thinking no-one would ever catch them. Who would ever look under an asparagus bed in a cottage garden? No-one was likely to trace the missing person to this out-of-the-way village. If investigators tracked the history of his mobile signal, as he'd seen in TV dramas, it would be no help to them. There was never any mobile signal out here. True, a neighbour had seen the young man, but she seemed satisfied with the story that Mrs McC had given her and would probably even give evidence that she'd heard him leave. The young man's last known whereabouts would appear to be the pub where Jason had left his car.

The second thought was his strongest motive for following the old lady's instructions. Namely, that if he hadn't done as she'd told him, she'd threatened to tell Bernie about how she'd caught him with Sarah, and that would be the end of their relationship.

'Jason,' said Mrs McCracken after she'd watched him distractedly eating his breakfast. 'Don't worry. There's no need to panic about this. It's all going to be fine. But I don't want Bernice hearing about it. Do you understand? Now we both have something we don't want her to hear about. We're even-stevens.'

2

The sight of his uncle hoovering his lounge upset Sam when he arrived at Terry's house.

'Thought you had a cleaner?'

'Shoes off, Sam. She comes Fridays,' said Terry. 'I was cracking nuts last night. Bits of shell everywhere. That can't wait until Friday. Needs clearing up.'

Sam took off his trainers and put them in the hallway. He knew Terry liked a clean house. He lived alone and kept his place like a show-home. In fact, it was an ex-show-home that he'd taken, fully furnished, from a firm of developers that owed him money. One of five executive new-builds on a plot just west of Wolverhampton. The pale sofas, chairs and bedding suited him fine. Even the pictures on the walls were from the show-room, brightly coloured abstracts, and moody-sunset landscapes. He'd put carpets down over the laminate flooring, though; a cream-coloured deep shag pile.

'So, what's up, Uncle Terry?'

'Yeah, I need you to do something for me, Sam. I sent Gregory on an errand yesterday and he's not called in since, and he's not answering his phone. I've been round to his flat and no sign, either.'

This didn't sound as urgent to Sam as the phone call earlier had suggested.

'I'll tell you what it is. You remember dear departed Henry? Well, it turns out his widow lives out on the other side of Bridgnorth. Ottershead. You'll have to Google it.'

'I thought Henry said his wife died ages ago?'

'Yeah, well, perhaps he got a new wife. Or perhaps it's not his wife, perhaps it's his sister or something. Either way, he left her a bung of money in his will. My money... our money... as it happens. Gregory went over there to find out what was going on and use a bit of gentle persuasion to get the money back.'

'How much money are we talking?'

'Substantial. Let's just say, substantial. He's a smart lad, Gregory. Perhaps a bit too smart. I'm just worried that he might have thought he could get away with making off with the money himself. If he has, then he won't know what's hit him. I can tell you that. Here's the address. Go over there, will you? Find out if he called there yesterday. Don't say anything to the McCracken woman about the money. Don't worry about the money at all. Just find out if Gregory showed up. Let me worry about the old lady and the money.'

'Okay, no problem. I'm on it,' said Sam, typing the address into his phone.

'No violence, Sam. Do you hear me?'

Sam smiled and left. He'd heard Terry's words, but in his heart, he knew that his mission was to return both Gregory and the money to the fold. He could just imagine Terry's grateful, beaming face when he frog-marched a bruised and beaten-up Gregory before him, carrying a sports bag, stuffed and overflowing with ten-pound notes. In Sam's experience, that was how money got transferred from one person to another: in a sports bag.

3

The population of the island of Sannah in the Inner Hebrides has peaked and dipped many times through the ages. There were certainly people there as far back as Neolithic times, and they dug many strange, steep-sided storage holes along the volcanic fault lines on the western side of the island. Experts have speculated that these holes were used as ancient prison cells, and that perhaps, the entire island was some sort of prison island, Scotland's own prehistoric Alcatraz.

Another theory is that early Christian settlers in the sixth century AD used the holes as monastic cells; places where monks could sacrifice comfort and liberty in order to gain a deeper contemplation and a closer relationship with God. When the Vikings arrived in the area three hundred years later, some believe that the holes were used for hiding loot, pillaged from other islands. A more prosaic theory was that the Nordic invaders used the holes to dispose of their rubbish; old sheep carcasses, broken pottery and so on, a precursor to modern land-fill sites.

During the Napoleonic wars, Sannah experienced a sudden boom. Someone discovered that by burning seaweed, you could make soda ash, a vital raw material for making soap and glass. Sannah had a plenty of seaweed. The island's population grew, a church was built and a fine house for the minister, but when the war ended, the trade quickly became unprofitable and many of

Sannah's residents packed up their belongings and emigrated to Canada. Only a few hundred people remained, and numbers have dwindled ever since. The minister's house, Sannah House, was eventually converted to a hotel, but although Sannah has scenery to match many of the more famous Scottish islands, it has proved just a little too remote to attract a regular, sustainable tourist trade. Henry McCracken had picked the place up for a song when he was looking to squirrel away some money in the early 2000s.

The two dozen or so current residents of the island would probably love to attract more visitors to the island, but what they lack in prosperity, they make up for in contentment. The CalMac Ferry calls in the island's little harbour twice a week, bringing a handful of tourists during the summer and they can usually be persuaded to buy a painting from the local artist, and a shawl from the local weaver. When the tourists leave, the island life quietly continues, sunny days followed by rainy days, in an endless succession as it has always been.

'Gracie!' shouted Sandy, the manager of the hotel. 'That's the Widow McCracken I've just been talking to. She's changed her plans. She's coming early.'

Gracie, the hotel's only other full-time employee, descended from the first floor where she'd been changing bed linen. A Hospitality Management graduate from the University of

Greenwich, she'd taken the job of General Manager at Sannah House eight months ago based on the job title alone, and without properly researching the island, the hotel or the actual duties. It was a bit of a shock when she found out Sandy wanted her to 'just generally manage things'. But the island of Sannah had been kind and provided a rare, glorious summer, and she'd fallen in love with the place. She'd made friends with the locals and adopted the island's laid-back lifestyle. Now, the news that the owner of the hotel had invited a group of people from London with a view to making over the hotel had reignited her ambition.

'Oh my God! Are they all coming early? Or just Mrs McCracken?' she asked, breathlessly.

'Just Gillian tomorrow,' said Sandy. 'But she said that two new extra guests would follow on Wednesday. That's on top of the five that were already coming: Mr Richards, that TV chef and all. Heaven help us!'

'So. Look. It's totally not a problem,' said Gracie. 'I've got all ten rooms ready anyway, so Mr Richards and his crew can inspect them as much as they like. If they're thinking of buying the place, they won't want to see the rooms all stripped down and moth-balled for the winter. And two more guests, you say? Fine. We'll just have to get some more food in, that's all. That's the only scary bit, to be fair. Jack Tang coming to inspect our kitchens! If he gets all Gordon Ramsay with me, I don't know what I'm going to do.'

'Don't worry, lassie. They're not expecting anything grand,' said Sandy. Gracie looked hurt, so he quickly added, 'I mean "grand" as in "fancy". What you serve our guests is fantastic! They'll not be disappointed. Best local ingredients, hardly a food mile to be seen, traditional highland and island recipes, — that's way better than any "grand and fancy" Michelin-starred muck! It's authentic!'

'Hey, I can do fancy,' protested Gracie. 'I can *jus* with the best of them. I'm quite happy to call a prawn a langoustine, if that's what floats their boat.'

The phone rang in the hall and Sandy left Gracie as she started pulling recipe books from the shelves. It hadn't been his intention to spur her on to raise her culinary game, but somethings couldn't be helped. He had a smile on his lips and a twinkle in his eye as he picked up the phone.

'Hello, Sannah House Hotel, Good Morning, how can I help you?'

'Hello, can I speak to Mr Sandy Lamb, please?'

'Speaking, Can I ask who's calling?' Sandy had quite a practised telephone manner.

'It's James Wilkes. We were at school together. The Flora Stevenson School, Comely Bank, Edinburgh. Have I got the right Sandy Lamb?'

'Aye, well, Flora Stevenson School.' Sandy spoke cautiously. 'That's right enough. What did you say your name was, again? Wilkes? Let me think... Wilkes.... not Jimmy Wilkes? Oh, my word, it's never you?'

'You remember me, then?'

'Just about, Jimmy,' said Sandy with a laugh. 'It's been a long time. How are you keeping?'

'Yeah, I'm fine. Like you say, it's been a long time. I can't say I remember those days very well. I remember Mrs Mickey, the teacher, and one or two of the lads we used to hang out with in the gang hut. Do you remember that?'

'Well, I remember the gang hut,' said Sandy, 'But I never used to hang out there. I was always playing soccer, if you remember.'

'So you were, so you were. Yes, that's right. Listen, Sandy, I'm really trying to catch up with Henry. Henry McCracken, do you remember him? I lost touch with everyone from Flora Stevenson, but I met up with Henry when he moved down this way. We were good pals for a while, but our paths separated when I got married. Anyway, I'm trying to track him down. You don't happen to be in touch with him, do you?'

'Och, I'm awfully sorry, Jimmy. I was in touch with Henry, regularly you might say, but I'm afraid he passed away just last year. It's the strangest thing, Jimmy. I've just this very minute been talking to his widow on the telephone. Would you believe that?'

'His widow? No, you're right. I don't believe it. Isn't that strange? How is she?'

'Gillian? Aye, she's coping,' said Sandy. 'She's coming over here to stay awhile, as it happens. She and Henry used to come every year, so it's nice she's still able to come.'

'Oh, that is nice, yes.' There was a brief pause. 'Listen, Sandy, this is a bit spur of the moment, but you don't have a spare room at Sannah House Hotel, do you? I'd really like to see Gillian. Surprise her, like. I've got some old photos of Henry I think she'd like. It's a bit mad, but you'll understand me. At our time of life, Sandy, if you don't take your chances when they come... well, they may not come again.'

'Now that's a real shame, Jimmy. We're actually fully occupied that weekend, believe it or not. But I could put you in touch with the bed-and-breakfast by the quay, if you'd like? It's the only other place on the island, but they're sure to have room. And they'll no mind you taking your meals up here, so you can chat with Gillian.'

A few minutes later, Sandy interrupted his General Manager as she browsed through an old copy of *Larousse Gastronomique*.

'If you're going to be ordering langoustines, Gracie, you'd better ask old Billy to pull a few more out of the sea...'

4

Julia needed another cup of tea. It was all getting too much to take in. She had BBC News 24 on the television and every update she saw seemed to bring worse news. The death toll in Italy had risen above a thousand. Macron had closed all French schools. Trump had banned travel from twenty-six European countries. There had only been twelve deaths in the UK, so far, but Boris Johnson was saying it was probably going to be the worst public health crisis in a generation. He was calm, though. He said his government had a strategy to get the country through. She hoped he was right, but the BBC kept finding scientists to talk to who were calling for stricter measures and something called 'social distancing'.

As well as coronavirus, there was something else on Julia's mind: all the comings and goings at Gillian's house. She'd seen that young man, Jason, leaving in his flashy white sports car at about nine. And then, at about a quarter to eleven, a taxi had turned up and Gillian had left the house with two suitcases! Where was she off to? Julia wondered. She wished Gillian would tell her neighbour when she was going away. She'd be more than happy to keep an eye on the house for her.

And now, what was this? Another young man in a shiny black car had turned up. This was the third one in twenty-four hours! Julia peeped around the curtains to watch this one leave his car and approach Gillian's door. Heavier built and more scruffily dressed than the other two, in a red tee-shirt and grey jogging bottoms. He knocked on the door and waited, then peered through the sitting-room window. Oh dear, he might be casing the joint! He might have heard that Gillian had gone away and come round to break in. She'd have to intervene.

'Hello, can I help you?' she called, leaving her doorway and crossing the narrow road. She had her headscarf around her face and was wearing her sunglasses again. The man looked at her distrustfully, and held his arm up, as if to prevent her coming too near. 'It's alright, I haven't got it. Just taking precautions,' she said.

'Got what? The bag?' he asked.

'I'm sorry?'

'This is McCracken's house, yeah?

'Mrs McCracken lives here, yes,' said Julia. 'She's just popped out. Can I help you?' *There's no way I'm telling a random stranger she's gone off with a couple of suitcases.*

'When's she back, love?'

'I'm not sure. A few days, I expect.' *Damn him for asking such a direct question!* 'But I'm keeping an eye on the place for her. Who shall I tell her has called?' *Oh Julia! You're not on the bloody phone, you fool.*

'She with anyone?' the man said, ignoring her question. 'A friend of mine called here yesterday.'

'Ahh!' said Julia. *Thank God! Not a burglar then. Just someone connected with yesterday's visitors.* 'Would that be Jason, or the windows man?'

'Jason? Jason Tranter?'

The man looked suddenly angry.

Oh dear, I'm getting a bad feeling about this again.

'I don't know his second name. Look, would you mind telling me your name?'

'What was he driving?'

'I don't know, a white sports car.' *Just go away. I don't like this.*

'That's him. Right.'

The man strode back to his car, got in, and sped off.

Well, a 'thank you' wouldn't have cost anything. Young people!

5

When Jason set off for Bernie's flat at about 3 p.m., his head was already buzzing, and he wondered how safe it was for him to drive. He'd tried to get an hour's sleep before the two-hour drive to Cambridge, but visions of the dead body in its makeshift grave and thoughts about his eventual arrest and prison sentence would not let him lie still and ended up feeling worse. So he decided to cut his losses and get on the road. He'd be able to sleep at Bernie's.

He wished he was in his old Ford Focus, not the Aston Martin DB5 he was leasing. The Aston was designed to be exhilarating rather than relaxing, and even though Jason was quite proud of his driving skills, it still took a lot of mental energy to keep control of that powerful V8 engine. Seeing a police car in his rear-view mirror, he panicked briefly, even though he was only doing seventy. The car overtook him, and he prepared to be pulled over, but it sped on, chasing some other prey. As usual, on the M6 and A14, the car was attracting the attention of young men in BMWs or Audis who felt they had something to prove. One such driver was playing tag with him today, following close behind, occasionally overtaking and nipping in just in front. Evidently trying to show it wasn't always about how powerful or expensive a car was, it was about how well you drove it. Jason wasn't interested. Normally, when he was driving to Bernie's, he enjoyed opening up the throttle when the road was clear and he knew there weren't any speed traps waiting, but today, especially, he just wanted to get to Cambridge and rest. He craved the comfort of Bernie's sofa, a pizza from Deliveroo, a few beers and some deep sleep.

He pulled up outside her house, but one look at Bernie's face as she opened the door told him that none of that was going to happen. She looked flushed and anxious.

'I've just come off the phone from Aunty Gillian,' she said, even as he was walking through the door. 'She says we've got to go up to Sannah House straight away. She says things are too dangerous. You look like shit, by the way. Are you okay?'

'I'm okay, just tired, thanks,' said Jason, confused. What was this now? He thought the arrangement was that Bernie wasn't to be told about what had gone on. So why had Mrs McC said that things were 'too dangerous'? What had happened in the hours since he'd left the cottage?

'What exactly did your aunt say?' he asked.

'She said that she'd heard that this virus is worse than the Government is saying. Some medical friend of hers told her. We're to get up to Scotland as quickly as we can — tonight.'

'Oh, that's just rubbish,' said Jason, relieved. 'We're perfectly safe here.'

'She knew you'd say that, and she told me I should tell you, from her, that you had to do as you're told.'

So that was a clear message from Mrs McCracken then. Something had happened. They were in danger of being found out, and now they were on the run. He wasn't sure he was going to be able to cope with this.

'I can't drive now,' he said. 'I'm too tired.'

'You don't have to. It's okay. I've just booked tickets on the sleeper from London to Fort William. It'll be romantic!'

6

As soon as he heard Jason's name, Sam Flint knew Tranter was involved in the McCracken thing. And the neighbour had said that he drove a white sports car, so that proved it. It must be personal. Tranter's company had been sniffing around Sam's security business, and now it seemed he was involved with some scheme to swindle Terry out of money.

He sped through the country lanes from Ottershead to Hambourne, following the instructions from his satnav. Tranter must have hooked up with Gregory, he thought. That was it, of course. He'd never really trusted Gregory, with that superior smile of his. Too clever for his own good. Gregory knew all the businesses on Sam's security rota and must have fed them to Tranter so he could sabotage the business.

It was about two in the afternoon when Sam pulled up in the road, just in time to see Jason Tranter leaving his house and getting into his white Aston Martin DB5. The sight of it raised his anger levels another notch, but he stayed in his car, watching. Perhaps Tranter was on his way to meet Gregory. Catching the two of them together would be sweet.

Sam pulled out a few moments after Tranter. He mustn't make it too obvious that he was following. But then again, why not? In Sam's experience of dealing with people, things usually worked out better when the other person was feeling nervy and intimidated. It wouldn't hurt to be a nagging presence in Tranter's rear-view mirror. As it happened though, it was a tough job keeping on Tranter's tail. Not that they were driving fast, but other cars kept getting in the way at junctions. Lights changed, buses pulled out, all met with curses from Sam. As he'd predicted, Tranter seemed to be taking a route towards Bilston where Gregory's place was. But he drove straight through and onto the M6. It occurred to Sam that this might turn out to be a long journey. He checked his petrol gauge - there was just under half a tank. The question was, how much had Tranter got?

It was easier to keep behind him when they were on the M6. Even that made Sam mad, though. What was the point in having an Aston Martin, for chrissakes, if you stayed under seventy? Tranter was clearly the same wuss that he had been at school. Sam even tried to goad him into a bit of sport. Along the A14, he overtook and slid in front of Tranter's car and then applied the brakes. When Tranter started to overtake, Sam raced him side by side. But it was too easy. Tranter couldn't be encouraged to do more than eighty, however many times Sam tried the stunt. Whenever they were level with each other, Sam looked across at Jason, his face screwed up in an angry snarl. But the ginger bastard kept his eyes on the road ahead, concentrating like a bloody learner driver.

Time dragged for Sam. His ex-girlfriend, Letta, had left one of her CDs in the car. Ed Sheeran. He hated it, but played it anyway to pass the time. God, he'd like to punch that guy!

After about two hours, Sam checked his petrol gauge again. He only had about fifty miles left in the tank. If Tranter carried on much further, Sam would have to abandon the pursuit. The idea came to him, however, that if that looked like happening, he'd just get right behind Tranter's poxy Aston Martin and shunt his rear end. Sod the damage to both cars. He wasn't insured anyway. Who cared? He'd just punch up Tranter a bit and run off. There didn't seem to be a downside.

As he was pondering this, Jason indicated to turn off the A14 towards Cambridge. Sam became curious again. Where was he going, then? Was Gregory in Cambridge for some reason? He followed the car right through the city centre. This was alien territory to Sam. So many parks and open spaces in the middle of the city, old churches and colleges and far too many cyclists. If the long car journey had calmed Sam down at all, the cyclists with their trailing scarves and exaggerated ideas of how much road space they were entitled to topped up his anger again. Eventually they turned down a residential road lined with Victorian houses, trees and hedges. Sam saw Tranter pull up onto a paved-over garden of one of the houses. He cruised along the road, looking for somewhere to park nearby. It was a residents-only parking area, but that wouldn't have troubled Sam, had there been any spaces free to park. He drove up and down the street, looking in vain for a gap in the cars. He tried the next street along, but it was exactly the same. How did people live like this? Stuck up, stupid, selfish morons!

He found himself outside the residential area again, back on a road he had been on previously, with a large green playing field on one side. He was about ready to drive his car straight onto the grass and leave it there, but then he saw a sign for a multi-storey car park on his right. Sod it then, he thought, and drove through the entrance. He needed to climb three levels before he found a space. Sam felt hot, clammy, and frustrated by chasing after his prey for so long, only to be humiliated at the end by the parking conditions of Cambridge City Centre. He got out of his car, stretched himself and shouted 'Bastards!' as loud as he could into the echoey concrete car park. It made him feel better. A couple who had also just parked got back into their car quickly and locked the door. A young mother with two children hurried down the stairs to get away from any trouble.

Emerging back into the daylight, it was now a question of re-finding the road where Jason Tranter had parked. Sam had a pretty good sense of direction, but it all looked different on foot. He found the residential area, but he couldn't remember which street it had been, and they all looked similar. He tramped up and down streets, looking behind hedges for the white Aston Martin. Nearly forty minutes had passed since Jason Tranter had parked up when, standing at the end of one street, Sam caught just a flash of a ginger head of hair, about fifty metres away.

'I don't fucking believe it!' he muttered to himself. Tranter was just leaving the house with the same woman he had seen him with outside his house in Hambourne. She was locking her front door.

'So, she's in on it too!' No-one could hear him, but Sam wasn't even aware that was speaking his thoughts aloud. 'Shit! When they drive off. I'm going to lose them.'

But they didn't get in the car. Instead, they walked down the pavement, towards him. He nipped into a bus shelter and stood next to two ladies.

Less than a minute later, Tranter and the woman walked past the bus stop. The woman was pulling two suitcases on wheels. Tranter had one suitcase and a sports bag.

'Terry's money,' said Sam, under his breath, but still audibly. 'He looks a bit handy, but I reckon I could have him... if he was on his own. She's only a woman, but she might make a difference. I'm not having Ginger Tranter and his stupid girlfriend get one over on me. That is not happening, not today.'

The ladies at the bus stop listened to him, raised their eyebrows to each other and gripped their umbrellas firmly, but thankfully, Sam was already off following the couple.

7

'OK Robin, 3 p.m. then. Old Turn Junction. Jenny'

Sarah checked the phone message. It confirmed that she was in the right place and at the right time, and it reminded her that for the next hour or two she was reverting to her true identity, Robin Towers, rather than Sarah Headly. It was a mental switch that required some effort these days.

She scanned the scene. On a summer's day, the Birmingham canal basin would be a lively place with plenty going on: alfresco dining and tourists queuing for the Sea Life centre. But on this misty, wet Friday in March, there was hardly anyone about. She checked the few people she could see, making sure there was no-one she knew, no-one acting suspiciously, and no-one watching her. Jenny had been almost angry with her when she'd turned up at the pub last Christmas Eve, and she knew he'd be expecting her to be more careful this time. Meeting her commanding officer in person was a risk; if the wrong person saw them together, it could blow her cover. Sultan and Stuart, for instance, had met Detective Inspector Jeremy 'Jenny' Wren last summer. If either of them was to see her with him again, now, it might raise some tough questions. Still, she was pretty certain that Stuart would be at his office with Deepa, and it was a school day, so Sultan would be teaching. And besides, perhaps it wouldn't matter for much longer.

There was no sign of Jenny. Robin was thinking about getting a coffee from the Costa on the other side of the canal, as much to keep her hands warm as for something nice to drink, when she heard a sharp whistle coming from a narrowboat that was chugging slowly towards her.

'Christ alive!' she muttered. It was him, standing at the stern of the boat, next to a woman in a boiler suit and peaked cap who was holding the tiller.

'Ahoy there!' called Detective Inspector Jeremy Wren.

The boat pulled in towards the bank and slowed to a standstill a few metres ahead of her. Robin walked up and, taking Jenny's outstretched hand, stepped onto the boat. The woman at the tiller gave her a brief smile but was clearly more concerned with pulling the boat out away from the bank again.

'Let's go inside,' said Jenny, gesturing towards the cabin door.

'Bloody hell, Boss!' said Robin when they'd closed the door behind them. 'A narrowboat? Bit fancy, isn't it?'

Jenny laughed. 'It's my sister's. That's her outside. I just asked myself where could we talk privately in the middle of Brum? And I had this brainwave. Not bad, eh?'

Robin smiled. Jenny Wren liked to do things with a bit of flair. His sister did too, by the look of things. Robin felt like she had stepped into a museum piece, depicting how narrowboat life had been a century ago. A polished black stove pumped out heat, and traditional designs of flowers and castles decorated the wooden panels and cupboards. She sat down at a small table while Jenny poured a cup of tea.

'So what's up?' he asked. 'Something to report?'

Robin sighed.

'No, Boss. Nothing to report. That's kind of the point. It's been over a year now, and the only thing we've found out is that Sultan's brother was banged up for a failed attack on an airport in Canada. Sultan's made a new life here, and there's no evidence that he's any kind of threat. I've got to know him and he's a big softie. You know that - you even met him yourself. It's ludicrous. This all started because some paranoid fool raised an alarm because a few lads with beards were meeting in a pub, and the local wit had called them "The Taliban". It's been a waste of police time. I just think it's time to wrap up the operation, don't you?'

8

Jason was coming around to the idea of a dash up to Scotland on the night train. He was still deadbeat tired. Bernie had made him a restorative cup of tea, but there was hardly time to drink it before they had to get out of the door. He consoled himself with the idea that he'd be able to sleep on the train, as long as the waves of panic that still broke over him every fifteen minutes allowed him to snatch some rest.

Bernie seemed to treat it all as a great adventure. In her mind, this trip was all about avoiding the deadly virus that was about to sweep the country. Not that she was worried about the actual disease — it mostly affected the elderly and infirm, apparently. What appealed to her was the idea that they were acting on some inside information, unavailable to the general public, and taking steps to protect themselves. They were being the smart characters in a zombie apocalypse film, the ones that took swift action and were still around when the end credits rolled.

'Remember, we've got to be careful not to look like we're panicking,' she said as they put on their coats. 'We don't want to trigger mass hysteria or anything. We just need to keep calm and get ourselves out of danger.'

Jason thought about challenging her logic. If this really was going to be a serious medical crisis, what was the point of relocating somewhere where food supplies were sporadic and medical help was non-existent? And how long would it take before they could return to a post-plague England? They had only packed enough clothes for a week. But he didn't challenge her because he knew that Mrs McCracken's call wasn't really to warn them about the pandemic. It was a warning to him that there was some danger concerning the dead man that they had buried, or rather, that he had buried. Danger, coming either from the man's associates, or from the police. That felt like a much more real danger than the virus.

His mind span in turmoil. Part of him knew that at some point he was going to have to persuade the old lady to speak to the police. If the man was involved in organised crime, Jason didn't rate his own chances, or the old lady's, of outsmarting a vengeful mob. Eventually, they would catch up with one of them, or both. On the other hand, if Mrs McCracken had got it wrong, and the man wasn't a criminal, there was a much more likely chance that the police would come investigating a missing person. They *thought* they'd been careful, and that there was no way of tracing his last movements to Mrs McCracken's cottage, but in his present state of mind, he couldn't guarantee that he hadn't told someone where he was going. And if the police did turn up at Mrs McC's, what then? They *thought* they'd been careful to remove any evidence of him being there, but they hadn't been forensic about it. There might be fingerprints, fibres from his clothes, anything. Who knew what a thermal imaging camera trained on the asparagus bed would reveal? If they found the body, the police would never believe that he'd died shortly after falling down the stairs. Surely it would be better if he and Mrs McC confessed to the crime of unlawful burial of a body, saying that they did it in a panic, than being arrested on suspicion of murder?

These were the thoughts in Jason's head as they walked up the road. He didn't really notice the man who stared at him and then quickly nipped into the bus shelter. He really didn't hear the muttering as he and Bernie passed the shelter. Not consciously, anyway. But perhaps his subconscious noticed these things and turned up the dial on his anxiety. And then he *did* notice soft footsteps behind him, some way off but roughly in step with his own. As he quickened his pace, the footsteps quickened as well.

Bernie noticed the change in pace.

'Are you okay? We've got plenty of time...'

'I think we're being followed.' he said.

She turned and looked round.

'I don't think so. Why ever would you think that?'

9

'Well, hang on a minute, Robin,' said Jenny. 'Let's just wind this back. You say this has been a waste of police time, but remember how sensitive things were eighteen months ago? Planes getting grounded at Gatwick because of illegal aerial drones. And then we find that one of these lads is a bit of a drone expert. That set alarm bells ringing with the Governor. You know how worried she gets about Birmingham Airport. Okay, the idea of a terrorist cell operating out of a pub in Hambourne was unlikely, but what if we'd ignored a tip-off and then got burned? Heads would have rolled. Anyway, your early reports didn't dismiss the threat. If I recall correctly, you thought there might be something in the allegation.'

'Well, I was wrong,' said Robin. She stared at Wren, wondering whether she should admit that back last year she had swung the lead a bit, deliberately misleading her boss so that she could take it easy, while she recovered from her previous harrowing assignment. Wren stared back for a while, with a look suggested that she didn't need to admit anything; he already knew. He was playing with her.

He started again. 'And then one suspect suddenly starts flashing the cash, quits his job...'

'He'd won the lottery,' interrupted Robin.

'So he said!'

'We had it checked out,' she reminded him.

'Eventually, yes,' Jenny admitted. 'When he got himself involved in a hush-hush gang of millionaires in the South of France and there were people getting murdered left, right and centre. You can't say that was a waste of police time, Robin.'

'Jason and Sultan weren't responsible for any of that,' she said. 'They were the good guys, remember? You even bought them drinks.'

'But as I told you shortly afterwards, I had reasons for keeping your cover intact and continuing to observe them.'

'Really? Until I found out that Sultan was actually Jamil Khan, brother of suspected terrorist Reza Khan, you had no real reason to keep me there.'

'Apart from not being able to trace his records. But anyway, all that's changed. We sorted out the story of his change of identity, thanks to our friends in the Royal Canadian Mounted Police. They helped arrange Jamil's new identity after they arrested his brother.'

'So, all looking good then? Nothing suspicious after all.'

'Yeah, well, you say that.' Wren pulled a manilla file from his briefcase under the table. He opened it and showed Robin a handful of photographs. 'These come from a separate investigation we're running. A house in Lozells we've been watching.'

The photos showed a man approaching or walking away from a doorway in a modern terraced street. It was unmistakeably Sultan. The photos all had time and date stamps.

'So?' said Robin.

'Your friend has visited this house for the last three Saturdays. It's the house of Amina Bhuta, currently serving five and a half years for sharing extremist material online.'

'I see.' She stared out of the window of the boat for a moment. 'I guess we won't be wrapping it up just yet, then. That's disappointing.'

'I haven't heard you complaining up till now.' Jenny Wren had a twinkle in his eye. 'I thought you were enjoying hanging around Jason Tranter and his jet-set millionaire chums? Come off it, Robin. Most officers would kill you and climb over your dead body to get your job.'

'Yeah, well, it's not so easy spending time with Jason these days. He's got a new girlfriend, and he hardly spends any time with me... or the others.'

'Hmm... That's a shame. Is that why you've lost interest in this assignment?'

'No, boss!' Robin protested. But while she worked on suppressing a blush, her mind flashed back to the passionate fumble on Jason's stairs, a few days ago, when she realised that despite Bernie being on the scene, Jason still had feelings for her... or Sarah, at least... and unless she could end this operation, she was likely going to lose him.

The narrowboat's engine chugged on, filling the pause in conversation.

'So, look,' Wren started again, sounding more sympathetic. 'Just keep it up a few weeks more. We could just pull Jamil Ahmed... Khan... Sultan in, ask him to explain what's going on, what he's doing. But we're not ready to blow our surveillance of the Lozells house just yet. For now, I need you to keep tabs on him. Do you understand?'

Robin was looking down at her phone, where a message had just buzzed in.

'That's going to become difficult,' she said. 'Boris has just ordered all the pubs to close. Friday night at The Pig is cancelled!'

10

Sam Flint knew he had to concentrate on Tranter and his woman, but the thrill he got from frightening the two ladies at the bus stop still registered with him. It was a warm, familiar feeling, but also a dangerous one. He knew that was when he was this wired, he could easily lose the plot and indulge himself in a display of random violence. He mustn't get distracted.

'I'd better keep quiet,' he said, still audibly, to himself.

He was good at tailing people on foot. He remembered a trick he'd learnt from an old drug dealer in Oldbury when they'd followed a kid they suspected of being a police informant. 'Watch the ears,' he thought, without even moving his lips this time. Sure enough, something about Tranter's ears, a slight twitch or a pinkening perhaps, told Sam that Tranter suspected he was being followed.

'Quickening up, are you?' he thought, and smiled to himself. 'You ain't giving mc thc slip this timc.'

He saw the pair exchange words. 'They're gonna look round,' he thought, and sure enough, a second later, Tranter did. Just a glance, but long enough. Did he recognise him? It probably didn't matter.

Sam let the gap between them widen. The road was straight, and he had no problem following them as they crossed side-roads and turned at junctions until they approached the arched frontage of Cambridge Railway Station.

'Shit!' he said out loud. There were two problems now: first, the area in front of the station looked busier and it would be easier to lose them and second, he didn't know much about train stations and how they worked. He sprinted to catch up. He saw them enter the station and walk straight for the ticket barriers. The woman held her phone up to a sensor, and the barriers opened and let them through.

'Jump the barriers or get a ticket?' he wondered. There were too many people around to jump the barriers unnoticed. He looked at the ticket machines and the ticket office. There were queues and, he realised, he hadn't a clue where he was buying a ticket for.

'Sod it!' he said and headed for the barriers. A guard had just let a man with a pushchair and a small child on his arm through a wide barrier at the side, and Sam swerved and tried to tailgate. The guard blocked him.

'Okay mate,' said Sam. 'You don't want any trouble, do you?'

The look on Sam's face, his build, and how close he was standing all suggested levels of trouble that the tired, underpaid guard was not prepared to contemplate, and looking down at his shoes, he waved Sam through. He'd be someone else's problem at the end of the journey.

Sam Flint scanned the platform. Tranter and his girlfriend were nowhere to be seen. He could feel his anger rising as he thought that he might lose them again. A train was approaching the opposite platform and just before it obscured the people waiting to board, Sam saw Jason Tranter standing, staring straight back at him across the tracks.

11

As he'd expected, Jason felt a little more relaxed when he sat back in the train carriage. For the next forty-five minutes, he could 'let the train take the strain' as his dad used to say.

'I saw that bloke that I thought was following us at the station,' he told Bernie, who was leaning against him. 'He was waiting for the down train, though. Or the up train. Whichever one that is going the opposite direction to us. So you were right, I was just being paranoid.'

'I've not seen you like this, Jason. Are you okay?'

'I'm not sure whether I've been punched, bored or countersunk, to be honest. I guess I'm just over-tired.'

Bernie looked at him and frowned.

'It's an expression we used to use at the factory,' Jason explained. 'Do we get the Underground from King's Cross to Euston?'

'You must be joking,' she answered. 'This train's bad enough. The tube'll be a breeding ground for the virus. It's just a ten-minute walk. Will you be okay with that?'

Jason raised an eyebrow and gave her a hurt look.

12

Sam could just see Tranter and his girlfriend in the next carriage through the connecting door. It had been a mad sprint over the platform bridge at Cambridge, but now he could rest up. At each of the eighteen stops on the Thameslink route, he had to check that his quarry didn't leave the train, but they didn't, and a sense of unease grew in him as they approached London.

It was dawning on Sam that what he was doing was mad, even by his standards. On the spur of the moment, he had driven across the country following Tranter, left his car in a multi-storey in Cambridge and was now on a train to London. He had no idea how this day was going to end. At some point, he would presumably confront Jason, get his bag off him — the one with Terry's money. He'd probably do him over, depending on the conditions. He wouldn't do it here on the train. But if he could get him later on, in a quiet street or somewhere like that, preferably alone, then he could do a proper job. Then he'd have to get back to his car in Cambridge and get home. If he'd been back in the Midlands, all this would have been fine, but he wasn't comfortable being so far away from his home ground. This uneasy feeling was all Tranter's fault, and it made him more determined to see the thing through.

At King's Cross, he watched the couple get off the train and followed them at a safe distance towards the barriers. He could see two police officers standing on the other side. He glanced around him.

'Mate, can I just have a look at that?' he said to a man getting his ticket ready for the barrier and snatched the ticket. He ran for the barrier and pushed his way through the crowd. Emerging on the other side, Sam went straight towards the officers.

'Bloke back there is causing trouble, mate,' he said, pointing to the man he'd just robbed, then walked briskly into the station hall, scanning the crowds for Tranter and his girlfriend, while the police went to investigate the trouble at the barriers.

'There he is, the ginger bastard!' he said, spotting his quarry and following them out into the London streets.

It was easier tailing them in London than it had been in Cambridge. There were more people, but the noisy traffic meant that Sam could keep closer without being detected. After ten minutes, they walked into the entrance hall at Euston Station. Sam's limited knowledge of London was enough to tell him that this was the terminus where trains left for the Midlands, and Sam started to wonder whether Tranter was about to take his girlfriend back to Hambourne, via Wolverhampton.

'The evil bastard!' he said. His anger had been reignited, and he was thinking out loud again. 'He must have clocked that I'd tailed him to Cambridge and now he's trying to shake me off by going back home on trains. I'll fucking kill him.' A shiver went through him, as he realised it wasn't just a turn of phrase. Something had snapped. He needed to punish Jason Tranter hard for this stupid goose chase. Killing him would be fine.

'Or his girlfriend,' he said to himself.

But Tranter didn't go towards the platform where the Wolverhampton train waited. He walked to the end of the great hall, to Platform One, where screens displayed that the Caledonian Sleeper service was boarding.

'Where's this train go to?' Sam asked the guard, as he watched Jason and the girl walk down the ramp towards the train.

'Scotland, sonny. Heard of it?' the guard replied, but looking at Sam's face, added, 'Glasgow, Edinburgh, Fort William, Inverness and Aberdeen, sir.'

'I need to get on it,' said Sam.

'You'll be lucky... I'm afraid the train is fully booked, sir.'

'I don't think you understand,' said Sam, rubbing the knuckles of his right hand.

'You can try the ticket office, sir,' said the guard, making eye contact with a police officer standing ten metres away. 'They sometimes get last-minute cancellations. The train doesn't depart for another thirty minutes, so you may get lucky. They'll be able to look after you better than I can.'

Sam saw the police officer, considered his options, and walked over to the ticket office, where he asked for a ticket for the sleeper train.

The assistant winced and said, 'Which destination?'

'Scotland. All the way,' said Sam.

The assistant explained the train split at Edinburgh, and three portions then went on to Fort William, Inverness and Aberdeen. 'So... er...?'

'The last one.'

The assistant looked doubtful but punched the keys again. 'Well, you are in luck! We've had a cancellation for Aberdeen. It's a club cabin, so you should have a very comfortable trip.'

It meant nothing to Sam, but he got out his credit card and paid his fare for the first time that day. The guard at the end of Platform One looked disappointed to see the man in the red tee-shirt and grey jogging bottoms again.

'Coach G, sir,' he said, with something less than his customary cheerfulness.

13

'Are you there, Sarah?'

'We can't hear you.'

'Can you hear us?'

'We can see you, but we can't hear you.'

'You need to come off mute.'

Sarah stared at her laptop. She could see three panels on the screen, one showing Sultan sitting in front of a bookcase, another showing the tops of Stuart and Deepa's heads — they appeared to be sitting on a sofa, but their camera was tilted at the wrong angle — and the third showing her own face. She could see a line of icons and menu options, but it wasn't immediately obvious how to stop herself from being muted. Eventually, she found how to do it, and joined her first ever Zoom call.

'Thanks for organising this, Stuart and Deepa,' said Sarah. 'So, is this it then? Is this what we're reduced to? Remote drinking sessions? Cheers, everyone!' She held up a glass and a bottle of wine in front of the camera.

'Cheers,' said Sultan, holding up a mug decorated with the words 'World's best teacher'. 'Tea for me. Never have alcohol in the house. Drinking alone is a slippery slope, Sarah.'

Sarah ignored the jibe. She was too busy trying to work out if there was a way of getting a screen grab of Sultan's picture. She wanted to inspect the view of the bookcase behind him more closely.

'You alright, Sarah?' said Stuart. 'You look as if you're having problems.'

'Sorry guys,' she said. 'No, it's fine. I'm just getting too old for new technology, I think.'

'Rubbish,' said Stuart. 'Sultan managed it and he's way older than you.'

'Hey! Hold on there. I'm a spring onion, me,' said Sultan.

'You mean spring chicken,' chipped in Deepa.

'I know what the correct saying is, Deepa, but kindly respect my vegetarianism, please. It's what keeps me so lithe and trim. Not like some people who might struggle to step onto a canal boat.'

He beamed. His eyes stared directly into the camera, and Sarah knew he was aiming his look at her. Her mind raced. He'd seen her in Birmingham then. Had he seen Wren, too? If so, had he recognised him? Was her cover blown after all, then?

'You what?' she said and grinned back at him. There was no need to panic. 'You spying on me or something? Were you doing in Birmingham yesterday, then? What were you doing there?'

'Helping out with a school trip to the Sea Life centre,' said Sultan. 'Penguins and shit. I was right then? I thought it was you! Very mysterious, Miss Headly, stepping onto boats on a Friday afternoon. What's that all about?'

'None of your business, really, but I'd been doing some shopping and was just wandering along the canal, thinking of getting a coffee, when a narrowboat pulled up and an old friend called for me to jump on board. Did you see him?'

'Maybe,' said Sultan. 'There were a couple, weren't there?'

Sarah decided that Sultan probably hadn't recognised Wren. She'd left an opening for him and he hadn't taken it.

'Yes. The boat's lovely. I had a happy hour chugging along. I must tell Jason about it. It would be right up his street... so to speak. Perhaps we could persuade him to buy one.'

'Where is his Lordship this weekend? Anyone know?' Sultan asked.

Sarah felt relieved that the subject had moved on; she could feel her heart resuming its normal beat. Her cover was probably still intact.

'Stuart had a message from him this evening, didn't you, Stuart,' said Deepa. Stuart looked too deep in thought to answer, so Deepa added, 'Apparently, Jason and Bernie are off on a trip to Scotland on the sleeper train.'

'Well, we all know where they're headed, then,' said Sultan.

'Scotland?' suggested Sarah.

'Gretna Green,' said Sultan. 'Eloped. It had to happen. She's whisked him off for a quickie wedding. You watch.'

'Eloped?' said Sarah in a higher voice than she had planned. 'Why would they need to elope? They're both adults. And eloping's just not a thing anymore. Anyway, Jason's not going to get married. They've only known each other since Christmas.'

Sultan was grinning again.

'She'll move quick,' he said. 'That Bernie's no fool. She won't want to let him slip through her fingers. I'm really worried about him.'

Sarah was about to say that he didn't look really worried, but just then, her phone buzzed on the table. 'Talk of the devil. That's him now. I'm just going on mute again.'

'I've just thought of something,' said Stuart while they watched Sarah silently talking on the phone. 'If Jason does buy a narrowboat, he should let Sultan drive it. Then he'd be the spring onion bargee.'

'I never had you down for a racist, Stuart,' said Sultan with a mock look of hurt on his face.

14

The Club Class 'onboard host' showed Sam to his cabin, explained how the key card worked and started to go through the features of the room: the climate control, the power points, the USB adaptors, and was just about to describe the en-suite toilet that doubled as a shower when Sam decided enough was enough.

'Alright feller, piss off!' he said.

'I'm sorry sir?' He put on an indignant voice as Sam pushed him back into the corridor, but he wasn't really shocked by the young man's brutish behaviour. The Club Class passengers were frequently ruder than those in the Standard seats.

Once alone, Sam threw himself onto the double bed for a moment and stared at the ceiling. He didn't know what he was going to do next. Jason Tranter was somewhere on the train, but he had no clue where, and no idea which station he would get off at. He didn't know much about the train at all. He looked at a guide to the train that had the host had left on the bed. There was a lounge car where they served drinks. Sooner or later, Tranter would make his way to the bar; that stood to reason. So best make his way to the lounge car then. But first the toilet. Sam wished he'd let that old codger explain how the en-suite toilet worked.

Ten minutes later, as the train was just pulling out of Euston Station, Sam was sitting in the lounge bar with a can of beer. It was a smart, soulless place that seemed designed to discourage people from lingering. It gradually filled up with passengers, all rather more smartly dressed than Sam, in his customary hoodie and jogging bottoms.

A smartly dressed, middle-aged man dressed in a shirt and tie and a tweed jacket approached the table where Sam was sitting.

'Good evening. This looks like the only seat left in the carriage. Would you mind if I joined you?'

The beer must have already had a calming effect on Sam's mind, because instead of letting out an abusive stream, he gave a bored flick of his head to suggest that he didn't mind.

'Thank you very much,' said the man. 'That's very kind of you. F William or Abba?'

Sam screwed his face up, not understanding the question.

'Your destination, Fort William or Aberdeen?' explained the man. 'Actually, let me guess, Aberdeen?'

Sam had forgotten; the two names meant nothing to him. He fished in his pocket for his ticket.

'Yeah, Aberdeen,' said Sam, displaying the ticket.

'I thought so. I can usually tell. Silly game of mine. The clue is in the build, you see. Thin, wiry chaps are usually off trekking the Highlands and Islands from Fort William, while strong well-built chaps like yourself are bound for Aberdeen. Are you in oil?'

Sam looked at the man as if he was mad.

'On the rigs, I mean. I don't mean like a sardine!' The man laughed. 'Here, can I get you another beer? It's the least I can do after I've spoiled your peace and quiet. In fact, we ought to order some food, you know. They'll be really busy later and it will take ages. They do a good chicken supreme, very cheap. Let me pay. It's nice to have someone to talk to."

Sam didn't object. This bloke was a bore, but a free meal was a free meal and if he was planning to stay in this bar for the duration of the trip, or at least until Tranter showed up, then he might as well eat.

'Cheers. When does the train get to Scotland then?' said Sam after the food had been ordered and the drinks had been served.

'Well, we cross the border shortly after midnight, and then, of course, the train goes on to Edinburgh, where it splits in the small hours of the morning, while we are all tucked up asleep in our cabins. And that's where we part company, I'm afraid...' He pointed to the rear of the train. '... your portion of the train goes on to Aberdeen...' and then to the front carriages '...and my little portion goes on to Fort William, arriving at about ten in the morning. There's another portion that goes to Inverness, but that's a different story. They've got their own lounge car and everything.'

'So wait,' said Sam, who was struggling to take in the implications of this information. 'There's two bars on the train? And three bits of train? Two bits share this bar, and another bit has its own bar?'

'You've got it,' said the man and went on to describe exactly how the three-way split of the train worked and gave details of the shunting procedure at Edinburgh. He was, apparently, something of an expert.

Sam didn't listen. He was processing the information he already had. If Jason didn't show up in the club car, it meant he was headed for Inverness, wherever that was. If he came into the carriage using the rear door, then his cabin or seat was in the portion of the train headed for Aberdeen, the same destination as Sam. And if Jason came in from the door at the front of the carriage, that meant he was headed for Fort William, like Mr

Tweed Jacket here. Sam just needed to be in the right portion of the train when it split in Edinburgh.

'I only really know the Fort William journey,' the man was saying. 'I've got a little cottage near there, so I'm a frequent traveller, you might say. It's not what it used to be, this train, I'm afraid. All new rolling stock, you see? Not as cosy as the old train. And they've stopped the shared cabins, haven't they?'

'If you say so,' Sam mumbled, and took a swig of his beer.

'Oh yes, it's ridiculous. Only people booking tickets together can share a cabin now, so if you're travelling alone, you have to book an entire cabin to yourself. Very comfy but extortionate! They used to let people of the same sex share a cabin. Much better. I've never objected to roughing it with a stranger.'

Sam's attention was caught by the swish of the front carriage door. For a brief moment, Jason Tranter was standing in the doorway, and their eyes met. Then Tranter turned away and was back off up the corridor. Back to his cabin and locking his door, he guessed.

The food arrived.

'You could show me your cabin, after,' Sam said to the man.

'My pleasure,' said the man, smiling.

15

'Okay, so let's just walk up the hill and I'll show you, yah?'

At first Dodge Mhlongo wondered whether she was taking the piss. Was she trying to mimic the South African accent with the 'yah' and an upward inflection at the end of the sentence? He'd heard people do it before. But as Gracie led him along the track, he realised that she really spoke this way. British accents were confusing.

'You from the island, then?' he asked.

'God yes,' she said, striding ahead up the hill, carrying one of his bags. She was fit. He'd give her that. 'I mean no, I was like born in Guilford, but I've been here eight months now, so practically a local, y'know. What about you?'

'Born in Bloemfontein'

'That's Africa, right?'

'South Africa, yes.'

'Yeah, but Africa — amazing! You know that there is a deep connection between the Celtic and the African peoples, right?'

'Honey, there's a deep connection between the African people and every other bugger on the planet when you look into it. But how about you and me making a deep connection?' He didn't say any of this, but the words ran through his head automatically, from force of habit more than anything else. He didn't make these sorts of remarks out loud anymore.

'Oh yah,' she went on, 'one per cent of Scots have DNA that is shared with Berber and Egyptian peoples, and the Gaelic language has African roots. And the music, obviously. So some of your ancestors might be here, you might meet them. Isn't that totes amazing?'

It's totes bollocks, he thought, but said nothing. He was too out of breath. He'd let himself go a bit these last couple of months, but he reckoned that life on a Scottish island would soon tone him up again, blow away the cobwebs.

'And here it is, Keeper's Cottage,' she said. 'Not a bad location, eh?'

A perfect location, he thought. A vantage point where he could keep his eye on what was going on amongst the scattering of houses and outbuildings that accounted for most of the dwellings on the island of Sannah. Especially the big house; that was the brief, after all. Security for the latest potential Rara Avis acquisition. That, and sussing out the opportunities for game. Behind the cottage, the hills and moorlands looked promising. But more than anything else, the seclusion appealed to Dodge. Set apart up here, no-one would disturb him, and that suited him perfectly.

Gracie's tour of the cottage didn't take long. The front door opened into a lounge with a kitchenette in one corner. There was a door leading to a small bathroom at one end of the room. At the other end, a drawn curtain marked the entrance to the bedroom.

'So, that's it basically,' said Gracie. 'Now, is there anything I can help you with? Anything at all?'

'No thanks.' There was a time when Dodge Mhlongo wouldn't have been able to resist an open goal like that, but lately he had no appetite for overtures, still less for actual liaisons. It was a change he hadn't adjusted to yet, almost as if a limb had gone missing or his hair had dropped out.

He watched Gracie walking back down the hill, then stepped into the cottage, closing the door behind him.

'Oh Beccy. Oh Beccy, Beccy, Beccy.' he moaned softly.

16

Bernie was already asleep on the upper bed of the cabin when Jason returned and locked their door. Should he wake her up to tell her who he'd just seen? Surely, there could be only one reason that the man who appeared to be waiting for a different train at Cambridge Station was here, on this train? He must have been following them. But Jason knew she would reassure him, say it's just a coincidence, that he was being paranoid and that he should get some sleep.

That was easy for her. She hadn't buried a man. She wasn't wanted by gangsters, or the police. She could sleep easy, not knowing anything about this.

He lay down on the lower berth, trying to calm himself down and think rationally about his situation. Could it be a coincidence? No, he didn't think so. Life wasn't like that. And anyway, that stare the man had just given him from the club car - that wasn't the stare of a random stranger. It was a triumphant stare. But who was he? Who was he working for? The gangsters or the police?

The man wore a hoodie and jogging trousers and looked roughly the same age as Jason. He looked mean. His hair was cut short in one of those styles that make it look like it was done for a dare. Gangsters or police? He could be either.

He was dining with someone; Jason had only seen him from behind, but he looked older and smarter, wearing a jacket. Perhaps it was foolish to think in stereotypes, but that man didn't give off gangster energy. Police then. A plain-clothes officer and his superior. Could that be right? Two of them following Jason up to Scotland? Surely, if they suspected him of being involved in a missing person case, they would just question him, not follow him? But the actions of the police were a mystery to Jason, especially since he'd found out that his best friend, Sarah, was an undercover cop, investigating who knew what?

The train sped on through the darkness and Jason lay awake. For the first time since winning the lottery, nearly a year ago, it felt like he had a problem that his money couldn't help him with. He'd done something stupid and criminal, and it left him feeling frightened and ashamed. He needed to talk to Sarah. Time to come clean.

He slid out of his bed again and opened the cabin door as quietly as he could. Quickly, he scanned the corridor to check there was no-one in either direction. He walked quickly in the opposite direction to the club car. There was a communal toilet at the end of the carriage and Jason slipped in, unseen, and locked the door. He found Sarah's number on his phone.

'Sarah?'

'Oh, hi Jason! Hang on a minute...'

Jason thought he heard voices for a second, as Sarah fumbled to mute her Zoom call.

'That's better. Are you okay, Jason?'

'Not really, no. I've been stupid, I think.' He paused, staring at himself in the toilet mirror. God, he looked a wreck! 'Look, first of all, can you just tell me? Do you know any reason the police might be tailing me?'

'What? No! Don't be silly. What's going on?'

'Don't be silly'. The words, and hearing Sarah say them, had a dual effect. On one hand, here was the reassurance he'd been looking for. Yes, he probably was being silly. Coincidences do happen, and the bloke he'd seen at Cambridge was probably just as surprised as he was to be face-to-face again on the Caledonian Sleeper. Now that he thought of it, the look on the man's face could have been one of incredulity rather than triumph. On the other hand, as he stared at himself in the mirror, he knew there was no way he could tell Sarah how silly he'd already been; how he'd buried a body in Mrs McCracken's asparagus bed.

'Oh, it's probably nothing. I'm on a train going up to Scotland.'

'Nice. Any particular reason?'

'Ah... just a short break. You know.'

'And you've rung me because...?'

'Sorry, yes. The thing is, I had this creepy feeling I was being followed. I've had it all day, but it's bollocks. I can see that already.' He described the man in Cambridge, how they'd clocked each other across the railway tracks and how he had just seen him again in the Club Car. and how the strange look he'd given him had shaken him.

'And you're sure it was the same man?' Sarah sounded interested.

'Yes, but you know — just a coincidence. I guess I noticed him because he was just wearing a hoodie. Everyone else had coats on.'

'Wait, what colour hoodie was it?' asked Sarah.

'Purple, why?'

'Probably nothing... just trying to get a picture. Look, here's what I want you to do...'

17

Sarah rejoined the Zoom call, looking a bit flushed.

'You okay?' asked Deepa.

'Yes, thanks,' said Sarah 'Sultan, did you just say you were really worried about Jason?'

'I did,' said Sultan. 'I think the boy is about to be fleeced.'

'Great,' said Sarah. 'Well, that makes two of us. And I need your help. Can you drive over? We're going to rescue him. Oh, and Stu, can you remember back just before Christmas when that bloke came into your office and assaulted you? Can you remember what he looked like?'

'Erm...' said Stuart.

'Tall, well-built, short hair, shaved round the back and sides, grey jogging pants and a purple hoodie,' said Deepa.

'Deepa, you're a star,' said Sarah.

Thirty minutes later, Sarah and Sultan were heading north on the M6.

'No way,' said Sultan. 'That's way further than Gretna. I'm not driving all the way up there! Are you mad? How far is the next exit? We're heading back.'

Sarah had only just told him that their destination was somewhere in the Western Highlands of Scotland.

'It's okay. I'll share the driving when I've sobered up a bit. Luckily, I've only had a couple of glasses of wine. I'll be okay in an hour or two.'

'Where are we going to sleep? I haven't even got a toothbrush. How long are we...'

'I don't know. I haven't thought it all through. I'm making it up as I go along.'

'But this is crazy! You are a crazy woman! What are you hoping to achieve?'

'Come off it, Sultan! You must have known that Jason and I had a bit of a thing going, last year. Out on the boat, in the Med.'

Sultan grunted in a non-committed way.

'So, we both thought it was just a holiday fling — the result of too much sun, sea and Sambuca, you know,' continued Sarah, 'And we didn't want to mess up a friendship, so we called a halt to it. But just lately... well, let's just say we haven't quite resolved everything.'

'Aye-aye. So you think you're going to crash their elopement then?'

'Something like that. But they're not "eloping", as we've been through. They're not even getting married as far as I know. But she's not right for Jason.'

'Hmm. Why were you asking Stuart about the bloke that punched him?'

'Okay, well, that's why Jason called me. He thought someone was trying to intimidate him on the Sleeper train. His description sounded familiar, that's all.'

18

Sam Flint became aware of someone touching his feet. He lay still and heard the rhythm train slowing down. He opened his eyes.

'We there, then?' he said.

The man in the tweed jacket nodded. His face was streaked with tears.

Sam checked the clock on his phone. It was just after nine-thirty in the morning. He got up off the cabin bed, pulled on his hoodie and trainers and splashed some water over his face in the little sink. The train was slowing down to a halt.

'Okay then,' said Sam. 'You stay here till someone finds you. If you say anything, I promise you, I will find you and I will kill you. You know that, don't you?'

The man in the tweed jacket nodded vigorously. Sam left the cabin and closed the door behind him. The man, still in the tweed jacket he'd worn all night, gagged by a towel and with his hands bound behind his back with his own necktie, sobbed quietly at last. Something he had been too frightened to do while Sam was in the cabin.

Sam was by the door as the train pulled into Fort William station. As soon as the doors were released, he jumped down and scanned up and down the platform. He was the first passenger to leave the train. He walked towards the station building at the end of the platform and found a quiet corner where he could watch the other passengers as they disembarked. A few other people were also standing around waiting to meet the new arrivals; friends, family, taxi drivers. Gradually these patient onlookers met up with their respective travellers, exchanged greetings and departed the station, until only one woman and Sam remained. He looked over at her. A bit posh for him, he thought, but he wouldn't say no. She caught his glance, gave him a superior smirk, and turned towards the train.

The stream of travellers had dwindled to a trickle. Cleaners were boarding the train.

'Come on, Tranter,' thought Sam. 'Him and his bird have overslept. A toss-up now whether someone finds them or that sad bastard first. I ought not be here when they find him, though.' He shuffled from one foot to another and looked around for potential routes he could take if he suddenly needed to leave the station in a hurry.

The posh woman fiddled with her phone, keeping one eye on the train and occasionally glancing at Sam.

There was a commotion by one of the carriages. A cleaner was calling for the station guard to come over. A few minutes later, the guard escorted the man in the tweed jacket along the platform towards the station hall.

'No, it's quite alright,' the man was saying. 'It's not a problem... my own mistake, really. Most embarrassing. I've learned my lesson now. It won't happen again.'

As they reached the hall, the man saw Sam standing waiting. He blanched a little but carried on talking slightly louder.

'Thank you, so, so much,' he said to the guard as he passed through the hall. 'I would rather this was kept quiet... I'm sure you would too. We'll say no more about it, eh?'

Sam watched the man leave the station and climb into a taxi, and his lips formed a brief smile. The woman seemed to notice it and looked at him quizzically, but Sam turned and looked back at the train. No more passengers were emerging. His smile reverted to a scowl.

'Seems like they've given us both the slip,' said the woman.

Sam turned back to her.

'Who?' he asked.

'Bernie and Jason,' she said. 'That is who you're waiting for, isn't it?'

'No!' said Sam, and then, 'How do you know?'

'You've been following them since Cambridge,' she said. 'I saw you there. And at Euston. You're quite... noticeable... you know?'

'Where are they, then?' Sam demanded.

'How should I know?' said the woman. 'They've given me the slip, too. I'm sort of following them as well — not deliberately — and a little more unobtrusively than you, I'd say. They must have got off the train at an earlier stop.'

'Shit!' shouted Sam loudly. The whole futility of the last twenty-four hours had come crashing in on him. His car was in Cambridge, he was somewhere in Scotland and his only reason for being there had gone up in smoke. He had no idea where Tranter was, and no hope of finding him. He punched a nearby temporary display sign, and it fell to the floor with a clatter.

The woman walked towards him, grabbed him by the arm and made him walk towards the exit, just as the station guard came out to investigate the noise.

'Don't get upset, sweetie,' she said to Sam, as they walked out into the car park. 'I know where they're headed. I'm headed there too. So if you want to see them, you'll just have to stick with me, won't you?'

They walked across the car park and through a subway that led to the centre of Fort William. Sam was bewildered. He wasn't used to being pushed around by a woman. Who was she, and what was she doing, following Jason Tranter?

'The thing is,' said Rebecca Leyden-Fuller, 'I've been sat in a freezing reclining chair for the last ten hours, and before I go any further, I need a warm shower and an hour or two on a bed. I've just booked a room in that hotel, over there. Care to join me?'

Sam cheered up. It was the second such offer he'd had recently, and this time he was inclined to accept.

19

'I can't believe you have no music in your car,' said Sarah, somewhere near Carlisle.

'Oh! Pardon me. I'm sorry that the car you've hijacked doesn't quite meet your specifications, Madam. If I'd known we'd be driving all night, I'd have swapped cars and driven the Jaguar tonight. The Panda is just a runaround for when I pop out to the shops, doncha know?'

Sultan seemed to have settled into the situation and was happily teasing Sarah again.

'But no CDs? No Bluetooth? And the radio doesn't work. What's that about?'

'Kids snapped the aerial off, didn't they?'

'Tsk. So if you did have some music, what would it be?'

'Dunno. Never listen to music. Waste of time.'

'What? You must like some music. Bhangra? Classical Indian?'

'And here we are, straight into the racial stereotypes. What next? Bollywood soundtracks? No Sarah, I'm just not into music, okay?'

They drove on in silence for a few miles, with Sarah regretting her clumsy attempt to get Sultan to open up about himself.

'Actually, there is one type of Asian music that I enjoy, from time-to-time.'

'Oh yeah, what's that?'

'K-pop.'

They pulled into a service station at about two o'clock in the morning and refuelled. Sarah took on the driving and three hours later they had cleared Glasgow, driven up the west bank of Loch Lomond, and arrived at their destination, Tyndrum, at five a.m.

'We've got three hours to wait,' said Sarah softly. But Sultan was already asleep. She carefully reached over and covered him with a coat from the backseat. His phone was propped up in a recess in the dashboard. They'd been using Google Maps as a SatNav for the journey, and she went to switch it off. But she checked Sultan was still asleep, then quickly looked at the Recent Destinations tab. An address in Lozells, Birmingham, yesterday. And yet when she'd asked him how he'd spent Saturday, he'd said he'd been at home all day, marking homework and planning next week's lessons. She typed the address into her own phone, then tilted her own seat back and closed her eyes.

After his phone call with Sarah, Jason felt a little calmer. It was worrying that she had pretty well confirmed his suspicions about being followed, but at least she had provided a plan to deal with it. Things were going to get better. He made his way back to the cabin and slipped into the lower bunk without waking Bernie. It was doubtful that he'd sleep, but he set an alarm on his phone, anyway. He dozed on and off for a few hours, but was awake in time to cancel the alarm just before it sounded. He slid out of the bed and washed and dressed as quietly as he could.

'Hey, Bernie?' he said softly, gently rocking her shoulder. 'Time to get up. We need to get off the train soon.'

'What? No, can't be!' Bernie grumbled.

'I've got a surprise for you.'

Bernie climbed down from the top bunk. Jason kissed her hair and gave her a brief hug, then guided her through the mechanics of brushing her teeth and putting on some clothes. She was still barely conscious when they left their cabin with their modest luggage just as the train was pulling into a station.

'Wait! This isn't Fort William, you jerk!' she said. 'We don't get off here!'

'Change of plan,' said Jason, smiling and opening the carriage door.

They alighted, and Jason was relieved to notice that no one else left the train at Upper Tyndrum. The platform was empty except for the two familiar figures of Sarah and Sultan, who walked up to greet them.

'Ahoy there, mateys!' called Sultan. 'Elbow bumps, please. No hugging!'

'I don't understand,' said Bernie, looking at Jason.

'These guys had the same idea as us,' said Jason. 'Head for the Highlands! I saw a message on WhatsApp last night and suggested we meet up. We're only an hour and a half away from Fort William, and Sultan can drive us there, and we get to go through Glencoe.'

'But first, we have breakfast,' said Sultan. 'Proper breakfast, not train food. There's a great place a couple of minutes away.'

They drove the short distance to the Real Food Cafe, Jason in the front passenger seat next to Sultan, Sarah and Bernie in the back. Sarah smiled at Bernie, and received a weak smile in return, but they didn't speak.

The cafe lived up to its billing. A full fried breakfast hit the spot for Jason and Sarah. Sultan had the vegetarian version, which included meat-free haggis, and Bernie had a steaming bowl of porridge.

'How was the train, then?' Sarah asked Bernie.

'It was fine, thanks,' said Bernie. 'I didn't see much of it, just our cabin. We slept through it all, didn't we, Jason? Well, I did, anyway. Jason was obviously hooking up with you guys.'

After they'd eaten, and while Bernie was using the toilet, Sarah said: 'Sultan and I need a few things before we go on. Like a change of clothes. There's a shop just up the road. Nothing expensive, of course, but...'

Jason took the hint. 'Take my credit card. Don't go crazy.'

Sultan and Sarah walked up the road to investigate the Green Welly Stop, a huge shop that offered 'Whisky, Wellies, Gifts and so much more', and left Jason and Bernie having a second cup of coffee. The conversation was stilted.

'I would have appreciated being asked first, Jason.'

'I'm sorry, I nearly woke you, but you looked peaceful.'

'Where are they going, anyway?'

'Same place as us. They've just changed their arrangements. It will be fine, I promise.'

'Oh, why not? The more the merrier! So much for our romantic getaway!'

'Bernie, it was never going to be that; your aunt is going to be there, Richards, Jack Tang and Paige....'

'Just as well, it will be someone for me to talk to while you are giggling with your mates.'

'Hey, don't be like that. I know you're just jealous of Sultan.'

Bernie exhaled loudly and picked up a newspaper to read. Jason drank the rest of his coffee in silence.

Sultan and Sarah were soon back, laden with bags from The Green Welly Stop.

'Wax jacket,' said Sultan proudly. 'Plaid shirt and get a load of these... tartan underpants!'

20

'So, what are you up to, Samuel?' asked Rebecca Leyden-Fuller. She was lying on her side, watching the rapid rise and fall of Sam's chest. He didn't answer. He was still out of breath.

'Following Bernie and Jason, I mean. What's that all about?' she tried again.

'Er... old friend from school. Gonna surprise him, like. What about you?'

'Similar, really. I'm an old friend of Bernice. We did our PhD's together in London. Shared a flat. Shared a bed, sometimes. Those were the days. Young, free, and up for anything. All great fun, actually. Those were the days when you could go out, get completely ratted, and not find pictures of yourself all over Twitter the next morning.'

Rebecca Leyden-Fuller rolled onto her back and stared at the ceiling.

'Anyway, halfway through my course I got an offer I couldn't refuse for an editorship of a magazine, which launched my career. I abandoned my PhD and Bernie and I kind of drifted apart. She became boringly respectable; got her doctorate — now there's a story — and eventually ended up as "Head of" something or other at Cambridge. Whereas I went on a different path. You know my story, right? ... I mean, you know who I am...?'

Sam snorted in a way that could have meant either yes or no. Rebecca Leyden-Fuller decided it meant no. She was amused rather than offended.

'I'm on the TV enough. Question Time? Newsnight? The Pledge? Loose Women? I guess they're not your shows. And I won't ask you what paper you read. Anyway, congratulations, you've just shagged a celebrity. But be a darling, and don't go trying to sell your story, will you? It won't do you any favours. "I Bedded RLF" is up there with "Strictly Star Cheats On Partner" as non-story of the week, to be honest. And it just distracts the nutters. I spend a lot of time working on which stories I want my followers and detractors to engage with. I'd rather have them cheering me or slagging me off for standing up for free speech, or personal freedom than worrying about what happens in my bedroom.

'Which brings me back to Bernice Tenant. She dropped me like a cold kebab as soon as I started getting famous. I really couldn't care less, but then I was invited by some students to speak at Cambridge University, where she teaches. And at the last moment, I'm suddenly cancelled, and I'm pretty bloody sure I know who was behind it. Look, I'm not daft. I know I won't be able to ride this celebrity thing forever, so I don't like it when opportunities are suddenly taken from me. You never know when the next one might arrive.

'So I did exactly what you are doing. I secretly followed her on a jaunt to South Africa, so I could give her a bit of a Christmas surprise. It was just devilment, really; I was at a loose end, and I find that if you follow your instincts, it can lead you to some interesting places. In this case, it led me to a party of millionaires, living it up on safari, including your mate, Jason Tranter. Then when I do a bit of Googling on the guest list, it turns out that these millionaires are all rather a secretive bunch. Well, except for Jack Tang, who couldn't really be less secretive, but there you go. I figured there might be a story somewhere in this secret millionaires' club, but the organiser persuaded me not to go digging. He reckons he might have a role for me in the organisation, instead. Sounds interesting, so here I am. This time I'm invited to join them on a remote Scottish island that they're sussing out as a potential hideaway location for their members. Shit! I probably wasn't supposed to tell you all that!'

But there was no need for Rebecca Leyden-Fuller to worry. Sam Flint had been asleep for some time now.

Part 3

1

When they woke up on Sunday morning, many people in the UK tuned into the news to track the progress of a virus that had originated in China, spread to Europe and had already caused over fifty deaths in the UK. Hospitals were declaring 'critical incidents' and there was a sense that there was a lot worse to come. Sandy Lamb, however, was more worried about the progress of an area of low pressure making its way across the Atlantic. His rigid inflatable boat could make the trip from the mainland to Sannah in less than forty-five minutes in calm weather, but when the wind whipped up and there was more of a swell, the voyage became a daunting one for even a seasoned sailor like himself, and an inexperienced passenger would probably be terrified.

It was all okay for the moment though, and his elderly passenger seemed to enjoy the exhilarating motion of the RIB as it bounced across the waves in the early morning sunlight, throwing up occasional salty splashes onto her face. Then she dropped her bombshell.

'You'll be able to pick up my niece and her friend later this morning, won't you, Sandy dear?'

'Ach, Mrs McC,' said Sandy. 'She'll be better waiting for the afternoon ferry. The weather's coming in fast. It's going to make things a bit bumpy.'

'Oh Sandy,' replied Mrs McCracken, 'I'd really rather you pick them up. They've been travelling all night on the sleeper train. They'll be safe in your hands; Henry always used to say what a wonderful boatman you were.'

'Aye, well, we'll see. No promises, mind.'

It was a worried-looking Sandy that greeted these new passengers a couple of hours later, and he frowned when he saw there were four instead of the two he was expecting.

'What's this? Your Aunt never said anything about extra passengers? Where will they stay? There's no room at Sannah House. We're awfully busy this weekend.'

'Yes, sorry, it is all a bit last minute...' Bernie began.

'It's okay, I've just spoken to a lady at the hotel... Gracie... and she says she can squeeze us in,' said Sarah.

'Oh, she did?' said Sandy. 'Well, listen, I don't know about this. It's getting a wee bit choppy out there. I shouldn't really be taking you out on the RIB in this weather. The CalMac Ferry would be a lot safer. It sails this afternoon. I don't know... it would be bad enough drowning two of you, but drowning four would look really bad, y'know?'

Jason looked at his friends. Sarah and Bernie were both looking uneasy, but Sultan had obviously enjoyed the joke.

'I'm sure we'll be in safe hands,' said Jason, 'And we'll give you something extra for your trouble.'

Sandy smiled. 'Well, it will take us a wee while longer than usual. Have you all eaten? That's a shame. I hope you've all got strong stomachs, is all I'll say.'

When the rigid inflatable set off, bouncing across the dark grey waters, Jason, Bernie, Sarah and Sultan all experienced the same exhilaration that Mrs McCracken had enjoyed earlier in the morning. But before long, the rise and fall of the boat grew less enjoyable and Jason looked at his companions' faces and guessed they were regretting the trip. He felt Bernie lean into him, resting her head on his shoulder. Her romantic dash to the Highlands had been ruined, not so much by this, but by Sarah unexpectedly joining them.

Had he been wrong to ask Sarah, he wondered? He'd felt such a sense of relief when he saw her walking up the platform at Tyndrum. She was going to help him sort out this business of the buried body; he felt sure. He hadn't told her about it yet, but she'd know what to do. Somehow, he'd have to work out how to get some time alone with her to talk about it. That wouldn't be easy with both Bernie and her aunt about. He didn't like the idea of going behind his girlfriend's back. He was ashamed enough of what had nearly happened the last time he and Sarah were alone together.

It amused Jason to see that Sarah had chosen Sultan to help her drive up to Scotland. That way, she could legitimately claim she was still keeping up her surveillance if her bosses asked what she was doing in Scotland. Seeing Sultan, Jason imagined how his friend would react if he told him his story about the body buried in Bernie's aunt's garden. Maybe he would treat it like a joke, the way he treated most things, but realistically, it was all too serious and macabre to be made a joke of. It was one more thing that he couldn't tell his friend about. Another secret to be kept.

It was two hours later that the RIB tied up at the short Sannah pier. The four passengers stepped ashore gingerly, as if they were worried that the ground would give way under their feet. Their faces were ashen, and they were silent. Sandy, on the other hand, was cheerful and helped with their luggage as they walked the short distance up to the hotel.

Gracie was ready to greet them.

'Welcome to Sanna! Now it's a double room for you,' she said to Bernie and Jason.

'And a twin room for you,' she added, addressing Sarah and Sultan. 'If you follow me, I'll show you all to your rooms.'

'Unless you follow me to the bar,' said Sandy, 'In which case, I'll join you in a restorative wee dram. It'll help you find your land legs.'

Neither Bernie nor Sarah was interested in this offer, and they followed Gracie upstairs to their rooms. Jason and Sultan decided that the man who had steered them to safety across a perilous sea probably knew what he was talking about.

2

Sandy went behind the bar while Jason and Sultan sat on comfortable leather-topped bar stools and surveyed the room. An oak-panelled wall displayed various sets of deer antlers mounted on wooden shields. There was a grand stone fireplace with thistles carved into the stonework. On the mantelpiece sat a stuffed pine marten, reared up on its hind legs and showing an incomplete set of claws. Sultan stared at it in disbelief. Its misaligned glass eyes and shabby fur gave it a faintly comical appearance, but he felt sure it would haunt his dreams that night.

A small old-fashioned electric heater stood in front of the fire, but some scorch marks on the carpet suggested that a proper fire was occasionally lit. A pair of dark, heavy curtains surrounded the window that looked out across the bay. The sky outside was now a dark grey, but even a sunny day would struggle to light up this room.

'Not quite the same as Isola Gallinara, Jason,' observed Sultan, referring to the luxury private island they had visited the previous year. The bars on that island could rival any cosmopolitan bar for both ambience and variety of drinks on offer. The bar at Sannah House displayed only half a dozen bottles, but something had caught Jason's eye, and he was transfixed.

On a shelf next to the bottles was a small stripy wooden cup with two handles. The cup stood on a wooden plinth that bore an indistinct inscription.

'Are you whisky drinkers, gentlemen?' asked Sandy.

'It's usually a sweet sherry for me,' said Sultan, 'But when in Rome...'

'That'll be great,' said Jason, 'Thanks. That's an interesting cup on the shelf there. Could I take a closer look?'

'Och, that old thing,' said Sandy, taking it off the shelf and passing it to Jason. 'I've never understood it myself. A wooden cup? It's not hygienic. A "friendship cup", I think they call them. You're supposed to pass it round or something. It'd never touch my lips; I can tell you that! Old Henry liked it, mind. He used to like to take a dram in it when he was up here, God rest his soul. I can picture him now sitting in the window over there and smiling to himself. I can't see anyone using it now.'

'I'd be prepared to buy it off you,' said Jason. 'I've read about them, but never seen one.'

Sultan noticed that the tips of Jason's ears were pink.

'How much do you want for it?' asked Jason.

'Well, now,' said Sandy, looking suddenly serious. 'I don't know. It's a shabby old thing, but it's old. Could be an antique.'

'What if I offered you a hundred pounds?' said Jason.

Sandy did his best not to look surprised but took a sip from his own glass.

'I was thinking a bit more,' he said in a quiet voice.

'A hundred and twenty,' said Jason. 'It'll have to be my final offer. It's all the cash I have with me. Unless you can cash a cheque? I'm guessing there isn't a cash machine anywhere on the island?'

'A hundred and twenty it is then,' said Sandy, beaming. 'I'll take your cash. Don't worry, there's nothing else to spend it on here in the next few days.'

Jason handed over his notes. Sandy went to put them in the till and then paused and closed the drawer.

'I'll just put this safe upstairs,' he said. 'Look, I'll leave the bottle here. If you gentlemen feel like another, just help yourselves.'

He left and Jason cradled the cup in his hands. The stripes resulted from the cup being made of two types of wood, light and dark in alternate bands. It must have taken some craftsmanship to make it. He rubbed the inscription on the cup holder with his thumb and, taking some of the grime away, confirmed his first suspicion. The words were 'Weel Watch'.

'For a moment there, I thought I was part of a daytime TV show,' said Sultan. '*Cash in the Attic*, *Antiques Under The Hammer* or something. What have you bought, matey?'

Jason smiled.

'Well, I'm not sure,' he said. 'I've been reading a lot about these cups. There was a feature in my Whiskey Club magazine. Some are very rare. It's a real long shot, but I think I might just have made a bit of a killing.'

The smile left Jason's lips suddenly, and his face reddened. He paused for a while and then, in a quiet voice, said, 'It's good to see you, Sultan. Are you okay?'

'I'm fine, matey. A bit bloody tired, to tell the truth. So if you don't mind, I'm going to put my head down for a while.'

'Oh, yeah, good idea,' said Jason.

Sultan finished his drink, slid off his bar stool, and went off to find his room, leaving Jason alone with the bottle.

'.... made a bit of a killing...' thought Jason as he poured himself a refill. 'Did I really just say that?'

3

He wiped the cup with a paper napkin and poured some whisky into it.

'Cheers, Henry!' he said to himself.

It wasn't the best whisky he'd ever tasted, but it was hitting the spot for Jason. He could feel a cosy numbness descending on him and he started to relax. There were twenty miles of ocean separating him from the mainland; over twenty miles from whoever was following him on the train, and hundreds of miles away from that asparagus bed and its gruesome contents. And now he had this cup. He knew it was only a temporary relief he was feeling, but it was welcome just the same.

'Ah, there you are,' said a voice from the doorway. It was Mrs McCracken, without the smile that she usually had for Jason.

'Hello,' said Jason.

Gillian McCracken looked around and walked up close to Jason.

'Just what is she doing here?' she asked in a low voice. 'She's the woman I saw you with the other day, isn't she? I just saw her on the stairs... I couldn't believe it! What's she doing here? What do you think you're playing at, young man?'

'It's not what you think, Gillian,' said Jason. 'Sarah came with Sultan... my friend from Hambourne. I think we were being followed up here by someone... the police, possibly. He was on the train, anyway. Sultan and Sarah helped us give whoever it was the slip.'

'How nice! Well, they're not needed here, now, are they? They can head back on the next boat, can't they? Listen, Jason. I'm not having you upsetting Bernice. That woman leaves on the next boat, or I'll be obliged to tell Bernice what I saw... for her own protection.'

'That's blackmail, Mrs Mc C,' protested Jason.

'All's fair in love and war. Look, I'm doing this for both of you. Either you are serious about Bernice or you're not. And if you're not, she needs to know now.'

'I am serious. What you saw the other day was a silly mistake and it won't happen again. But Sarah and Sultan are my friends and have travelled the length of the country to help me lose whoever it was who was following me. I can't just turn them back. I'm sure they'll be leaving soon, anyway. Sultan will need to be back at school. Anyway, there's a more important thing we need to be discussing. Someone was following me. You know what that means. Somebody suspects something. It could be the police, or it could be someone who knew the poor bloke who's lying underneath your asparagus bed. Listen, Gillian, this is crazy. We need to stop this. We need to come clean about the whole thing with the police. It'll be bad at first, but...'

'Stunning views! Yes, The Sutherland is the best room in the hotel. You'll love it.' Mrs McCracken was speaking loudly and smiling broadly again.

Jason looked up and noticed that a woman had entered the room.

'Ah, Gracie,' said Mrs McCracken. 'I was telling Jason how lucky he was to have The Sutherland Suite.'

'Totally,' said Gracie. 'It's like our best room. Are you both okay here? Can I get you any more drinks?'

'No, thank you dear,' said Mrs McCracken. 'In fact, you can clear these away, please. We can't have you getting tipsy, can we, Jason? There's no knowing where that would lead!'

Jason grabbed the cup he had just bought before Gracie could take it away.

'I've just bought it off Sandy,' he explained.

Gracie looked surprised but cleared away the bottle and glasses. Jason drained his wooden cup.

'Still drinking?' said Bernie, entering the room. 'Come on, Jason, we're going for a walk. Let's get some fresh air before the rain really sets in.'

4

There was consternation in the waiting room at the Mallaig ferry terminal. Rumours were circulating that they might cancel the Small Isles ferry. Jack Tang went to the ticket office to see if he could find more information, leaving Richards standing awkwardly with Paige.

'I'm glad you could join us for the trip,' said Richards. He sounded weary. The journey up had been more tiring than he'd expected.

'It's my pleasure,' said Paige. 'Bernie and Jason are going to be there, right? I'm looking forward to another Rara Avis get together.'

'Yes, I understand they will be joining us,' said Richards. 'But this isn't one of our regular events. Gillian McCracken has offered Rara Avis the chance to develop her island hideaway as a location for future club events. Jack and I arranged to meet Gillian over there to assess its potential, but I'm afraid it's rather basic accommodation, as it stands.'

The door to the waiting room opened and a draft of cold air blew in with Rebecca Leyden-Fuller accompanied by someone Richards didn't recognise.

'Well, hello there,' said Rebecca Leyden-Fuller.

'Hello, Rebecca,' said Richards. 'You made it then. You remember Paige, of course?'

It was meant as a prompt for Rebecca to introduce her companion, but she ignored it.

'Where's the delicious Jack Tang, then?' she asked.

Jack returned from the ticket office by way of an answer.

'Hey, guys! Oh, hi!' said Jack, looking puzzled to see their party had grown. 'So, here's the thing. The ferry is running this afternoon, but they are warning passengers that this might be the last sailing for a while. It's the virus. They're expecting an announcement from the government sometime soon and there might be a travel ban. They don't want people to get stranded, so they're advising only essential travel.'

'So where does that leave us?' asked Paige.

'Essential travel,' said Richards. 'I haven't come all this way to be turned back now. This will all blow over. Anyway, the hotel manager has his own boat, I gather. He can bring us back if they stop the ferry service.'

'That's my man, Richards!' said Rebecca Leyden-Fuller. 'Fortune favours the brave, I always say. Let's crack on.'

Richards looked at her, then at her companion, who'd moved over to a window and was watching the harbour. Then he turned back to her with a quizzical expression.

'Oh, yes,' said Leyden-Fuller. 'This is Sam... don't know his surname, only met him this morning. He's a friend of Jason Tranter's, apparently. He's coming along for the ride.'

'Has he booked into the hotel?' said Richards. 'I think they may be a bit squeezed.'

'It won't be a problem,' said Rebecca Leyden-Fuller with a grin. 'He'll be shacking up with me.'

Richards, Jack and Paige all raised eyebrows, but Rebecca Leyden-Fuller didn't notice because at that moment, Sam walked briskly back from the window and grabbed her by the arm.

'Are we getting me a ticket, then?' he asked.

'The ticket office is just through there,' said Jack Tang, pointing to a door. 'Hi, I'm Jack...'

But Sam Flint was already marching Rebecca Leyden-Fuller towards the office. As they left the waiting room by one door, the other door opened with another bluster of cold sea air and a heavily built man in a navy reefer coat entered. He stood apart from the others and blew into his hands to warm them up.

5

'Weather could be better,' shouted Jason as he struggled to walk upright along a stony road that wound its way inland through grassy moors. He shouted to be heard above the raging wind. Sheep, huddled together in ditches and hollows, stared at the two figures as they walked by.

'It's not raining yet,' shouted back Bernie. 'That means this is technically good weather. Any weather that's not snow, sleet or rain is technically good weather out here.'

'Okay. I'll start enjoying it then. Hmm! Lovely! There, can we go back now?'

'Trust me, Jason,' said Bernie, 'When that rain comes in we'll be stuck inside the Hotel for heaven knows how long. You'll be thankful that we've had this quick walk. The views up there are stunning. Especially when it's blowing like this.'

Ahead of them, the green of a small hill seemed to glow underneath the dark grey clouds that were rolling in fast. One side of the hill appeared to be missing; black cliffs rose up, marking perhaps where the shoreline had once been before some prehistoric readjustment of the landscape.

They trudged upwards against the wind, Bernie holding Jason's arm. He bit his lip. He knew she was trying to encourage him, but the effect of her holding his arm was actually to make progress up the hill slower.

'Besides, this way we get some time alone together.'

Now he frowned. Bernie famously didn't 'do romantic'. It was unlike her to say something like that.

'Have you been missing me, then?' he asked.

'I just know what you'll be like, now your friends are here with you. It'll be "Sultan, come and look at this..." and "Oh, Sarah, how about..."'. She left the phrase hanging.

'How about what?' Jason asked.

'Nothing. I just mean that you get excited to see them. Let's face it, first chance you got you were propping up the bar with Sultan.'

'And in doing so, I got the bargain of the century,' said Jason.

'Aw, come on!' said Bernie. 'That old cup? It doesn't look much to me.'

'You saw the inscription. You, of all people, would know what that means.'

'Okay, you get full marks for knowing that "Watch Weel" was the motto of Sir Walter Scot. I'm impressed. But Jason, there's all sorts of commemorative tat, printed up with those words, all over the place. There's nothing to suggest that cup was his.'

'Maybe not. But here's the thing. I read this story in my Whisky Drinker's Monthly. Walter Scott used to collect these old whisky cups. They're called quaichs... I don't know if I've pronounced that correctly. He had loads of them and used them to serve whisky to his guests. There was one made out of the wood from an oak tree that stood on the battlefield of Waterloo. Another was made from the tree that William Wallace hid in — you know, Braveheart.'

'I know who William Wallace was, thank you.'

'And another was supposed to have belonged to Bonnie Prince Charlie. A seven-banded wooden quaich. Anyway, back in the nineteen-nineties, art thieves raided the Scott family home and stole loads of these quaichs, plus other treasures like a brooch belonging to Napoleon and a lock of Nelson's hair. The thieves were never caught, and no-one knows what happened to all the gear. Probably sold to private collectors, was the verdict at the time, and people thought they'd never be seen by the public again. But a month or two ago, the Waterloo Oak Quaich turned up at a car boot sale in France. Suddenly, people have become very excited about the possibility of finding other pieces from the collection. So you never know! My cup might be the Prince's Quaich. I just need to get back and get on the internet and see if I can find any pictures to compare it against.'

'Well, it can wait till we get back. If you're so interested in history now, I've got something else to show you.'

They walked on up the track and then up a path that took them to the top of the small hill. They could now see most of the island, and some of the other nearby 'Small Islands'. Coming in from the west, heavy clouds rolled in but between them, occasionally, shafts of light shone down, highlighting patches of grey green ocean or silvery sandy beaches. The shapes were endlessly shifting, and they stood in the wind, staring at the view.

'Not bad,' said Jason, and Bernie smiled triumphantly.

'Down here,' she said, pointing to another path down the hill. They came to a field surrounded by dry-stone walls. In the centre was a tall standing stone, irregularly shaped and about two metres high. There was a small hole just below the top of the column.

'Put your thumb in there,' said Bernie.

Jason looked at her, doubtfully.

'It's called the Punishment Stone,' she said. 'It's believed that in olden times, criminals were led here, and had their thumbs wedged in the hole. They were made to stand there for days until they had atoned for their misdeeds.'

'What do you think my misdeeds are?' asked Jason. He had a pretty good idea himself what they were and didn't think that any amount of standing around with his thumb stuck in an old rock was going to ease his conscience.

'I haven't decided yet,' said Bernie. 'Perhaps a more serious punishment may be called for. Come on, there's more.'

She led him out of the field, and along rough ground towards the coast. There was no path, and the going became difficult. The sound of waves on the beach below competed with the roar of the wind, but they couldn't see them yet. Bernie held Jason's arm again.

'Is that to support me or you?' he asked.

'Both of us. It gets dangerous from here,' she said.

'Let's stay away from the edge then,' said Jason.

'It's not just the cliffs that are dangerous,' said Bernie. 'Here, look down there.'

She guided him to a hole in the clifftop, less than two metres across and about three metres deep. The sides of the hole were rocky and steep, almost vertical. At the bottom of the hole, there were just wet stones.

'Woah!' said Jason. 'Who put that there? And shouldn't there be a warning sign?'

'There's more like it,' said Bernie, leading him away and showing him another hole, not as deep, but with even steeper sides. 'There's twelve of them, apparently. Nobody knows quite how they got here. Some say they were formed naturally, a geological thing. Others say they were dug by twelfth century smugglers to hide loot in. Others say they were used as prison cells, or that monks used to entomb themselves down as preparation for purgatory, or something like that. Weird, huh? So, it's a toss-up between the Punishment Stone or the Prison Holes for you. Which do you prefer? Hey, are you okay? You look terrified! I'm only joking.'

'Yeah, fine. I think we should get back now. The ferry gets in at three. Richards and Jack and Paige should be on it.'

'Oh, is Paige coming too? Fantastic. Sorry you didn't like the Prison Holes. Let's go back then.'

'Cool,' said Jason, glad to get away from the tomb-like holes.

Back in Sannah House, Sultan and Sarah were resting in their twin room. Or at least, Sultan was. When they'd left Sultan's car at Mallaig, Sarah had noticed Sultan scooping an A4 notebook from the car boot into the 'Green Welly' carrier bag that held his new clothes. Curious to find out what it contained, she lay on her bed with one eye watching Sultan, waiting for him to stop tossing and turning, grunting and groaning, and fall at last into a deep and restful sleep.

She found herself fighting her own tiredness. Her head swam with the events of the last 24 hours and the strange sensation of being on an island she'd never heard of until a few hours ago. She wrestled with the idea that the man she's spent the last eighteen hours with could be involved in activities of interest to the West Midlands Counter Terrorism unit. Apart from the first hour of grumbling, he'd been great company, and he was clearly a good friend to Jason. She thought about Jason, how ill and worried he looked. Was someone really following him? She thought about their last meeting at his house and wondered what it all meant.

She awoke with a start. How long had she been asleep? Just minutes, surely? She checked her watch to find it had been nearly an hour. Sultan was quiet. It was now or never.

She eased herself off the bed and found the plastic bag on the other side of the room. It was the sort of plastic that rustles — of course it was — and the slower and more carefully she tried to look inside it, the louder the noise she made. Her fingers found the A4 pad, and she eased it out of the bag. On the front cover was a B12 post code written in ball-point pen and circled multiple times. Sarah was pretty sure it was the same one she'd seen in Sultan's Google Maps history. She opened the cover of the pad and exclaimed, albeit in a whisper.

'Shiiiiit!'

Sultan stirred. She pushed the pad back into the bag.

'What are you doing, Sarah?' said Sultan sleepily.

'Knickers.' said Sarah. 'I can't find the knickers I bought at Tyndrum. I thought they may have ended up in your bag.'

'What exactly are you accusing me of?'

'Nothing, Sultan. Don't worry.'

But she was the one that was worried. The image of the page she had just glimpsed was burnt into her brain. Arabic handwriting, around a crude sketch of an aeroplane, with its trajectory marked by a curved dotted line that arched across the width of the page. A trajectory that ended at a cluster of skyscrapers labelled as 'Birmingham'.

6

Dodge Mhlongo propped himself against the outside wall of Keeper's Cottage and trained his binoculars on the ferry that had just arrived at the jetty. The first passengers to disembark walked purposefully up the ramp and headed directly to their nearby homes or else to cars that were waiting for them. Locals, determined to get out of the rain as quickly as possible. Then came the people less familiar with their surroundings, looking around, getting their bearings — visitors.

He recognised Richards immediately.

'Careful, boss,' he muttered to himself. 'You don't want to get that sexy hair wet.' And as if he heard, Richards pulled an umbrella out of nowhere and sheltered as he looked back at the ferry and waited for others to join him.

His binoculars scanned the jetty. Here was another figure he recognised. Jack Tang, struggling with two suitcases. He was wearing an expensive-looking skiing jacket. Too bright perhaps for the Scottish Highlands, and with its drawstrings pulled tight, framing his round face, it made him look ridiculous. And there was his girlfriend, Paige, was it? Running ahead to get under

Richards' umbrella. She was cute, but a little too perfect, he seemed to remember.

And then there she was. Rebecca Leyden-Fuller. Dodge's breath quickened and became shallower. It shocked him to see her, but he realised that he'd been half-expecting this moment all along.

It wasn't exactly the first time he'd seen her since she'd left Molatedi. In those dull, listless days after her departure, he'd messaged her seven or eight times and when she didn't respond, he Googled her and found that her claims to being a media personality were not unfounded. There she was, on panel shows and in articles about the 'culture wars'. It felt odd to see her in that context. He'd known her as a woman with spirit, someone as straight-talking as he was and with opinions and appetites that matched his own. And there she was, raising all kinds of hell in the UK. Dodge missed her. He'd never missed anyone before.

He'd expected the feeling would soon blow over, but then one day he saw news on Twitter that she'd hooked up with an outspoken and out-of-work actor who'd set up his own fringe political party. He felt wounded. What was she doing with him? From what Dodge could see, he was a fully certified, attention-seeking jerk. But there he was, pulling a stupid face while she looked at him adoringly. Pundits were referring to them as 'The Cancelled Couple' Both of them happily adopted it as a hashtag and both gained followers from each other's fanbase.

But then the bloke made some dumb comments about how there was no such thing as white privilege and how he'd actually been the victim of racism himself once, when a black actor had beat him to the part of Hamlet in a production that he said, 'should have been re-titled, "All's Well That Ends Woke".' Dodge was relieved to read that Rebecca Leyden-Fuller had dropped her new friend as quickly as she'd picked him up. And he wondered whether her decision had anything to do with the brief couple of weeks she'd spent with him. Did she ever wonder about him?

He watched her walking up the jetty to join the others and then pausing and looking back at the ferry, waiting for someone. A man ran up to join her, wearing just jogging bottoms and a T-shirt. In this weather? Jeez! What a dickhead! And he ran up to Rebecca, took her arm and leant into her as if somehow she'd shelter him from the rain. What the actual f—?

Dodge lowered his binoculars and wiped his eyes. He'd been staring too long. When he raised them again, he saw that party were all making their way from the harbour up the road a short distance to Sannah House. The guy was still right up close to Beccy, and Dodge didn't want to watch them anymore. He scanned back to the ferry. One straggler, a guy in a dark reefer coat, was leaving the ramp. He looked around, noticed the party headed for Sannah House, and stood watching them for a while. When they reached the house and went inside, the man started walking himself, but disappeared into a giftshop.

7

Bernie refilled the bath and lit the tealights she had brought in from their room. 'I'll get him a small glass of whisky as well,' she thought, as she looked at the warm, dimly lit, steamy bathroom she had prepared for Jason. 'Perhaps he'll be able to relax.'

Her own bath hadn't been relaxing. She'd made the mistake of getting in the bath while the water was running, and it had taken ages to fill. She'd shivered as the water slowly crept up to cover her properly, and she'd worried about Jason. He'd been acting strangely ever since he'd arrived at her flat in Cambridge, less than twenty-four hours ago. He seemed preoccupied and distant and wasn't making the usual goofy jokes all the time. Admittedly, his sense of humour could get irritating at times, but its sudden, unexpected, and unexplained absence bothered her. It didn't help that Sultan and, especially, Sarah had turned up on the scene. She preferred having his undivided attention.

She walked back along the corridor to their room and noticed the door was slightly ajar.

'I've run you a bath, Jason. Thank me, because it takes for-bloody-ever...' she said, entering the room, and stopped suddenly.

'Umm... Yah, so I was just turning down the bedcovers,' said Gracie. She was holding Jason's whisky cup. The bedcovers were untouched.

'What are you doing with that?' asked Bernie.

Gracie blushed and her eyes darted around the room as if looking for inspiration. When she looked back at Bernie, there was a fierce defiance in her eyes.

'Okay, so Mr Tranter shouldn't have taken this from Sandy,' she said.

'Jason didn't take it. He paid for it. From where I'm standing, it looks like you're the one who was about to take it.'

'Okay. So, the thing is, it wasn't really Sandy's to sell. Actually, I think it belonged to old Mr McCracken.'

'And I'm Henry McCracken's niece, so hand it to me please, and we'll say no more about it.'

That the cup had belonged to her uncle was news to Bernie, and she suddenly felt the same way about it as Gracie did. Jason had no right to pay Sandy a pittance for what was probably a valuable family heirloom. And given its Walter Scott connections, she felt sure that it was an heirloom that would have naturally passed to her. No, she wasn't going to let him get away with that.

'I mean it,' she said, as Gracie handed her the cup and turned to leave the room. 'We'll say no more about it. I won't say anything about finding you with the cup, and you won't say anything about what you've told me. And if Mr Tranter finds he is no longer in possession of the cup, we won't say anything about that, either. Do you understand me?'

Flustered and confused, Gracie just nodded and slipped out as quickly as she could.

8

Built in 1855, Sannah House was just high enough up the hill to boast superb views over the bay, but the architect had designed the house to provide a refuge from the wild landscape rather than a window onto it. Thick walls kept the elements out. Iron railings on a high stone wall around the property kept animals out. People too, if necessary. Once inside, it felt like time, too, was denied access.

The décor was Victorian, not because that was the current nostalgic fashion for Scottish country homes and hotels, but because the original fittings remained, or at least had been replaced like-for-like since the house was built. Innovations like electricity and central heating had been introduced, eventually; but many decades after they had swept the rest of the country. Sannah resisted change. The word 'makeover' had never been uttered within its walls until now.

The new guests stood in the entrance hall, shaking the rain from their coats — those that had such a thing. Jack Tang was the first to speak.

'You weren't joking then, Richards,' he said. 'This place is like a museum.'

'It has charm,' said Richards quietly, looking around. 'Something we can build on.'

'It has a real fire somewhere,' said Rebecca Leyden-Fuller. 'I can smell it. Lead me to it.'

Sandy Lamb appeared from an adjoining room.

'Good afternoon, ladies and gentlemen,' he said. 'Welcome to Sannah House. I'm sorry your journey has been delayed today. I'm pleased to say that we'll be serving you a good hot meal in an hour's time. So we've got time to get you settled in your rooms and for you to freshen up — or dry off. Some of the rooms have en-suites, but I'm afraid some of you will have to use the shared bathroom, so perhaps you'd like to arrange who's taking turns and when.'

Richards frowned. Shared bathrooms weren't the usual arrangement for Rara Avis locations. That was one thing that would have to change. 'Is Mrs McCracken about? I'd like to talk with her.'

'She's in her room resting at the moment. I'm just about to take her a hot toddy. I'll let her know ye've arrived.'

Jack Tang was more concerned about what was meant by 'a good hot meal'.

9

'Any good neighbour would check the place over while the occupier is away,' said Julia to an empty garden. The headscarf tied round her mouth muffled her voice. Her mirrored sunglasses reflected the doors and windows of Mrs McCracken's cottage as she scanned them. The sun had barely risen, and three crows flew out of the orange sky and alighted on the garden wall. Their heads swivelled as they joined in the appraisal of the little cottage and its grounds. Their attention settled on a raised bed at the back of the garden where asparagus spears broke through the soil.

'That's early for asparagus,' said Julia, following their gaze. 'It's only March. I wonder how on earth she does it?' She walked over to the bed.

'Cor!' One of the crows seemed to be in agreement.

Julia bent over the bed to inspect more closely. The tips of the asparagus started to quiver.

'Cor! Cor...'

The greenish-purple stems were waving more wildly. They seemed to be growing upwards while she watched. The ground around them started to break apart. And then the asparagus fell to the side as a soil-strewn head rose up from the bed and the figure sat up.

'Corpse!' called the third crow.

And suddenly, Jason was that corpse. Everything was black, but warm... and wet. He turned his head and saw a narrow stripe of light — a pathway, maybe? This was death then. But something wasn't right. He could move, he could feel water around him. Had he drowned himself... in the bath? The bath, yes. Now he remembered where he was. He must have fallen asleep and now he'd woken up in darkness. He could hear his own shallow breathing. So he wasn't dead, and he hadn't been buried; he'd had a nightmare about that garden. But why was it dark? The candles must have burned out. He looked closer at the pencil thin stripe of light that was stretching across the floor. It must be leading to the door, and he figured the light switch would be by the door.

Disoriented and slipping about in the darkness, he climbed out of the bath and then walked cautiously along the strip of light. Not cautiously enough, though; his face banged against a wall, exactly where he didn't expect one to be. Panicking, he shuffled along the wall, feeling with his hands for the light switch.

'Where the hell...? Help! Where is the sodding thing?'

At last, he found the door.

10

At four o'clock Sultan and Sarah went downstairs for afternoon tea in the lounge bar. Richards was there, and he looked surprised and disappointed to see them.

'Mr Ahmed, Ms Headly, I didn't realise you'd be joining our party.'

'I didn't realise it was a party,' said Sultan. 'I'd have worn a brighter shirt, applied some glitter.'

'It's nice to see you again, Mr Richards,' said Sarah. 'What brings you here? Are you on the run from the virus, too?'

'There's a party of us here to assess whether Sannah House is a suitable location for Rara Avis events,' said Richards. 'Jack Tang is reviewing the kitchens. We have someone to make proposals regarding the décor. Someone else to look into security.'

Last year, Sultan and Stuart had somehow got themselves the job of security consultants for Rara Avis's super-yacht, but if Sultan felt put out about missing out on the gig this time, he didn't show it.

'Is that Jason's job now, then?' asked Sultan.

'No,' replied Richards. 'Mr Tranter is... attached to the McCracken party. Mrs McCracken being the owner of Sannah House.' He looked at Sarah, curious to see what effect his reference to Jason's 'attachment' had on her.

Sarah smiled. 'Is there enough to do on this island? For your millionaire set, I mean.'

'It's a good point Ms Headly. But we think the remoteness will appeal to some of our members, particularly the older ones. The odd day walking in the hills, taking in the views and fresh air, followed by a whisky in the library, and rounded off with a venison banquet, might suit some, I think. We hope to offer shooting and fishing, maybe some whale-watching excursions, for the more activity-minded. And, I have to say, there is some excellent bird life on the island.'

'How convenient for you,' said Sarah, raising an eyebrow but still smiling pleasantly. 'I remember your fondness for the old birdwatching.'

'Indeed. It is most fortuitous.'

Gracie entered with a tray of tea things. Sultan looked at a plate of shortbread biscuits.

'Any chance of something a bit more substantial?' he said with a cheerful smile and an affected voice. 'I must confess to being rather peckish. Plate of chips perhaps?'

'Aww... look, I'm so sorry,' said Gracie. 'Normally, we'd do whatever we could for the guests. But we're preparing for the big meal tonight, what with Jack Tang being here, and I'm really not sure I can —'

'—Big meal? Oh well, that sounds okay.' Sultan reached for a shortbread.

'The meal is for Rara Avis,' interjected Richards. 'I expect the normal menu will be available for the other guests.'

'Er... no,' said Gracie, blushing. 'Actually, it'll be the special menu for all the guests. It'll be one sitting at seven o'clock, with everyone around the table in the formal dining hall. Sorry, we thought that would be more in keeping...'

Richards huffed. 'I see. Well, that's that, then. I'll see you both later, in the formal dining room. I hope you've brought your evening wear!' he said and walked briskly out of the room.

'So, Sultan, did you pick up a tuxedo at the Green Welly Cafe?' asked Sarah, when they were walking back to their rooms, having drunk their tea and demolished the shortbread biscuits.

'No, but I find that when I'm wearing my tartan pants, I'm accepted in most places. How about you? Did you remember to pack your little black number?'

'Why, of course! And luckily, I grabbed my best pearls as we left Hambourne, barely eighteen hours ago.'

'Indeed. That is most fortuitous.'

Sarah laughed and was once again struck by how easy, how natural, it was to play the role of Sultan's friend, even though the evidence that he was involved with terrorists was mounting by the day. Her laughter, feigned or otherwise, was cut short by a panicked cry coming from a door they were passing. The door opened and a dripping wet, naked Jason Tranter staggered out into the corridor.

Gillian McCracken stared at a picture on her bedroom wall, a print of Edwin Landseer's '*The Stag at Bay*'. Two Irish wolfhounds attacking a magnificent stag against a stormy highland backdrop.

'Oh, Henry,' she sighed. 'You loved this picture, and I couldn't bear it. "Nature red in tooth and claw," you used to say. Perhaps. But you were such a peaceful man. How did you get mixed up with those... dogs?'

She heard a commotion coming from the bathroom that was next to her bedroom. Someone was shouting, and then there was a shrieking from the corridor. She went to investigate.

'Jason Tranter! What are you thinking? You've gone too far this time,' she exclaimed, on seeing the naked man standing with his two friends.

'I can explain,' said Jason.

'I'm sure you can. We spoke about this, Jason. I'm going straight to see my niece.'

'There's no need, Mrs McCracken. This isn't what it looks like... I don't even know what it looks like. Bernie ran me a bath — a candlelit bath — and I fell asleep. When I woke up, the candles had gone out, and it was pitch dark. I panicked and couldn't find the light switch. Sarah and Sultan were just walking down the corridor as I opened the door.'

'Happens all the time in Channel Four sitcoms,' said Sultan, enjoying the situation.

Sarah, having just popped into the bathroom, handed Jason a towel.

'So, you fell asleep in the bath? That's all the whisky, young man,' said Mrs McCracken in a cracked voice. Her face was flushed with anger rather than embarrassment.

'I fell asleep because I've been on the go since Friday. I couldn't sleep last night because I was on a train and I was being followed, and I thought I was going to be murdered in my cabin. And before that, I was up all the previous night in your —'

'—Jason, I've no time to stand listening to your moaning,' Mrs McCracken interrupted. 'Go back to your room, and for God's sake, put some clothes on.'

11

When they were standing in the hotel reception and Sam Flint heard Richards ask to see a 'Mrs McCracken', it took him a few moments to remember where he'd heard that name before. It was just yesterday morning, although it felt about a week ago already. Terry had told him he'd sent Gregory to retrieve money from this McCracken bird, but he'd disappeared off the radar. So Sam had driven over to McCracken's place in the back of beyond, but nobody was there. And then McCracken's weirdo neighbour had talked about Jason Tranter, and he'd forgotten about Gregory and switched his attentions to his old school 'friend'. He'd seen Tranter carrying the sports bag — the one with the money in it. He must have taken the money off the old girl and be taking it to Gregory's place. But Tranter had driven all the way to Cambridge, then caught the train to London and on up to Scotland. And he, Sam, had followed him all the way. Pretty smart, actually.

And now, confusingly, it looked like Tranter was taking the money back to McCracken. So he's not hooked up with Gregory; he's on McCracken's side. Is Tranter bringing the bag of money to McCracken then? Has he already delivered it? Time to find out.

'Be with you later,' Sam said to Rebecca Leyden-Fuller, after they had checked in and she was jangling the room keys at him. She answered silently with a face that said 'Suit yourself,' and headed off to their room.

While the other guests checked in and dispersed, Sam loitered in the reception, the lounge, and even the dining room, looking at the assorted weaponry displayed on the walls. As well as a mounted set of shotguns and pistols, there was an enormous pair of crossed swords — claymores — above the fireplace. He pictured himself swinging one around and nodded appreciatively. 'Heavy duty,' he thought. After a few minutes, Sandy Lamb passed through reception carrying a tray of tea things. Sam followed him upstairs.

Gillian McCracken was back in her room, staring out the window, wondering about her niece. She'd always had a soft spot for Bernie and allowed herself the credit for the young woman's academic success. Bernie's parents weren't great believers in education, and it had been the aunt's job to supply the child with books for Christmas and birthdays. As a teenager, Bernie had spent much of her school holidays with her and Henry. Mrs McCracken's natural inquisitiveness had rubbed off on the girl and she'd done well at school and studied English Literature at the University of East Anglia. She followed that up with a PhD at University College London, and it was there that she'd shared a flat with, amongst others, Rebecca Leyden-Fuller. And it was there that the trouble had started.

Mrs McCracken had kept in close contact with Bernie during her courses, following her academic progress. But when she was in London, the phone calls had become less frequent, and Bernie had become evasive when her aunt asked how she was doing with her research. Until one weekend when Bernie had arrived unexpectedly on the McCracken's doorstep in floods of tears, worried that she'd barely started her thesis, and her supervisor had threatened to throw her off the course. After much tea and sympathy, and some gently worded advice that she might need to rein in her social life and concentrate on her work, Bernie had felt able to return to London. The advice must have worked, because, of course, Bernie had got her PhD, with flying colours, and soon had a plum job with Cambridge University.

Even so, Mrs McCracken continued to worry about her niece. She never seemed to hold down any personal relationships. She was smart and attractive. Neither Gillian nor Henry could understand why she didn't have young men queuing up for her attention. Or young women; Gillian wasn't prudish. Anyway, she was very pleased when Bernie and Jason started 'stepping out', as she still described it. He wasn't bad looking, he was polite and kind, and that he was one of the 'Secret Millionaires' was a lucky bonus.

But was he to be trusted?

'What do you think, Henry?' she murmured to herself. 'Is he going to break Bernie's heart? What should I do?'

A knock came at the door, and she wiped away a tear. She opened the door to the grateful sight of Sandy, bringing a tray of tea, along with the news that the other guests had arrived.

'You're my saviour,' she said to him. 'I've got an awful headache, and I really couldn't face anyone downstairs just at the moment.'

'Ach, I'm not surprised. You've had a long journey getting up here. You and I are of an age where we can't just zoom about the world without its taking its toll anymore.'

'Oh, it's not that, Sandy. I've just got rather a lot to think about at the moment. I want to make a good impression on Mr Richards and his friends. If Rara Avis take on Sannah House as one of their venues, it'll mean the place will get refurbished and developed in a much better way than I would ever manage.'

'So you'll be selling the place, then?' The tea cup rattled in its saucer as Sandy brought it over.

'No, I want to keep it, but Rara Avis will take a share in the place in return for their investment.'

'Like in Dragon's Den, then? Off the TV?'

'That's the sort of thing, yes. I think I'd make a splendid old dragon, don't you? Don't worry, Sandy, I'll make sure that you and Gracie come out of this alright. You've been a wonderful friend to me, and to Henry before me. You've kept the place going all these years, since Henry bought the place.'

'Ay, and all the while you never knew your husband had bought it, did you? Even when he brought you up here? Just a wee holiday at a place run by his old school pal, Sandy, eh? Did you really never know that he was the owner? That's strange, that is.'

'Henry had his reasons for keeping quiet about it and I'd really like it if we continue to keep that side of things quiet, Sandy. As far as Rara Avis know it's been in Henry's family for generations. All adds to the charm, you see. If we play our cards right and they take the place on, I'll see that they look after you. And don't worry about your job. I expect there will be new people coming in, but if you want to stay on, I'm sure we can arrange something. So if anyone asks about the history of the place... it's best if you know nothing. Just leave that to me. Is that okay, Sandy?'

'Oh, that's fine,' said Sandy. 'Now I must be getting back to help in the kitchen. Don't you worry, Mrs McCracken. It'll all turn out dandy.'

'I hope so. Thanks, Sandy.'

And as Sandy left her room, she added, 'I really hope so.'

The deal with Rara Avis was only part of her worries. She had the problem of the dead body in her asparagus bed to worry about, and the threat of retribution from the gang that the body belonged to. And then she was concerned about her niece's relationship with Jason Tranter. Should she tell Bernie what she saw at Jason's house, with that woman who was now at Sannah House? If she did, what would Jason do, and how would that affect the dead body situation?

Another knock at the door.

'Who is it?' she called, but the door opened and a young man in a red tee-shirt and grey jogging bottoms entered the room.

'Excuse me, young man?' said Gillian McCracken.

'Now why should I do that?' said Sam slowly. He walked into the centre of the room and looked around at the walls and windows, but never looking directly at McCracken.

'Who are you? Leave my room at once!'

'I used to play golf with your husband, Henry. Nice man. Quiet.' Sam walked over to the window and stared out at the rain. 'But it's the quiet ones you have to watch out for, isn't it? He owed us money... but you know that, of course.' He turned to look at her. 'Where's the bag, then? Has Tranter given it to you already?'

'I beg your pardon? Whatever do you mean?'

'The bag of money. Tranter's brought it here. Has he given it to you, or do I have to go pay him a visit?'

Gillian McCracken stared at him, her brow furrowed. Then she smiled.

'I see what's happened here. You're another one of Terry Flint's men, aren't you?' said Gillian McCracken.

'What do you mean?'

'I mean you're talking about Terry Flint's money. That's what you're here for, isn't it?'

'Might be...'

'Which can only mean one thing. Oh, dear! How unfortunate!'

She was still smiling. Now it was Sam's face that was troubled.

'What do you mean? I haven't got time for this.'

'I'll say you haven't. I'd say you need to catch up with your colleague, pretty sharpish. Two days ago, a young man came to my house and explained that my husband may - ahem - not have settled his financial affairs before he died. It wasn't a surprise to me. There was an unexplained suitcase of money, you see. I found it when I was clearing out Henry's things. Such a lot of money. I knew it couldn't be right. So I kept it hidden in the cellar and tried not to think about it. Sounds silly, I know, but when you get to my age... you must understand that I'm quite comfortable. I don't need much, just the occasional holiday really and I've got enough...'

'What happened to the money?' Sam interrupted.

'That's what I'm explaining. Your colleague came round asking for the money, rather brusquely, and so I... I let him have it.'

'You what? So Gregory's got the money then?'

'That's right. And if you work for Terry Flint, and you're up here chasing the same money I gave to your colleague — Gregory, you say...? Well, that rather suggests to me that Gregory has run off with the money, wouldn't you say?'

Sam raised his hands to his head.

'Sssshii...' He couldn't bring himself to complete the expletive. 'So what's Jason Tranter got to do with it, then? Why's he here?'

'Jason? No, he doesn't know anything about it. He's my niece's boyfriend. They've come up here for a break.'

Sam Flint turned back to look out of the window, his face darker than the clouds outside. He banged his fist down on the windowsill and then stormed out of the room.

Gillian McCracken's headache felt like it had lifted a bit.

12

Paige Fellows sneaked into the dining hall before the others and stood squinting at the furnishings. A long table was set with ornate silver, china, and glass. Above it hung two large crystal chandeliers. Old portraits in gilt frames hung on deep red walls, and the carpet was a tartan of blues, browns and greys. It was kitsch, and she knew that nothing in this room would never have found a place in any of Jack Tang's restaurants, but taken altogether, and applying the blurred filter that squinting provided, she had to admit it had something. It spoke of a different way of life in a different time. This would have been the height of highland luxury once, and it still felt special. It exuded an ambience that spoke of privilege and power, and essentially, that was the brief that Rara Avis had given her. She opened her eyes wider, however, and noticed that the silver was tarnished, the china chipped, and the tartan carpet was threadbare. Still, they could all be replaced, like-for-like, with quality furnishings. The paintings could be restored; this whole room could be restored to its original glory.

Jack Tang joined her.

'Hey Baby. Wow! Clear this junk out, right?'

'Au contraire, Jack.' Paige smiled at him. 'Leave the décor to me. Your job is to work out what can be done with the food.'

Jack pulled a face. 'Oh listen, Baby. I'm gonna need your help. Do I really have to say nice things about the meal tonight? You know I won't like it.'

As he said this, Gracie ushered the other guests into the room. Paige glared at him, warning him to keep quiet.

Mrs McCracken entered, holding her niece's arm. 'From the way everyone was attacking those peanuts in the bar, I think we've all brought a healthy appetite with us. I have every confidence in you and Sandy, Gracie.'

Richards was talking with Jason, but Jason looked distracted. His eyes darted round the room and his hands nursed a beer that he'd carried in from the bar. Any peace that his candlelit bath had restored to his shattered nerves had been blown apart again by the recent naked encounter with his friends in the corridor and the argument he'd had with Bernie in their room just afterwards.

'There's an opportunity for you here, Jason. I don't know how you feel about going into a venture with Mrs McCracken? Thing is, this place is going to need capital investment. The rough draft business plan I've had drawn up shows that there could be a very attractive return on the investment here. Obviously, as a Rara Avis venue, there will be some income from the events we hold, but with the connections we have, we could get interest from a lot of other exclusive clients. Still, I recognise that given your relationship with her niece, you may have reservations about becoming Gillian's "partner in crime".'

The phrase broke Jason into a cold sweat. Richards had a reputation for knowing everything about everyone, but there was no way he could know about what had happened in Mrs McC's garden, could there? If he did, it would be typical of him to drop it casually into a conversation like that. 'No,' thought Jason, 'I'm just being paranoid.' Richards carried on talking about the business prospects for the Sannah House. Jason tuned out and looked around the room.

Bernie had walked over to join Paige, and the cloud that had hung over her since rowing with Jason had dissipated. 'Paige has that effect on people.' he thought. He remembered the effect she had on him, when he first met her out at Molatedi, when he'd mistakenly thought that she was someone Richards had wanted him to meet. 'What would life have been like if I'd ended up with Paige rather than Bernie?' he wondered. He'd not be in this mess with Mrs McC. He'd only agreed to burying the body because he wanted to protect his relationship with Bernie. But what was that relationship? He loved the lifestyle that he and Bernie had carved out together. Who wouldn't love that lifestyle? Travelling around the world, doing everything he'd ever wanted with his money. Life was simple and life was fun. But was it just the lifestyle that he loved? What about Bernie herself? She made him happy, didn't she? Well, he wasn't happy at the moment. He couldn't imagine ever truly being happy again. Not with the weight of his secret weighing around his neck.

'... the expected exponential growth in Chinese tourism could provide a reliable income stream...' Richards was saying.

Sarah and Sultan walked into the dining room and, seeing Richards in full flow with Jason, made their way over to join Bernie and Paige.

Jason winced, and Richard noticed. 'Ah, you think this pandemic thingy might affect the tourist trade? A temporary blip, I promise you.'

Jason watched Bernie as Sarah approached. He saw her angry cloud return, but somehow, to his relief, Paige was all smiles and eager to meet the newcomers. Sultan started talking to Jack. They'd met once before, at Tang's restaurant in Birmingham, and Jason wondered if Sultan would be more polite this time. He watched Sarah, dressed in jeans and a white shirt, standing with Paige and Bernie, who were both in sparkling eveningwear. 'That can't be easy,' he thought, 'but she probably doesn't even see it as a problem.' And it struck him in that moment that Sarah was where his sympathies lay. In his ideal world, he would be with Sarah, enjoying the lifestyle that he'd had with Bernie. Of course, that couldn't happen because Sarah — Robin really — was so wedded to her job. A job which involved investigating his best mate. If she could only take the casual approach to her career that he'd had at PKR. 'But being a police officer, being in public service, is different to being a webmaster,' he supposed. 'And she's just not that sort of person. She's solid. Dependable. If I could just talk to her about this nightmare... this problem... the body I buried. She's good at making problems go away. Could she make the crime of unlawful burial go away? Possibly not. The law's too important for that'.

He looked at Sultan. He was wearing a T-shirt with the words 'Never Stop Believing' and a small silhouette of the Loch Ness Monster. His hair was shiny and combed, his beard trimmed, and he looked at ease with himself.

They were all seated by the time Rebecca Leyden-Fuller and Sam entered the room. Rebecca, in a black jumpsuit with lacey sleeves, looked more in keeping with Richards' idea of formal dinner wear, but Sam looked completely out of place. Rebecca had asked Sandy if he could find spare a jacket for Sam. Sandy had found an old ill-fitting dinner jacket and Sam wore it over the red t-shirt, along with a thunderous scowl.

'Oops! Are we late?' said Rebecca with an unconcerned smile, as they sat at the end of the table.

Sam looked briefly at Mrs McCracken and then bowed his head and stared a hole in his placemat.

Jason panicked. He gripped the table with both hands and pushed his chair back a little. It was an involuntary reaction; his nervous system was telling him to escape, get out of the room as quickly as possible. This was the guy he had suspected of following him in Cambridge and on the night train. Somehow he'd followed him all the way here, despite the diversion they'd taken. He looked at Sarah across the table and tried to convey this information by a frown and a series of half-nods in Sam's direction. Sarah looked puzzled. The cloud hanging over Bernie had turned thunderous when she saw Rebecca was also a guest.

When she noticed the exchange of glances between Jason and Sarah, she looked even more annoyed. Mrs McCracken sat quietly, watching them all.

Gracie wheeled in a trolley laden with bowls of steaming soup, which she distributed around the table.

Mrs McCracken broke the silence. 'Ms Leyden-Fuller, perhaps you should introduce your... friend? Although I think Jason may know him?'

'W... what?' stammered Jason.

'Of course,' said Rebecca Leyden-Fuller. 'Everyone, this is Sam. Old school friend of Jason's, apparently. I think this was supposed to be a big "surprise, surprise" moment, but it seems to have gone off a bit half-cocked. Heigh-ho. Say hello to Jason, Samuel.'

'Yeah, hello Tranter. Surprise, surprise. Remember me?' Sam spat the words out.

'Sam? Sammy Flint? Oh my god! What are you doing here?'

Mrs McCracken's eyes widened.

'Just thought I'd say hello,' Sam mumbled and stared at the bowl of the soup that had been placed in front of him.

Everyone in the room remained in awkward silence during the exchange. It felt like there was more to be said, but nothing was forthcoming from either party.

'Ten more deaths today, apparently.' Richards opened up the conversation.

'Oh, you believe all that, do you?' said Rebecca in a tired voice.

'I see no reason not to. Why, do you think there are more?'

'No, I think it's just the usual mainstream media scaremongering.'

'It's not the media who are going to put the country into lockdown tomorrow, Rebecca. It's the government. Now I don't think they'd be doing that if there wasn't a serious threat.'

'Lockdown?' This was Sam. Everyone turned to look at him.

'My understanding,' said Richards, 'is that there will be an announcement tomorrow, banning unnecessary travel, but there'll be a lockdown soon where we are told to stay in our homes, you can be sure.'

'What are they calling unnecessary travel?' asked Sam. 'Cos I need to get off this sodding island.'

Rebecca Leyden-Fuller rolled her eyes. 'The chap at reception told you that there's no boat likely until Tuesday. Sea's too rough.'

'Never mind, mate,' said Sultan. He'd rejected his soup on account of it having visible signs of chicken, but uncharacteristically, he had not caused a fuss about there not being a vegetarian option. 'You can spend some time catching up with your old school pal, Jason. I bet you've got some stories you'd like to share about him, eh?'

'No,' said Sam, soaking a bread roll into his soup and stuffing it messily into his mouth.

Sultan smiled broadly and sat back in his chair, enjoying the awkward atmosphere that this latest addition to the party was causing.

Quiet conversations began again around the table. Jack Tang was saying complimentary things about the soup to Richards. Paige was praising the décor to Bernie and Mrs McCracken.

Jason appeared to be concentrating on his soup. His hand was still shaking slightly, making progress difficult, but he felt a little calmer. So Sam Flint had tracked him down. Well, something like that was always going to happen, he supposed. Some old acquaintance turning up out of the blue was always going to be a possibility since his lottery win. It would be awkward to turn down the inevitable request for money, but he was relieved that it wasn't a police officer or a member of a criminal gang that had followed him up here. He avoided looking at Sam and poured himself another glass of wine.

Rebecca Leyden-Fuller called across the table, 'Hi Bernice, fancy seeing you again! What brings you here, I wonder? Same as me, I guess. There's something very rewarding about hanging around with millionaires, isn't there?'

Bernie ignored her and quietly asked Paige about her journey up to Sannah.

'We're being ghosted, Sammy-Boy!' said Rebecca. 'Jason won't look at you and Bernie won't look at me. Mind you, it's not the first time I've been cancelled by her. And I know why.'

She spoke loudly, inviting Bernie to respond, but it was Sultan who spoke.

'Is it your repellent views on immigration?'

Jason looked up from his soup. Sarah put down her spoon.

'Sorry, because I've only just remembered who you are. But some things stick in the mind, like being called "a cockroach" for instance.' There was fire in Sultan's eyes.

Rebecca Leyden-Fuller looked pleased with herself.

'Ah, the article I wrote three years ago. Still being talked about... amazing! As a matter of fact, I didn't call anyone a cockroach. I said that a group of people were like cockroaches. There's a difference. If only we had a respected academic from the English Faculty of Cambridge University to guide us on the niceties of simile and metaphor.'

This time, everyone turned to Bernie to see what her response would be, but Leyden-Fuller continued.

'Mind you, I did say "respected academic". Sorry, hun. Not sure you qualify. In fact, if the faculty knew what I know, I think the term would be "disgraced academic".'

'And what is that supposed to mean?' asked Mrs McCracken.

'It means that the thesis she wrote for her doctorate, the one that set her up for her academic career at Cambridge, was not her own work. And I should know, because I wrote it.'

Rebecca Leyden-Fuller sat back in her chair, triumphant. Bernie glared at her, red-faced but unable to speak.

Jason felt it was time to say something. 'Look, I know you make a living from winding people up, but please... please... just shut the fuck up.'

Sam saw Jason sticking up for his partner and felt the urge to do the same. 'Don't speak to her like that,' he said, and stood up and walked towards where Jason was sitting.

'Seriously?' said Jason, standing to meet him head on.

'Gentlemen, please!' Mrs McCracken's voice was stern.

Richards hid a satisfied smile as he bent over his phone and tapped to make a call.

Sam and Jason were now standing inches apart, sweat on their faces glistening in the candlelight from the table. They shuffled backwards and forwards, eyes locked, and somehow made their way to a clear space in front of the fireplace.

'Ja...,' began Bernie, but stopped when she saw Rebecca Leyden-Fuller glowing with delight at the prospect of the two men fighting. Bernie wouldn't urge Jason to back down in that case. Everyone else was silent.

Part of Jason expected, wanted even, someone to intervene, but another part of him was ready for his first fight since primary school. All the pent-up anxiety that had accumulated over the last few days had been transformed into anger, thanks to the catalyst of alcohol and the objectionable presence of Sam Flint. And thanks to the physical training of the last few months, he had confidence in his own strength and agility. This wasn't going to end like that old playground fight.

Sam's fist swung round in what seemed to Jason to be a slow-motion arc and landed on the side of his head. The force of the blow sent Jason staggering back to the table, bumping into the back of Mrs McCracken's chair. He glimpsed the stern look on her face, shook his head as if to throw off the pain that his left ear was feeling, and stepped back towards Sam Flint, this time with his fists raised.

Once again, the pair were toe-to-toe, red-faced, pulsing with anger, both taking exaggerated sniffs of the air. And then Jason jabbed downwards, towards his opponent's belly, creasing him in two, and followed up quickly with an upwards cut that landed directly on his mouth, and suddenly Sam was lying crumpled on the floor, his head level with Jason's shoes.

Sam couldn't process what had happened. He stared glassily at the shoes. Brown leather, that brogue pattern he hated, and pointy toe caps that irritated him. Smug bastard shoes. Sam craned his head forward and bit into Jason's shins.

Jason was as surprised at being bitten as he was at having floored Sam in the first place. The pain was an electric jolt shooting up his leg, but he was already feeling victorious. All he had to do was bring his other foot down on Sam's head. He lifted it in the air but hesitated. Was stamping on a head going too far? Could you kill someone like that? He had no sympathy for Sam, but he didn't need a murder or manslaughter charge right now. He found himself staring into Mrs McCracken's faintly smiling face.

'Hold it, buddy,' came a familiar voice from the doorway. It was Dodge Mhlongo. 'That's enough, don't you think? What's going on precisely?' He walked up to where Jason was standing, his foot resting firmly, but gently, on the side of Sam's head.

'Thank you for coming so quickly, Dodge,' said Richards. 'This is the situation. These gentlemen have had a bit of a disagreement.'

'Started by her,' said Bernie, pointing at Rebecca Leyden-Fuller.

Dodge turned. He hadn't clocked anyone else in the room, yet alone the woman he still held a torch for.

'Becky!' he said hoarsely.

'Two guys fighting over my honour,' said Rebecca. 'What can I say? It happens from time to time.'

Dodge grunted and turned back to Jason and Sam.

'Okay, buddy,' he said, gently pushing Jason out of the way, 'I'll take it from here.' He grabbed Sam by the collar of his red t-shirt and pulled him to his feet. 'Alright Mister, I believe you've been showing disrespect to the lady over there. I want you to apologise to her.' He man-handled Sam over towards Rebecca Leyden-Fuller. Sam's lip was bleeding and there was snot dripping from his nose.

'Well… no. He was the one standing up for me,' said Rebecca, looking amused.

'Actually,' said Richards. 'I think there may be a long-term rivalry between him and Mr Tranter. Things got overheated.'

'Sam Flint has been behaving obnoxiously since he arrived with Ms Leyden-Fuller.' said Gillian McCracken.

'They're a thing,' added Bernie, coolly, to drive the point home.

Dodge looked shocked. 'What, this piece of shit? Becky, really?'

'Um… as my grandmother used to say, "you have to settle for scrag end of lamb when you can't get beefsteak."'

She lowered her head and looked up at Dodge coquettishly. Sam's fate was sealed.

13

'Who are you calling a piece of shit, you piece of shit?' said Sam, shaking himself free from Dodge Mhlongo. Then he turned to the rest of the diners. 'What a fucking crowd you lot are, heh? Millionaires. You think you're the dog's bollocks, don't you? A bit of money, so you can hide away from the world on your manky little island, stuck out in the arse-end of nowhere. Pathetic.' He walked towards Jack Tang and gripped the back of his chair. Tang shot up, thinking Sam was about to up turn him, or hit him or something, but Sam merely took the chair.

'And the moment there's any trouble, what do you do?' he continued, as he walked with chair and placed it by the fireplace. 'You call in this guy, your security boy, to deal with it for you.'

Dodge breathed in sharply and walked towards Sam, who calmly stepped up onto the seat of the chair. There he stood still for a second, looking down on the diners, and a smile came to his bleeding lip. 'You have no fucking idea, do you?' he said, and spun round to the wall above the fireplace and unhooked one of the huge claymores and lifted it down from the wall. He stepped down from the chair and, gripping the handle in both hands, began swinging the sword from side to side, his face contorted in an angry snarl.

Dodge had reached him now, and he raised both arms wide and started a dance where he kept a fraction longer than a sword's width from Sam. The diners rearranged themselves so they were all on the other side of the table from the pair, who shuffled back and forth by the fireplace. Then Sam realised Dodge was now standing by the chair. Sam glanced up at the remaining claymore on the wall and realised he may have made a tactical mistake. Dodge might get his own sword, and Sam didn't know how to sword-fight. Never mind. If Dodge got on the chair, Sam would take him out with one swipe across the knees. He raised the heavy claymore back over his shoulder, ready for a killer strike, and said, 'Don't even think about it.'

Dodge swooped up the chair and hurled it at Sam's legs. It was enough to topple him and fell onto the floor, releasing his grip on the sword. Dodge was swift and before people could take in what was happening, he was kneeling on Sam's chest with the dull blade of the claymore across his throat.

'Never call me "boy",' he said.

There was a collective exhalation around the room.

'Is there somewhere we can lock this feller up?' asked Dodge. 'Let him cool down a bit?'

'The rooms all have locks,' said Sandy, who had come in to take the soup plates away and found the commotion.

'He'll trash the place if he's left alone,' said Rebecca Leyden-Fuller.

'I don't think he will,' said Mrs McCracken in a quiet but commanding voice. 'Between us, I'm sure we can persuade him to behave himself. I've dealt with schoolboys twice as awkward as this one. Come on, Mr Mhlongo, let's get this gentleman to his room, and have a quiet word with him.'

Dodge looked at Richards questioningly, but Richards shrugged, and Dodge obeyed instructions.

When they returned, about ten minutes later, Dodge took Sam's place at the table, next to Rebecca Leyden-Fuller, and the meal resumed. As Sandy served the main course, he apologised for the effect the delay had had on the presentation. 'Gracie's distraught,' he said, 'but I told her you'll all have to just accept that the vegetables are no longer as perky as they were.'

'Tell her not to worry,' said Jack Tang. 'Everything will be fine.'

'Is he alright?' Rebecca asked Dodge.

'He's fine. Quiet as a lamb. I don't know what the lady said to him — she asked me to leave the room — but he's calmed right down. Don't expect any more trouble from him. I told him what I'd do to him if there was any trouble, just to be sure.'

Rebecca smiled and poured some wine into Dodge's glass.

'Is that it then?' said Jason. 'He's just going to be allowed to stay here and everything goes back to how it was?' Jason still didn't quite have full hearing in one ear, but after a swift glass of red wine, he'd mostly recovered from his tussle with Sam. 'Shouldn't we inform the local police?' He avoided eye contact with Sarah.

'There's only one special constable on Sannah,' said Mrs McCracken. 'And I'm not sure it's the best idea to get him involved. There's virtually no crime on the island, you see. There just isn't. About ten years ago, someone stole all the knitted hats from the gift shop, and it made all the London papers, because it was a quaint story about a crime free island where they don't even lock the doors of the shops. If another story breaks, we might get a surge in publicity. I imagine Rara Avis would really rather not have that.'

'Definitely not,' said Richards. 'I think we just need to get Mr Flint off the island as quickly as possible.'

'That won't be easy,' said Mrs McCracken. 'They've cancelled all the ferries while they work out what they're doing about the virus, and Sandy's not taking the boat out in this weather. He'll have to stay a couple of days, at least until the weather clears.'

'Well, news just in,' said Rebecca Leyden-Fuller. 'I don't intend to let him sleep in my room. He's clearly unstable. I mean...'

'That's alright, Becky,' said Dodge. 'There's my bothy just up the hill. I don't mind swapping with him. He'll be fine up there. And I'll be...'

'... fine down here,' Rebecca finished for him.

14

Paige Fellows sat up and looked across at the twin bed where Jack Tang was snoring away in his purple satin pyjamas. Another disturbed night. She picked up her phone from her bedside table, its hi-res camera showing her reflection in unforgiving detail. Despite the expensive preparation she'd applied before retiring to bed, her skin looked tired and washed out. There were hints of bulges beneath her eyes. This room didn't help. It was stuffy and smelled of damp. Jack had tried leaving the window slightly ajar, but the gale outside whistled through the gap with a noise that they both agreed was incompatible with sleep. She looked back at Jack, snoring in utter oblivion. She filmed him briefly for evidence. Her phone's weather app told her that the morning winds would still be strong, but rain wasn't expected until late morning.

She sent the video she had just taken to Bernie's WhatsApp. 'Can't take any more of this. Fancy a brisk morning walk?' she added to the message.

Not waiting for a reply, she slipped into the en-suite, washed and did her best to repair the night's damage. When she returned to her phone, a message was waiting.

'Yes! Can't see video. Phone battery not good. Let's meet at 10.'

15

'Is this what Scottish people live like?' thought Sam Flint. 'Poor bastards!'

He'd woken in the bothy and looked around him, seeing it properly for the first time. Last night, the South African security bloke had brought him here and left him with a pathetic little battery light that had faded quickly. He'd been so cold that his only thoughts had been to get himself cocooned in the sleeping bag that was laid out on a camp bed. As soon as he'd warmed up, he'd fallen into a deep, drunken sleep.

The light streaming through the bothy window revealed a room that was far better appointed than most bothies in the Highlands, and better than some flats that Flint Holdings let out to migrant workers, where he sometimes collected rent. It had a washbasin, a cupboard, and a bookcase with a dozen paperbacks and a pile of magazines that were intended for helping guests build a fire in the grate at the other end of the room from his bed. There was a table and two chairs.

'What a dump,' he thought, still wrapped up in his sleeping bag, now damp from a night's perspiration. His head was aching, but that was okay. That was because of the wine he'd put away last night. His jaw felt painful too, and that was not okay. That was from the punch that Jason Tranter had landed on him, and the indignity hurt more than the bruise. He'd taken some damage at the hands of the security bloke as well, but that didn't bother him. With Tranter, it was personal. A score needed to be settled.

He got up, walked over to the washbasin, and bent his head over to drink some water from the tap. Through the window, he saw a female figure striding up the hill about twenty metres away. Tranter's girlfriend.

16

Bernie wasn't sure why she had picked up the quaich before she left the house — just another impulse that she didn't understand. There were so many of those lately. As soon as she had woken and seen Jason splayed out on the bed, his head partly under a pillow and one leg hanging out of the covers, she knew she had to get out of the room and into the fresh air. Perhaps that would help clarify her thoughts. She slipped out of bed quietly so as not to wake him, not out of kindness, but so that she didn't have to talk to him or explain where she was going. As she left the room, she saw the quaich on the dressing table and it irritated her. She didn't like the way he'd come by it, and she didn't want him to wake up, see it and feel smug about it. She put it in her pocket.

She didn't know where she was going. She'd pulled on some clothes, but probably not the right ones for the weather. Jeans, a top and a light jacket. Trainers. Well, it wasn't raining at the moment and a short, brisk walk would keep her warm. Maybe it would turn into a long walk. She certainly didn't feel like joining the others for breakfast. The salty, fresh morning air was an excellent substitute for the shower she would normally have taken to banish any sleepiness. She took long strides up the hill at the back of the house and the exertion felt good.

Last night had been horrible. First, there was the bombshell from Rebecca, when she finally dragged the skeleton out of the closet; Bernie's doctorate thesis, 'Everything on Evidence - Implausible Reality in the Victorian Novel' had been written by Rebecca, when they were living together. It had all been a question of expediency. Bernie had been struggling with her studies and was in danger of crashing out, while Rebecca wanted to quit college anyway to take up a media career. 'Why waste a good thesis?' Rebecca had said. And now she was threatening to expose her: '*If the faculty knew what I know...*'. If she followed through on that threat and told them, it would mean the end of her career. The surprising thing was that she hadn't done it before, when there was the row about the cancelled debate in Cambridge. There must have been something holding her back. Perhaps she didn't want to draw attention to her own elite education. Her core fanbase were quite hostile to experts and academics.

Then there was Jason's fight with that thug. He'd stood up for her, putting Rebecca in her place, and he'd floored the other chap pretty quickly. So shouldn't she feel proud of him? No, some other feeling was drowning out any pride.

'Shut the fuck up!' Jason had told Rebecca. That was the drink talking. And that was what had led to that drunken brawl. It was so unlike him. In her experience, Jason could handle his drink. Whenever he'd been even tipsy before, it had just made him daft, which could be quite endearing. She was seeing a different side to him lately. She suspected it was a side that was more familiar to Sarah and Sultan. Perhaps last night's coarseness was an example of how they all behaved on those nights they used to spend in that pokey pub in the West Midlands.

Why did he always insist on going back to that dingy public house? Since they had been together, she had shown him so many better places — places they had discovered together. The Paradiso in Barcelona sprang to mind, and The Connaught bar in London, where Jason had impressed an American film star with his knowledge of single malts, and his ability to stand rounds despite the exorbitant prices. God! That night! She felt that something had clicked with Jason after that. He'd finally stopped feeling guilty for being wealthy and started enjoying the lifestyle that his fortune could buy. That was the deal. That was why she felt no shame in being with a guy so much richer than her. She had the knowledge, the initiative, and the appetite to help him get pleasure from his money. They'd only just begun to see the world, and now borders were closing, and the world was locking down. She hated it, but she had a feeling Jason didn't mind at all.

And then Paige's message arrived: '*Can't take any more of this. Fancy a brisk morning walk?*'

Can't take any more of what? Bernie wondered. Frustratingly, the bright sunshine made it impossible to make out what the attached video was about. Typical, actually: she'd been picking up signals from Paige ever since they'd met, and she was always unsure if they meant what she thought they did. It would be great to have a walk with her. It would be easier to talk. She felt the lump of the whisky cup in her pocket. There was something she wanted to do before meeting up with Paige. She texted back to suggest they met up in an hour's time.

She quickened her pace, reached the top of the hill, and the view of Sannah was exhilarating. Clouds were racing across the sky and complicated patterns of light and shade were moving across the land and over the wave-strewn sea. What if her suspicions about Paige were true? Would she do anything about it? There was no question. She knew she would. But would that mean betraying Jason? She wouldn't see it like that, but he would, she supposed. For her, a friendship with Paige could be completely separate from her relationship with him. She'd never told him about the other relationship she'd had with a woman long ago. Or it least, she'd never explained the nature of that relationship. As far as Jason knew, Rebecca Leyden-Fuller had just been a flat mate.

She pressed on with her mission.

Sam Flint didn't bother closing the door of the bothy as he left to follow Bernie Tenant on her walk up the hill. There was nothing belonging to him in there. He didn't expect he'd be going back. He didn't know where he was going later; the only thing going through his mind was catching up with her and then...

What did he know about her? First, she was Tranter's girlfriend, and that made him hate her. Sam thought about his own last girlfriend, Letta. Scruffy Letta. A good figure, but a miserable, scowly face, and she hardly knew any English. Her flat, in a back street of Willenhall. Compare that with the tree-lined street in Cambridge where he'd seen Tranter and his woman, Bernie. Bloke's name — typically posh. He'd never understand posh women. The way she'd looked down her nose at him, and the bitchy way she was with Rebecca. Mind you, she was no better. The way she'd dumped him for this other guy was out of order. No respect. Weren't these posh people supposed to be all about manners? And the clothes, of course. That dress Bernie was wearing last night, the jeans and jacket she was wearing today. Smart, pressed and no stains. Their neatness offended him. He badly wanted to do something about it.

Sam knew she shouldn't really be the target of his anger. It was Tranter who had floored him last night. It was Tranter who had somehow taken Terry's money — he was sure of it — and it was Tranter who had got out of line since the days back at school, when Sam had established the proper order of things. But Tranter was safe in the house somewhere, protected by his rich friends. And she was out here in the open. And just at the moment, he hated her just about as much as he hated Tranter.

Bernie made her way down the hill, towards the field surrounded by dry-stone walls, with its two-metre high 'Punishment Stone' in the centre. She wondered who it was that got punished here. Probably women, she thought. It was usually women. For being unfaithful, or letting the milk curdle, or gossiping, or something ungodly like that. They'd be the ones made to stand with their thumbs stuck in the hole for days on end. And how did that work? Why couldn't they just pull their thumbs out? Whereas she bet the men would get away with all sorts; drunkenness, sheep rustling, wife-beating, and so on. She imagined punishing Jason for his drunkenness last night. Marching him up to the stone and somehow coercing him to put his thumb in that hole. It didn't seem practical. The story of the Punishment Stone must be a myth.

She felt the weight of the quaich in her pocket banging against her hip as she descended the hill. No, she could think of a better way to punish Jason.

What had started as a walk for some fresh air had now become a mission. A secret mission. And suddenly she felt guilty, and she quickened her pace and walked with her head down, as if someone might be watching her misdeed. She passed the stone and made her way across the rough ground towards the coast.

'It won't be forever,' she told herself. 'He'll get it back, eventually. When the time is right. When he's sorry.'

The battle between the sunlight and the clouds had been conclusively won by the clouds. They gathered, thick and black, and the air felt colder and damper. Bernie reached the edge of the prison holes and walked carefully around them, looking for the best one to hide the quaich in. There were some that were only a metre deep and offered no hiding place. There was one which was steep and dark, and which she couldn't see the bottom of. It would probably still make an effective prison; you'd need a rope to get in and out.

She found one that she thought she could scramble down. It was maybe four metres deep, but it looked like others had climbed down before. There was litter at the bottom, a couple of cans, and a plastic bag. Someone might have thrown them down, of course, except that it looked like the cans were standing upright. She could almost trace a path spiralling down and jutting rocks should provide secure foot-holes. But it was madness, wasn't it, to climb down on her own, with no-one even knowing where she was? She checked her phone. She could read the screen now and she texted Paige. Now someone knew where she was.

The rain began as she reached the bottom of the hole. Just a drizzle, or a *smirr*, as her aunt might call it. Bernie was pleased with herself. She'd climbed down confidently and surely the climb back up would be even easier. She put the quaich into the discarded plastic bag and set it between the two cans of Irn Bru, left over from a kids' picnic, she supposed.

She started climbing back out of the hole. The rain was stronger, and the rocks were becoming slippy, but what could she expect in these shoes, really? Her fingers became numb as she gripped on cold wet rocks, but slowly, steadily, she reached the surface.

'Now, where do you think you're going?' said a voice, and Sam's foot came down on Bernie's hand.

17

'I have to hand it to you, lady,' said Dodge Mhlongo. 'You look quite at home with a shotgun.'

They were standing in a paddock to the east of Sannah House, an area that Mrs McCracken thought Rara Avis might want to develop for sporting use. She and Henry had been partial to a spot of clay pigeon shooting in recent years on their annual holidays at the hotel that Henry secretly owned.

'I've been shooting since I was a wee lass,' said Mrs McCracken. "Ran the Clay Society at Baschurch Girls' School and got the girls to the European finals in 2003. Pull!'

She'd tried to get Richards out this morning to convince him that the idea was worth pursuing. After last night's disrupted meal, she was worried that he might go cold on the idea of developing Sannah House. Unfortunately, Richards was busy with phone calls, so he suggested that Dodge Mhlongo went along in his place.

Dodge pulled back a lever on the old trap machine he was straddling and launched another skeet into the air. Mrs McCracken traced the arc of its flight with the barrel of her gun and fired, but the clay pigeon flew on, unharmed.

'Not really the weather for it today though, eh?' said Dodge. The rain from yesterday had stopped for a while, but the wind was stronger than ever, blowing the skeets off their intended trajectories. She had been shooting for fifteen minutes and hadn't hit one yet.

'No, but shooting at something is great for working out tension, don't you find?'

'Heh. Yeah, sometimes. Not so much if you miss, though. You're aiming ahead of the clay, which is good, but there's quite a headwind. Keep closer,'

'Hmm, perhaps you're right. Pull!'

She shot again and this time the skeet disintegrated satisfyingly in the sky. The next two went the same way.

'I thought you handled the situation with that young man very... efficiently last night,' said Mrs McCracken.

'Ah, he was well out of his depth. Too much drink, too many pills, not enough sleep. I've seen his type before. I checked on him first thing this morning, up at the bothy. Still sparked out.

Reckon he'll feel pretty sorry for himself when he eventually surfaces. I don't think we'll have any more trouble from him.'

'Hmm, I wonder,' she said. 'Would you like to take a few shots? I'll work the machine.'

'I dunno. I'll look a bit of a jerk if I can't hit them as well as you.'

'No-one's watching, and I won't tell.'

Dodge grinned and took up the shotgun, hitting the target every time.

Mrs McCracken was wrong, though. There was someone watching.

Gracie was still serving breakfast at a quarter past ten. Millionaires keeping London hours, she supposed. The porridge and kippers were easily prepared, but it was a pain to keep starting a new fry-up each time someone sauntered into the dining room and ordered 'The Full Sannah'. There was no way she was going to fry up bacon, sausages, black pudding and white pudding ahead of time and leave them sitting in a steamer. Gracie always cooked her breakfasts from scratch. Well, for this clientele, she would, anyway. And the head honcho still hadn't ordered his. Richards was standing in the bay window at the end of the room, on the phone. Paige, who seemed to appreciate the pressure Gracie was under, had taken the breakfast menu up to him, to nudge him into ordering, but he had waved her away while he continued talking on the phone.

'... yes. That's what I've heard... I know, it's hard to believe, but... actually, a virologist, good friend of mine, sound man... yes but he says the hospitals are going to be overwhelmed... well it's better to be safe than choking to death in some hospital corridor.' Richards maintained a calm tone, but his voice was becoming louder and Paige, Sultan and Sarah, the only other occupants of the dining room, could hear his half of the conversation clearly. 'Anyway, the thing is, I've had a dozen enquiries already and I think we need to lay something on. We need Isola Gallinara to prepare for thirty or forty guests for what might be an extended stay... I don't know... two months? Four? Who knows? All I know is that people want to ride the thing out in comfort... Yes, getting people there might be a problem... I know flights are being cancelled. We may have to use the *Rara Avis*. And we know some people with private jets, don't we? Anyway, can you just make a start getting the thing set up? I'll work on getting back to you as soon as I can. Irony is, there's a bunch of us here on this island, perfectly well isolated from the Great Unwashed, but truth is...' At this point he lowered his voice, '... there's no way anyone would want to stay here any length of time. Not yet, anyway.'

'What's this, Gus? We heading to warmer climes?' Rebecca Leyden-Fuller had just entered the dining room and caught the end of his phone call.

'You're not obliged to join us, Rebecca,' said Richards. 'I know you think coronavirus is all a hoax.'

'Still, no harm in topping up the vitamin D, is there?' she said. 'Doesn't look like we're going to get much sunshine here.'

Sarah's face had been getting redder. It was her turn to make a private conversation loud enough to be overheard. 'See, Sultan, that's my problem with Rara Avis. I don't object to them having fancy holidays and playing with expensive toys, but when it means they can escape something dreadful that the country should face together, well then you can count me out.'

'No-one was counting you in, Ms Headly,' said Richards. 'This service will be for Rara Avis members, their significant others, obviously. I gather you no longer fit that description, do you?'

'Me neither,' said Sultan. 'Never mind. I've got school on Monday, anyway.'

Outside, Mrs McCracken and Dodge Mhlongo were still taking it in turns to blast clay discs out of the sky. Something of a competition had developed between them, although Mrs McCracken thought her opponent was going easy on her. Meanwhile, Dodge was trying his hardest to create exactly that impression, whereas he was trying his very best to match the old lady's 'kill' count. Once she had hit her stride, she'd hardly missed.

A figure wearing a dark reefer coat walked heavily up from the house towards the paddock. He stopped by the stone wall and caught his breath while Dodge took a shot. Dodge saw the man from the corner of his eye and recognised him as the person who had been the last to disembark from the ferry yesterday. It was probably this mental distraction that made him miss his shot.

'Mrs McCracken?' The stranger said between laboured gasps for air.

Gillian McCracken turned to him.

'Good morning. Can I help you?'

'Jimmy Wilkes. May not recognise me. Been a long time. Sorry.'

'You'll have to forgive me. I've a terrible memory for names and faces.'

'Well, as I say, it was a very long time ago. An evening dinner-dance it was. Henry introduced us.'

'Ah, so you're a friend of Henry's.'

'Pals at school. Best pals.'

'Oh, I suppose you've heard?'

'Yes, Sandy told me. I was pals with him too, at school. I wanted to say how sorry I was to hear... and offer my condolences.'

'Thank you. What brings you to Sannah, Mr Wilkes?'

'Well, Gillian, — can I call you Gillian? — I suppose you could say it's a time of life thing. I'm retiring, you see. It's a big change for me. I've been in business all my life, and now I'm packing it all up and wondering what the next stage of my life is going to be. You might say that I am a free spirit. I thought I'd look in on some old friends, remake some connections, you know. I remember Henry talking about this place.' He looked back at the house and then scanned the view around.

'And what do you think about it, Mr Wilkes?'

'Call me Jimmy. Nice. Nice,' he said without conviction, and then added, 'Bleak, isn't it?'

Gillian McCracken laughed. 'Yes, you're not seeing it at its best, of course, and I have grand plans for the place. Imagine these grounds all tidied up, a formal garden by the house, and a golf course out to the west. Do you like golf, Jimmy?'

'I love golf. Do you play then?'

'Runner up in the Prestonfield Amateur Ladies, in 1975. My handicap's dropped back a little since then, but I can still put up a good show. Look, I think it's raining again. I think we'll pack it in now, Dodge. Would you like to join me for a morning coffee, Jimmy?'

Dodge watched them walk back down to the house and gave a long low whistle.

18

'Bernie?' Paige called and knocked gently on the door of Bernie and Jason's hotel room.

There was no answer.

'Bernie, it's Paige. Are you alright?' She knocked louder.

Still no reply, so Paige assumed the pair had gone out. She tried the door handle to confirm it was locked, but to her surprise, it opened.

'Bernie? Jason?' She stepped into the room timidly. The room was dark, and the air was stale. 'Hello?'

'Huh?' Jason's gruff voice came from the bed.

'Oh! Hi, Jason,' said Paige. 'Look, I'm sorry to disturb. I knocked, but I couldn't get an answer and... Do you know where Bernie is?'

'Paige... Hi... Um no. I mean, I thought she was... Has she gone down to breakfast? What time is it?'

'It's nearly eleven. I've checked downstairs, nobody's seen her. It's just that I had a strange text from her, and I've messaged back and called back, but I couldn't get a response and I was just getting worried.'

'Strange text?'

'She texted me earlier about meeting up to go for a walk at 10 o'clock. I've been waiting around for her downstairs, but then she sent another text, weirdly random, something about her bonnet being unscathed. Just gibberish, really. It was almost as if she'd pocket-texted me, you know, like pocket-dialling? Predictive text or something? I tried calling her but it's going straight to voicemail.'

Jason reached out of bed for his own phone and, despite his blurry eyes and uncooperative fingers, checked his messages. 'Nothing. Guess she's gone out for a walk. Somewhere where there's no signal. Or her battery...'

'Yes, but after last night, and with that man up in the bothy... I don't feel great about her being alone.'

Jason sat up. 'You're right. We should look for her. Can you go down to the harbour? I'll walk up to the bothy and check where Sam Flint is. I'll call you. Let me have your number.'

As soon as he left Sannah House, Jason knew he should have put a coat on, but he couldn't go back. He needed to check Flint was still in the bothy. If he was there, Bernie would be safe, and he could go back and dress better for the weather. The rain was coming down in buckets now, and the wind blew it into his face, making it difficult to find his way up to the bothy. Bonnet unscathed? What words would you have to mistype in order for predictive text to come up with those suggestions? His pounding head was in no state to even begin tackling that puzzle. He pushed on up the hill.

The door to the bothy was swinging open. Jason felt sick. He looked inside, and there was no sign of Sam. There were a hundred reasons both Sam and Bernie might be unaccounted for, but there was only one on his mind now. Sam was taking his revenge for last night. But he wouldn't have dared to come down to the house. Bernie must have walked this way, and Sam must have seen her. So where would she be going? The viewpoint at the top of the hill, maybe? It might be the best place to see her from, anyway.

He called Paige. 'Any sign? The bothy's empty. Can you get back to Sannah? Tell Dodge and the others? I should have thought of him before. I'm going up to the top of the hill.' His voice was shaky from the cold.

The rain was running down the hillside now as if it was one wide, shallow river. It made it difficult to negotiate the uneven terrain. He stumbled and fell flat on his face. 'Bernie Tenant, if you turn out to be holed up in some café, I'm going to be so pissed off,' he said aloud. He was back on his feet in an instant. Not a square centimetre of him was dry.

There was no view from the top of the hill, just rain and mist. Jason called out for Bernie, turning round, so his call would carry in all directions, but being exhausted, his voice was hoarse and blew away on the wind. He hung his head and tried to catch his breath and think about what to do next.

He'd have to go back. It was pointless searching like this. Dodge would know what to do. For all he knew, he might have already found her. He stood up straight again and checked his phone for messages. And then he saw her.

He hardly recognised her at first. She looked as drowned as he did, her hair flattened against her face, her clothes all sodden and covered in dirt. She was trudging up from the other side of the hill, her eyes set straight ahead, her mouth hanging open.

'Bernie! Here! Are you okay?' He ran to her, but she ignored him, marching on, reaching the top of the hill and starting the descent to the house.

'Bernie! It's me. What's happened?' He was beside her and tried to put his arm around her. She shrugged it away.

'Don't. I'm okay,' she said in a low voice. She hadn't even looked at him.

'You look frozen. Let's get you home.'

'No. I'm warm. I'm fine.' Her lips were blue. And Jason saw for the first time that there was blood running down the side of her face.

'Jesus! What's happened, Bernie? Did Sam do this?'

She carried on walking, but turned her head towards him.

'Sam? No. I fell. It's nothing. I'm okay.'

19

Jason and Bernie walked the rest of the way back towards Sannah House, side-by-side, without speaking. The rain looked like it had set in for the day. There were no breaks in the cloud and the wind was steady and cold. Jason's teeth chattered, Bernie shuffled her feet, and they both looked wet and miserable.

Jason had called Paige to let her know Bernie was okay, and that they were on their way back to the house, but the first person they saw striding up the hill to meet them was Dodge Mhlongo, dressed in his waterproofs and carrying a rucksack with a first aid kit, and an emergency insulation blanket inside.

'How are you doing, girl?' he called. 'How is she?' when she gave no response.

'I can't get much out of her. She said she fell, but that she's okay. She says she's not even cold, but...'

'Hypothermia, I reckon. Maybe concussion, if she fell. It's not much further. Let's get her home. You okay?'

'I'll be alright.'

As they reached the house, Paige and Sarah came out to greet them. Others were looking from the windows. Paige ran up to Bernie, and for the first time, Bernie looked up and focussed on her friend.

'Bernie! Thank God you're alright. Let's get you inside and warm.'

'Thanks... I'm so sorry.' Tears were mixing with the rain.

'You don't have to apologise, Bernie,' said Jason, but she ignored him. She took Paige's arm, and they went into the house.

'What's happened, Jason?' asked Sarah.

'No clue,' said Jason. 'I found her at the top of the hill. She's hurt her head but says it's nothing. Apart from that, she won't speak to me. We had a bit of a row last night.'

'What? After you defended her honour last night? She must need her head examining. The way you floored that bloke was well impressive.'

'She thought I'd drunk too much.'

'You probably had. Don't worry, she'll get over it.'

'I don't know, Sarah. I've got a feeling I've blown it,' said Jason in a tired, resigned voice. Then the shivers set in.

Sultan was waiting by the door of Sannah House.

'Hey, man. You look like one of them highland cows. You know, the big shaggy ginger ones?'

They led him to his room. Sarah left them and went to run a bath for Jason in the shared bathroom. Mrs McCracken was walking down the corridor and saw Sarah leaving Jason's room.

'It's not what you... I'm just going to run him a bath. Jason found Bernie out on the hills and brought her back. They're both in quite a state.'

'And they need you, do they?' said Mrs McCracken archly. 'Don't you think you've caused enough trouble?'

'Hey, listen, I'm...'

'No. You listen,' interrupted Mrs McCracken. She stepped close to Sarah, and even though she was the shorter of the two, the effect was intimidating. 'You need to stop interfering with my niece and her fiancé. I see what you're doing.'

'Fiancé? I don't think so,' Sarah gasped.

'You don't think so? Well, you don't know everything, young lady.'

'Well, I know that Jason's just this minute told me it's over between him and your gold-digging niece.'

Gillian McCracken's lips whitened, and her nostrils flared. She turned on her heel and stomped back into her room, slamming the door behind her.

Sarah stood with closed eyes for a moment, regretting what she'd just said. She walked a few paces down the corridor but stopped when she saw Paige Fellows coming out of the shared bathroom.

'I've just run a bath for Bernie,' she said. 'Listen, I need to go into their room to get her things while she has a soak. Bernie needs some time away from Jason. I'll look after her. Will that be okay? ... About getting her things, I mean.'

'Umm, sure. I was just going to... it doesn't matter, I'll sort out a bath for Jason in the other bathroom. Just give us ten minutes, will you? Then he'll be out of his room.'

'Great.'

20

Jason lowered himself into the bath carefully. It wasn't too hot. Sarah had taken care that it wouldn't burn his cold-numbed body. It smelt good, whatever she'd put in it. For the first time since he'd set out that morning looking for Bernie, his breathing felt calm, controlled.

He wasn't sure why Bernie was behaving the way she was. He'd found her and brought her home. Surely some gratitude would be the natural reaction? The argument last night hadn't been that bad, surely? But the look in her eyes told its own story. Their relationship was over. She didn't need to say anything, although some sort of explanation would be helpful. He felt shocked, dislocated. But, it surprised him to discover, not sad. Somehow, he felt he'd taken a small step towards sorting his life out.

Bang! The lights went out.

For the second time in two days, Jason found himself sitting in a bath in total darkness. No burned out candles this time; it must be the electricity failing. A fuse blown somewhere.

He reached to the floor for his phone and switched the torch on. He could hear voices elsewhere in the house. Panic, laughter and reassurance from different corners of the house. He waited for a short while, but no light returned, so he thought he'd better dry himself and get dressed.

As he dressed, he heard more commotion as people tried to sort out the situation. Richards' voice, irritably urging people to calm down. He opened the door, and still guided by his phone light, he made his way back to his room. He saw Paige banging on the door of the other bathroom.

'I can't get an answer.' She sounded panicky. 'She might have fallen asleep. I shouldn't have left her. Bernie! Bernie!'

Mrs McCracken came out of her room, holding an old-fashioned torch that shone upwards onto her face. 'What...?'

'Break open the door,' said Jason. 'I'll break open the door.'

He heaved his shoulder at the door, but it resisted. He aimed an unshod heel at the panel near the lock and this time the door opened, with the noise of splitting wood.

All three shone their lights into the bathroom, the beams finding focus on the wet skin of Bernie's back, as she lay slumped over the side of the bath. Water dripped from her hair onto the bathroom floor.

21

'First aider?' asked Paige breathlessly, the first to speak.

'I think Sarah...' said Jason quietly, almost to himself.

'Gracie. I'll get Gracie. She's trained,' said Mrs McCracken, and started back down the corridor.

Gracie was already at the top of the stairs, investigating the sound of the door being broken. She went straight into the bathroom while Jason and Paige shone the lights from their phones on the scene. She took Bernie's pulse confidently and then turned to the others and said, 'Lift her out of the bath, onto the floor. I'm going to perform CPR.'

'Do you know what you're doing?' asked Paige.

'First Aid module on my catering degree,' said Gracie. 'Someone call 999. They'll put you through to Evans. He's a First Responder. He's a special constable, as well.'

Richards had appeared on the scene and made the call.

With some effort, Jason and Paige laid Bernie out on the floor and partially covered her with a towel. Gracie knelt beside her, checked her airway, and then started chest compressions.

Special Constable Rhodri Evans drove up the drive of Sannah House in his van about fifteen minutes later. Sandy, who had by now restored electricity to the house, was waiting by the front door to lead him upstairs.

'Righty-ho, Sandy. Young lady, is it?' Evans grabbed a bag, including a defibrillator, out of his van. Sandy led him up the stairs, and as he walked, he pulled on a paper face mask and some disposable gloves.

He tutted as he entered the bathroom, knelt over Bernie's body and watched Gracie perform a few chest compressions. He attached the pads of the defibrillator to Bernie's chest.

'Step back now, Gracie. Three... Two... One...'

'Come on, now girl... Three... Two... One...'

'Three... Two... One...'

'How long did you say? Fifteen minutes?'

'Twenty.' said Gracie in an exhausted voice.

'Well, listen Gracie. You did everything correctly. You couldn't have done any more. I've done this more than a few times, back when I was Constable Evans with Dyfed-Powys Police. Some you win, and some... Do you hear me, Gracie? It's important that you know you did everything you could. Now, who's the best person to describe to me the exact sequence of events? Because now I'm Special Constable Evans with Police Scotland. And I'm going to need to report a sudden and unexplained death.'

Jack Tang stood with his arms outstretched as Paige re-entered their room. She glanced briefly at him, bowed her head and let him hold her. Her shoulders shook.

'Baby,' said Tang softly. 'I'm so sorry.'

Paige made no answer. She stood, enfolded by his arms, for several minutes until her sobs subsided. Then she said, 'The police officer wants us to go down to the lounge.'

Gillian McCracken wanted to be with her niece.

'Special Constable Evans says you can later,' said Gracie. 'He's just inspecting the bathroom, and he's on the phone to Mallaig at the moment. He says he'll come down to talk to us in the lounge when he's done. Shall we go there now?'

Mrs McCracken looked at her as though she'd suggested a swim in the harbour, but then said, 'I suppose so.'

Jimmy Wilkes met them on the stairs.

'Mrs McCracken. Gillian. I've just heard. I can't believe it. Can I do anything?'

He held out his arm, and Mrs McCracken let him steady her descent.

Jason was staring out of his bedroom window at the continuing wind and rain. Just an hour or two ago, he'd been out there, looking for Bernie, and he was thinking about how he'd led her back off the mountain. How he'd led her to her death.

Sarah knocked and entered.

'I think he's finished in the bathroom. Shall we go down to the lounge to hear what he's got to say? Are you up to it?'

'Why is she dead, Sarah? I mean, how did she die? Was the water too hot? Can that kill you, if you've been cold... hypothermic? Can the shock kill you? Do you have to warm up slowly?'

'I don't know, Jason, I don't think so. I don't expect the SPC will know either. It'll be a job for a coroner, or a procurator up here. But let's go down and see what he says. He'll want to talk to you.'

Special Constable Evans, still wearing his facemask and gloves, waited until everyone was in the room before he began.

'Now look, everyone. This has been a terrible tragedy.' He pulled off the mask. 'I don't think that's necessary. This isn't Covid-19. We can be fairly certain of that,' he explained.

'But before I say anymore, I've met Miss Fellows, Mr Tranter, Mrs McCracken, and I know Sandy and Gracie, of course. Who else do we have here, please?'

Richards spoke up. 'I'm Richards. And we have Jack Tang, Rebecca Leyden-Fuller, then there's two of Mr Tranter's friends, Sarah Headley and Jamil Ahmed, and... er...'

'Jim Wilkes,' said the unfamiliar man sitting next to Mrs McCracken and holding her hand.

Evans nodded to each person as Richards mentioned their name, and he wrote them down in his notebook. When he got to Sarah, he added a wink, which only Sarah and Sultan noticed.

'So listen,' said Evans. 'Strictly speaking, I shouldn't say anymore. My report will go to the procurator and he'll decide on the cause of death. But it only seems fair to me to let you know what I'm thinking. From what I've heard, Miss Bernie Tenant got caught out in the rain this morning, and when she returned, Ms Fellows ran her a bath, and after reassurances from Miss Tenant that she was feeling well, left her alone in the room. Miss Tenant locked the door, it being a shared bathroom and everything, and took her bath.'

'At about 1:30 p.m., the electricity supply failed, and the house went dark. Apparently, this is not an unusual occurrence in Sannah House. Ms Fellows went to check on Miss Tenant but couldn't get a response. Mr Tranter assisted in breaking the door of the bathroom where they found Ms Tenant lying across the side of the bath with one hand trailing on the floor. Can you confirm that, Mr Tenant? Does that describe Miss Tenant's position when you first saw her?'

Jason closed his eyes and the image of Benie's body in the torchlight came back so vividly, he winced.

'Yes. That's right.'

'One arm trailing on the floor?'

Jason nodded.

'Thank you. You see, what I think happened is that Miss Tenant stood up in the bath, and then maybe she slipped, or her legs gave way and she reached up for support. I'm afraid she reached and caught hold of the light hanging over the bath. It was that, you see, that caused the fuse to blow. And from what I've been able to tell, in discussion with my colleagues and experts back on the mainland, that is what caused the death of poor Miss Tenant.'

Sandy flashed a glance at Mrs McCracken, who looked as white as a sheet. 'Electrocuted, you mean? You can't be sure of that,' he said.

'Of course not... yet. I'm just letting you all know the lay of the land. The procurator will come out tomorrow. He'll be the one to sort out any liability or anything of that sort.'

Richards was quick to jump in. 'You might want to note down that nobody here is staying at the hotel on a commercial basis. We are all just staying as Mrs McCracken's personal guests. I think that's important to set that out from the start.'

'I see,' said Evans, raising an eyebrow. 'That's correct, is it?' he said, looking at Mrs McCracken and Sandy.

'Aye, it is,' said Sandy. 'You can check the books. No money has changed hands.'

Sultan coughed.

At that moment, Dodge Mhlongo entered the room, looking sweaty and damp with rain.

'I've been back to the bothy,' he said. 'And I've been all over the hills. There's still no sign of the little bastard. Nobody's seen him down at the harbour either. Just thought you should know. Hello?'

Dodge was surprised to see the man in uniform.

'This is Constable Evans, sweetheart,' said Rebecca Leyden-Fuller. 'There's been some trouble while you were out. Come with me. Let's get you dry, and I'll fill you in.' She walked him out of the room.

'Someone want to fill me in?' said Evans.

'Mr Mhlongo was looking for another guest, who's gone missing… temporarily. Out on the hills somewhere, probably, or perhaps, he's been lucky enough to find someone to take him off the island. Speaking of which, are we all free to leave? I'd just arranged transport for tomorrow.'

'Hang on a minute, Mr Richards,' said Evans. 'Do you want to report a missing person?'

'Not at all,' said Richards. 'He's just a stranger who blew in yesterday, but we can't find today. He's not a member of our party. Completely separate.'

Jason wasn't so sure. The feelings he'd been fighting back for the last few days were surging back. 'I don't know…' he began. His voice sounded manic.

Richards glared at him.

'It's just that… You all saw him last night. He was weird… violent… threatening. He was the reason I went out looking for Bernie this morning. She said she hadn't seen him, though.'

'So not connected then,' said Richards. 'Now, about leaving. Will this procurator need to see all of us? What time are they arriving?'

'No. We can't leave so soon,' said Jason before Evans could reply to Richards' question. He glanced at Mrs McCracken, who looked like a lost, confused lady, clutching onto the arm of this stranger, Wilkes. It was impossible not to feel sorry for her, of course; he knew how much Bernie meant to her. But here they were, with a police officer in the room. It felt like things were coming to a head at last, and Jason didn't want to let the moment go. 'And there's more...'

The words lined up in his head. 'There's a gangster's corpse in Mrs McCracken's asparagus bed. She made me put it there, because if I didn't, she'd tell Bernie about Sarah, who's actually a police officer. And she's called Robin, and I love Robin, not Bernie, even though Bernie is dead.'

And he looked at Sarah, and Sultan, and Mrs McCracken, and Richards, and he knew he couldn't say any of it.

'What else is there, Mr Tranter?' said Evans patiently.

'I had this quaich... a whiskey cup... valuable. I think it might have been stolen.' With that, Jason broke down and started sobbing. Sarah comforted him.

'It's all been a bit much for him. I'm sure we all understand.'

'Yes, of course,' said Evans. 'Don't worry. Not a problem. I think I'll ignore missing persons and stolen whisky cups for now and concentrate on dealing with Miss Tenant's unfortunate accident. Thank you for your help, Mr Tranter.'

22

The raging winds had subsided, but a grey mist still hung over Sannah island, and a chilling drizzle seemed to hang in the air. With its dark grey stone walls and its less than generous windows, Sannah House was always a dour place, but over the last couple of days, the sudden influx of guests and the prospect of regeneration had lifted the mood. Now an oppressive stillness hung over the house again. The slow ticking of the grandfather clock in the entrance hall seemed to stretch time.

Gracie and Sandy cleared out Jason and Bernie's room and laid her body on the bed there while they waited to hear how the procurator and an undertaker from the mainland would make their arrangements, given that the ferries were still not running.

'They didn't say anything about this in catering college,' said Gracie as they lifted her onto the bed.

'Aye, you never know what you may be called to do, true enough,' said Sandy, looking ten years older than he had at the start of the day.

Paige Fellows and Jack Tang sat in the lounge, looking at their phones. Richards stood by the window talking to his.

'And you're sure it can't be any earlier? ... Very well, tomorrow morning will have to do. I think there'll be about half a dozen of us... Oh, hang on, there maybe more. We seem to have picked up a few hangers on. Jason has his two friends here and Mrs McCracken has suddenly got a new friend. Just as well, really. I think he's being something of a support to her. I expected she'd want to stay on until everything was settled, but I've just been up to her room, explained the plan and she wants to come along — and bring this Mr Wilkes along as her guest, apparently. Who am I to argue? I'll have to ask Mhlongo what he wants to do. Best arrange transport for ten of us, plus luggage. There'll be room in the boat, won't there? Thank you, Smethwick.'

Jason had been sitting on the edge of Sultan's bed, head in hands, for almost an hour. Sultan and Sarah looked at each other, not knowing what to say, both feeling like a spare part, but neither of them wanting to leave it to the other to look after their friend. They'd offered to send for tea or something to eat, but Jason shook his head. Sultan was the first to weaken.

'I think I'm going to go outside and get some fresh air. Try my wax jacket out. That's if you're both okay?'

'That's fine, Sultan,' said Sarah. The thought of the A4 pad in Sultan's bag popped into her mind.

'Where are you going?' asked Jason, looking up. The first words he'd spoken for an hour.

'Dunno. Just for a walk, I guess.'

'I don't want to go back over the hills,' said Jason. 'How about just walking down to the harbour? I'll come with you. There's a bar down there.'

Sarah gave Sultan a worried look.

'I don't think drinking is a good idea just now, Jason.'

He stared at her, expressionless.

'Okay. I'll come too,' she said.

The Harbour Bar was really a small white cottage that had, at one time, served as a waiting room for the ferry. It didn't look very inviting; it was more of a functional place. When the three friends saw it, they almost turned back, but it was raining, and none of them particularly wanted to be back at the hotel. Jason just had his hand on the door when a familiar voice called out from across the road.

'The bar's shut, I'm afraid. New restrictions.'

It was Special Constable Evans.

The sight of the uniformed police officer almost made them feel they were being told off for attempting to enter the bar, but Evans crossed over the road with a conciliatory smile.

'To be honest, I only just remembered myself,' he said. 'I came down for a drink and a bit of company, after what's been a terrible day. Well, I don't have to tell you that.'

They acknowledged the truth of the statement with weak smiles.

'Listen, it's a bit irregular, perhaps, but why don't you come back to my little cottage? It's only just up the road there and I've got a bottle. We could take the edge off the day.' He looked at Sarah, and if he didn't quite wink at her, his eyes certainly twinkled.

'Oh, we really couldn't,' said Sarah. 'Thank you.'

'No, let's do it,' said Jason. 'Just one before we head back. It's very kind of you.'

They followed the Welshman back to his cottage, which looked a lot more welcoming than the bar had done. A log burner was already pumping out heat, and Evans sat them down in comfortable seats while he poured whiskey into tumblers and offered them around.

'Mr Tranter,' he said, 'and Mr....' He held back the glass while he struggled to remember.

'Ahmed.' said Sultan.

'Of course. But I remember your name, Ms Headly. Except it's not Sarah Headly, is it? Funny. I remembered where we'd met before, just after I left Sannah House. Wolverhampton, wasn't it? Emergency Life Support Training back in 2018. Never forget a face, I don't.'

Sarah froze.

'Towers. Police Constable Robin Towers, that's it,' said Evans, looking pleased with himself.

'You're mistaken.'

'I'm not, love,' said Evans, pulling his phone out of his pocket. 'I've been looking at the photos before I came out. Where is it now? Here. That's you, or I'm Richard Burton.'

He passed the phone to Jason, who glanced at it briefly, before Sultan snatched it out of his hands.

'Sarah?'

Sarah's eyes watered as she tried to think of some way out, but this time, words failed her.

'I think the game's up, Sarah,' said Jason, with a trace of a friendly smile on his otherwise despondent face.

'Okay then,' said Sarah, taking a deep breath and looking around the room. 'I am Detective Constable Robin Towers. Sarah is a cover name. I've been on a long-term operation. And Special Constable Evans has just blown it.'

23

Gracie was dreading her next task, which was simply serving a tray of tea to one of the bedrooms. But it was Mrs McCracken's room, the sweet old lady who'd lost her husband only six months ago and now tragically lost her niece as well. She couldn't imagine the pain that she was going through.

She took a deep breath, knocked and said, 'I've just brought some tea for you both.'

Jimmy Wilkes opened the door, and she came in and set the things on a table by the window, where Mrs McCracken was sitting.

'That's very thoughtful,' said Mrs McCracken. 'You're a kind girl, Gracie.' Her eyes were red, and she held a handkerchief, but her voice was calm, if lacking her usual enthusiasm.

Gracie couldn't think of the right way of expressing her sympathy, and so just said, 'There are some biscuits,' and left the room.

'I should leave you alone now,' said Jimmy Wilkes. 'I feel like I'm intruding.'

'Nonsense. I'm very grateful to you for being here. Why don't you pour us some tea? To tell you the truth, it's nice to have one of Henry's friends by my side just now. Someone from the old days. I'm sorry I don't really remember you, though. Isn't that dreadful of me? I just can't face the other guests at the moment.'

'Sometimes it can be harder to face friends than strangers.'

'Perhaps. Especially when one is feeling angry.'

'You looked angry when you saw that young man — Bernie's boyfriend — walking out with his friends just now.'

'I'm afraid I blame him for what happened. It was an accident, I know. The police officer said so. But Jason let Bernie down. I can't forgive him for that. To see him strolling off with his friends, especially her. Well, it upset me, I'll admit. He needs to show a bit more propriety, I think.'

'Do you want me to have a word with him?'

'Oh, Mr Wilkes... Jimmy, that's kind of you, but it's not necessary. It won't change anything now. The important thing now, for me, is to get away from here. You too. The country is moving into a lockdown, it seems. I'm worried we'll be stuck on Sannah for weeks if we're not careful. Richards is arranging a boat to get us back to the mainland. And he's offering to arrange an extended stay somewhere warmer. There's a little island in the Mediterranean he thinks will be ideal for sitting out any pandemic.'

'Mediterranean? Lovely. You should do that if you can.'

'What will you do? Where's home?'

'Anywhere I lay my hat, Gillian. I'm a free man. Retired, free and single. That's me.'

24

In Special Constable Evans' sitting room, four people stared warily at each other. Sarah looked at Jason, waiting for his reaction to the news that her secret was out. Jason was watching Sultan, wondering how long it would take for him to realise that Sarah had betrayed his friendship and that Jason was complicit.

Sultan was looking at Sarah, processing the news and its implications.

Evans eyed them all and realised he's stirred a hornet's nest.

'Oh, look, I'm dreadfully sorry,' he said. 'Me and my big size tens. I should have known better.'

'It's okay,' said Sarah, plunging the fingers of both hands through her hair. 'It was bound to come out eventually. I've been on an undercover operation, keeping an eye on Jason here. There's an investigation into the activities of Rara Avis, the society of millionaires that Jason has joined, and possible links to organised crime.'

There was a moment's pause while the three men absorbed this information.

'Bullshit!' said Sultan, more angrily than either Sarah or Jason had seen him before. 'I know exactly what this is. And I'm not having any of it.'

He stood up and stormed out of the room.

Sarah and Jason looked at each other.

'We've got to go after him,' said Sarah.

'Perhaps just the two of us,' said Jason.

'No,' said Sarah, 'I might need SPC Evans. I think I'm going to have to arrest Sultan.'

'What a bloody day! Let's go then,' said Special Constable Evans. 'And don't worry. We're on Sannah. He's not going anywhere.'

They caught up with him on the pier. Darkness was falling, and the drizzle had stopped. Sultan stood by the railings, looking out to sea, and, seeming to sense their presence, he turned round.

'Piss off!' he said.

'Sultan, listen mate,' said Jason. 'We're sorry. You've got a right to be angry. But Sarah was only doing her job...'

'I don't give a damn about her. It's you I'm angry with. It's obvious you knew who she was, and you didn't tell me.'

'Well, I wanted to. We argued about it. I knew it was a load of bollocks, but Sarah's senior officers told her she had to stay undercover even though she knew you were alright...'

'But it's not quite like that,' said Sarah. Her voice was low and calm, in contrast to the other two. 'Is it, Sultan?'

'No, Sarah, or whatever your real name is. No, you're right. It's never like that. Because I have brown skin, don't I? I have a beard and I can read Arabic. So that immediately makes me a suspicious character, doesn't it?'

'What makes you suspicious is that, like me, you live under a false identity. Only you're not working for the police. Your real name is Jamil Khan. Your brother is a convicted terrorist, Reza Khan. You've been seen, on several occasions, entering and leaving the house of Amina Bhuta, another terrorist currently serving time for disseminating extremist material. And back in your hotel room, you've got an A4 pad covered with calculations and plans for a terror attack on Birmingham. That's what makes you suspicious.'

Sultan nodded his head slowly and weighed up the situation. They stood in front of him; Sarah looking defiant, Jason looking surprised, and standing behind them both, Special Constable Evans looking excited. Sultan's mouth made the shape of a smile, but his eyes remained cold.

'When I'm helping kids prepare for maths exams, I always tell them to spend time at the end of the exam, checking their answers, and I say "Always assume your answer is wrong and look for the mistake you made, rather than assume it is right. Because if you assume it's probably right, it's harder to spot any mistake." They never listen, but it's good advice. It's called confirmation bias.'

SPC Evans looked restless. He was preparing himself to make an arrest, and he sensed the suspect intended making a long speech first.

'We should always check our confirmation bias,' Sultan continued. 'When my brother Reza was growing up in North Alberta, he was like any bored teenager with low self-esteem, rebelling against everything his family told him, convinced that the world was against him. His teachers told him to respect his parents. The local imam told him that instead of railing against the world, he should work peacefully to change the world. That sounded boring to Reza. And then he met some people who told him he was right. They said he was right to question his father, and the Imam, and his teachers. He was right to want to fight against the injustice in the world, by any means necessary. So who did he believe? The guys who were confirming his own thoughts, of course.

'I don't know how they convinced him that bombing a school was going to improve the lives of Muslim kids in Palestine, or anywhere else. It didn't improve mine. He was arrested, the neighbours shunned our family, and the police leant on me to tell them what I knew about Reza's friends. In exchange for what I could tell them, which wasn't much, they helped me change my identity, and I came to the UK to start a new life.

'You can move halfway around the world, but life catches up with you, doesn't it? I was teaching maths to kids in Dudley and some of them reminded me of Reza and I saw them fall under the same influences he did. I told my Head of School and quickly the authorities got involved. They's got this thing called the Prevent programme that works against radicalisation, and it's great... most of the time. Sometimes, in some families, the distrust about the Police and the system is so deeply ingrained that they really don't stand a chance.'

Sultan's voice was calm now. He leant back on the pier railings as he continued, and he might have been holding forth at The Pig on a Friday night.

'But there's another approach. With some kids, if you can just help build their self-esteem, it can make them less susceptible to bad influences. Maths is great for that. I can go to someone's house, give them one-to-one tuition and I don't have to talk about religion or politics or anything like that, but I can see them grow in confidence. I've done it for three years now with different children. There's a network of us and we work in families where we know Prevent aren't going to be able to do anything. I don't know if it's saved the world from any terror attacks, but it's not doing any harm. That's what I was doing in Amina Bhuta's house in the Lozells. Teaching her boy maths while she's in prison. And that A4 pad was our homework. Equations of motion. A plane takes 6 hours to fly from New York to Birmingham...'

'Are you hearing this, Sarah?' Jason interrupted. 'I think you owe Sultan a massive apology.'

'No, Jason. As you said, Sarah was just doing her job.' said Sultan. 'Which is looking for terrorists. All those things: Reza, the house in the Lozells, the stupid aeroplane diagram, just fed into her confirmation bias. No, it's you who owes me an apology. You knew who she was, and you let it go on for the sake of your peaceful, privileged, millionaire life. So I think that even if you apologise, I'm done with you, Jason. I've had enough.'

25

4 weeks later.

Everyone said they had never known weather like it. Day after day of calm, steady sunshine. It was like some divine compensation for the strange new world of lockdown. The TV showed pictures of empty roads and deserted city centres. People said that the birds were singing louder. A herd of wild goats wandered into a Welsh town. Fallow deer were seen on the streets of London. People lucky enough to live near green spaces were encouraged to exercise once a day, on their own, and experience the healing power of the natural world. Others had to make do with a workout in front of the telly with Joe Wicks.

For the inhabitants of Sannah, lockdown was less of a shock, in some ways at least. They were used to empty roads and living close to nature. But April was usually the start of the tourist season, and the islanders wondered how long it would be before that vital part of their economy would return, or if it ever would. The ferry now only came once a week, bringing vital supplies, but no visitors. The food that did arrive was subject to restrictions; flour and tinned goods were scarce. Still, they welcomed the fair weather.

Jason Tranter had made the island his lockdown home. He'd stayed on when, the day after Bernie's death, the rest of the visitors to Sannah House had left. He'd been there to attend to the visit from the undertakers and the procurator. And then, when there was no longer any need for him to remain on the island, he realised that there was no actual need for him to be anywhere else, either.

He quickly established a new routine; sleeping till midday, walking the island in the afternoon, watching spectacular sunsets before eating and drinking back at the hotel with Gracie and Sandy. He was the only guest and the distinction between guest and staff often blurred as they whiled away the evenings together. There was a long line of bottles of different whiskies on the Sannah Bar, and Jason embarked upon a project to get to know them all. When each bottle was finished, Sandy somehow found a new variety to take its place.

One evening, while he was still sober, he received an unexpected phone call from Jack Tang.

'Hey, man! Where are you?'

'I'm on Sannah, at the hotel.'

'Yeah, I heard you were still there. Crazy. But cool, actually. So here's the thing. I've just heard from Richards that the old lady... sorry, Mrs McCracken has decided to sell up Sannah House. As it is, lock, stock and barrel. It's going for a song and Richards thought I might take it on and develop it as per the original plan. And then he suggested you might want to be part of the action. Equal partner if you like. Share the risk.'

'What? I thought you didn't think much of the idea? Too old-fashioned. Too remote. Too cold?'

'Yeah, well, I didn't like the idea of working with someone so... traditional, so... fixed in her ideas. But if I can change things up a bit... as long as you're okay with my ideas, of course, then I think it might be cool. That's if you want in?'

'Oh Jack, I don't know. I suppose I might be interested. I'll have to think about it. But I guess there's no urgency. You can't exactly get any work done at the moment.'

'Oh, you'd be surprised, J-boy, you'd be surprised. Anyway, I'll send you some figures and I'll let you have a think about it.'

'Okay, thanks. So anyway, how are you? How's Paige?'

'Ah, she and I are no longer a thing. It all got weird after we left the island. She didn't want to be in my bubble. Her life has taken a different path. Takes a pandemic to find out who you are, I guess. But wow! So you stayed on the island! That can't be easy, right?'

'Easy? I don't know. You'd think that there'd be too many memories, wouldn't you? But no. Surprisingly few, actually. Those few days are a bit of a blur, to be honest. I guess that's one reason I'm still here. It's quiet and I'm hoping one day I'll make sense of it, but so far, I'm finding it hard to think about anything really... umm...'

Jason realised Jack was unusually quiet and then the penny dropped.

'... oh, you meant it can't be easy with Covid and the lockdown and everything, didn't you? Oh, sorry. Yeah, that's okay, really.'

'Oh no, how awkward! My bad, Jason. Of course, you've had a lot to deal with; losing B... Bar...'

'Bernie.'

'Yeah, Bernie. That's it. Sorry. So sad for you, man. You'll have to forgive me; it's all jumbled up in my head. Paige always told me I was self-obsessed. It's something I'm gonna work on. But you're right, that was a crazy couple of days. Hey, that weird guy that turned up and picked a fight with you... who was he and did he ever show up again?'

'Who? Sam Flint? Just a guy I knew at school. I think he had some old score to settle. He pinched my priceless antique whisky cup and I've not seen him since. Wasn't he on the boat that took you all off the island then? I guess he must have got off the island somehow.'

After the call, nursing a tumbler of whisky at the bar, Jason thought about Sam for the first time in ages. He'd become an expert in avoiding all the unanswered questions that had buzzed around his head in the days leading up to Bernie's accident. So why had Sam Flint followed him all the way up to a Scottish island? Surely not because of a childhood jealousy? Could it be, as he'd suspected all along, that he was in some way connected to the corpse buried in Mrs McCracken's garden?

Thinking about that body brought back the same nauseating shiver it always did, and he took a slug of the whisky. The more time passed, and it had been over four weeks now, the more it seemed likely that perhaps Mrs McCracken was right, and there wouldn't be any consequences to that unlawful burial. All the same, he was glad of the distance between Sannah and that Shropshire cottage garden where the body lay.

He hadn't contacted Mrs McCracken. The morning she left Sannah House, she'd blanked him. He knew she blamed him for Bernie's death. He blamed himself, too. And now came that other familiar feeling, from which only whisky seemed to provide respite. Loss.

He knew he'd lost Bernie before she even took that fatal bath. Had she lived, they would have separated anyway, he felt sure. That didn't lessen the feeling of a gaping void in his life. The memory of his time with Bernie was tainted. He could see now that they had never really been as close as he'd thought. The fun they'd had was mostly down to his fortune. If he'd still been a webmaster at PKR, she would never have bothered with him. But it was true she had shown him how to enjoy his wealth and opened up a world for him. That world felt closed now. Mind you, the world was in lockdown, and no-one knew what the future was going to be like, so perhaps he wasn't alone in feeling loss.

He'd also lost his friends, Sarah and Sultan. And when he thought about them, and especially if he'd reached his fifth or sixth whisky, his sadness turned to anger. Anger at Sarah, for initially allowing an obviously bogus operation to run on because it helped her get over a period of career burn-out, and then later for misinterpreting innocent behaviour as being suspicious in order to justify that same deluded operation. And anger at himself for allowing all that to go on.

26

Malcolm Dunnet came home after a night shift and opened the cardboard tube that the courier had delivered the previous day. He unfurled a large map of the world and gazed at it.

'Perfect,' he said and, after giving his wife a peck on the cheek, hurried upstairs to the spare room, or 'The War Room' as he thought of it. He'd set up his computer there and now he Blu-tacked his new poster to the wall. The task he was undertaking deserved a special room, he felt. After all, he was potentially about to join the ranks of Silkwood, Snowden and Serpico as one of the great whistleblowers.

Someone was stealing stuff from PKR Aerospace and from what he'd learned when he was roughed up in the car park, he was pretty sure that the management was allowing it to happen. But now he was on to them. On his rounds last night, he'd discovered that once again, thieves had cut through wire fencing and lifted several pallets of metal casings and large reels of cable. He was ready this time. Management might be prepared to turn a blind eye, but he wasn't going to. Two weeks ago, he'd spotted that more pallets had been left conspicuously by the perimeter fence. So he'd fitted the tracking devices he'd hired from Tranter Diall inside the cable reels and some of the casings. Now they were gone, but he was ready to trace their progress across the world.

He felt certain that this would be the work of an international conspiracy. PKR products were in demand worldwide, from Bogota to Borneo. Those casings would be precision-made, the cable would be extremely high specification. All military grade stuff. It was all probably destined to be spare parts for military juntas somewhere. He knew the PKR management was involved in this, but how high up did it go? At the top, the majority shareholder was an Eastern European oligarch. A far cry from the original owners, Purvis, Keane and Rudlings, who all came from Staffordshire, and built and repaired tractors.

He fired up the computer and ran the software that would locate the GPS tracking devices. He was looking forward to plotting their progress across the globe using stickers on his world map poster.

The tracking software showed all the devices in the same place. TF Scrap Metal in Bilston. Just three miles away.

Suddenly, it didn't feel like an international conspiracy anymore. Just a local gang knocking off some scrap metal. Someone at PKR was still involved, but Malcolm had misgivings about whether he really wanted to find out who. It would probably just end up with him losing his own job, and he didn't want to go through all that again. He felt foolish, pretending to be a whistleblower, with a War Room. Still, his wife had always wanted this room to be a study for all the family to use. Somewhere for their little girl to do her homework. She'd probably approve of the world map.

27

The sunsets on Isola Gallinara were even more breathtaking than the ones on Sannah. The Mediterranean Sea knew how to put on a good show, and the audience of millionaires temporarily resident on the island appreciated the views all the more, knowing they had bought their way out of the hardships of lockdown. Technically, the island was under the jurisdiction of Italy and hence should have been subject to harsh restrictions, but Rara Avis had a way of ensuring a different set of rules applied on their private island. Despite some circuitous supply lines and the occasional shortages, the island was still catering to the high standards its clientele expected. And unlike its Scottish counterpart, the distinction between staff and guests was still maintained.

A young waiter in a black t-shirt poured wine for a couple eating out on a terrace overlooking the moonlit bay. The couple ignored him.

'You're looking a lot brighter than when I saw you last, Gillian.'

'Am I?' said Mrs McCracken, sounding surprised.

'Yeah. Oh, I don't mean to say you've got over...'

'...It's alright Jimmy. You don't have to tiptoe around me. It was a great shock losing Bernie, and so soon after Henry as well. One doesn't get over things like that quickly. I'm not sure I feel any brighter, but I'm glad if I look better.'

'Hmm. Sorry. I find it difficult to know what to say. This place, though, eh? It's the spot for getting away from it all.'

'I'm very glad you could come out here. It's good to see you again. But what took you so long?'

'I had a bit of unexpected business to attend to. I managc this company, see. Imports, exports, warehousing, that sort of thing. Well, it was on its last legs, to be honest, what with one thing and another.'

He paused, screwing his eyes up and looking at Mrs McCracken closely. Then he relaxed and continued.

'But suddenly I was in a position to offload... I mean supply... some PPE, plastic gowns, gloves and masks to the NHS.'

'How wonderful to be able to help out like that!'

'Yes. It was very... rewarding. Anyway, that's all sorted, so here I am. It was a surprise to get your invitation, though.'

'Well, we had so little time on Sannah, but I've thought a lot about the conversation we had. It's a challenge, isn't it, to suddenly find oneself on one's own, at our time of life? Back home, I gather everyone is talking about setting up "support bubbles". I'm rather lacking in that department. Anyway, I just thought it would be good to get to know each other better.'

'Oh Gillian, that's very nice. I don't know what to say. Am I in your "bubble" then? Well, that's great! Listen, I didn't know... I mean I never came looking... I mean I'm just an old school pal of Henry. you know I never...'

'Now Jimmy, you remember the old school motto, don't you?'

'Oh yes.'

'Go on then...'

'Well. Er... what was it? Perhaps I've forgotten it after all. It's a long time ago.'

Mrs McCracken took a sip from her wineglass and looked at him over its rim, with large round eyes. There was even a hint of a flutter of eyelashes.

'I think we can drop the pretence, now... Terry,' she said.

Terry Flint screwed his eyes tightly again for a few seconds and then smiled.

'You know who I am, then?'

'Yes. I've known that for a long time.'

'And why I came looking for you?'

'I imagine you wanted the money that Henry had left me in his will.'

'That's my money. Henry stole it from me. That's naughty. Wicked, actually. And it's against the law.'

'Well now. Let's think about that. Is it your money? Did you come by it honestly?'

'Did *you*?'

'I think if you look at the financial records that Henry left, you'll find a pretty credible trail. My husband was a very skilled accountant, as you know. Whereas if the police ever investigated you... I think you'd have a hard job explaining such an enormous fortune. If you had one, I mean. The law would appear to be on my side.'

'Yeah, but I don't always rely on the law to sort my problems.' Terry Flint placed both hands, palms down, on the table.

'No, so I gather. But I don't think you'd try anything silly with a frail widow, would you? Not again?'

Terry Flint chuckled softly and relaxed again.

'Nothing frail about you, Gillian. You're right, though. I'm putting all that behind me. That was always the plan. Wind down the firm and chill out a bit in my old age. Start enjoying the finer things in life — like all this.'

He gestured to the sparkling moonlit bay.

'But then Henry pulled that stunt and left me without the means to put my plan into action. Still, what's been lost can usually be found again. I reckoned it would be easy enough to persuade you to hand back the money, but it seems I was wrong. I put my best man on the job and then I never saw hide nor hair of him again. Pay him off, did you, Gillian? Then I sent my nephew to see what happened to Greg. As far as I can tell, he seems to have lost the plot. Got into some row with your niece's boyfriend and followed him up to Scotland and made an arse of himself at the hotel. Excuse my language, Gillian. He's gone AWOL as well, now. Probably fallen in with Greg. He was never keen on my plan to wind the business down. Silly lad.'

Gillian McCracken listened with interest and nodded.

'What made you pose as Jimmy Wilkes? And how did you do it? You'd done your research, hadn't you? You fooled Sandy, and me, at first.'

'Ha! Quite proud of that, actually. You know, public libraries are marvellous places, aren't they? I can't use the internet and stuff — it's a closed book to me. But those libraries have digital assistants, people who help you use the web. They'll actually do everything for you if you're persuasive enough. Lady helped me out, found Henry's old school no problem. I told her I was just trying to get in touch with an old friend, you know. There's a website all about that school and loads of people going on a message board with stories from years gone by, listing all their mates, sharing photo's and everything. It was a doddle.'

'But why did you do it, Terry? Impersonate Jimmy Wilkes, I mean. You look nothing like him, by the way.' she said.

'I just wanted to meet you. Henry had mentioned you from time to time, you know. I always felt jealous of him, not having anyone myself. He told me you had died. Did you know that? It was so I wouldn't go looking for you, I suppose, whenever I discovered he'd cleaned me out. He'd got it all planned out.'

'Yes, I suppose he had. I have wondered exactly how much it was all planned,' she said in a low voice, almost to herself.

'You intrigued me. I wanted to see what you were like. Never done anything like it before. I must be going daft in my old age. Anyway, so I came up to the island, and saw you, outside the hotel, shooting clay pigeons. "What a woman!" I thought. Then you told me you liked golf. I couldn't believe it.'

'Terry, you're making me blush.'

'Obviously, what happened with Bernie, well that was a tragedy. I went back to the Midlands feeling... like I'd found a penny and lost a shilling. Then you phoned, inviting me out here. That put a spring in my step though, I don't mind telling you. Then this PPE contract came up, put some money in the coffers. And I thought, why not? I feel like a bloomin' teenager.'

'Let's not get ahead of ourselves, Terry. I like you, but I'm not ready for the dating game at the moment. I'm more interested in a business relationship.'

'Oh, dear! Sorry if I've made a mess of things... I'm sorry, Gillian.'

'Don't worry Terry. Here's my plan...'

28

Talking to Jack Tang had unsettled Jason. His evening whiskies performed their usual trick of getting him off to sleep quickly, but he awoke in the night after another vivid nightmare. He'd been watching faceless police officers exhuming a corpse from Mrs McCracken's asparagus bed, and as the soil fell away, it was Bernie's body that was revealed. Jack Tang and Paige Fellows were standing by the grave and Paige shouted, 'Look at her bonnet! It's clean!'

After that, he lay awake, and when thoughts about Bernie's accident inevitably came, this time, he didn't push them away. He thought about the sequence of events leading up to her death. He remembered Paige had woken him that day, knocking on his door, looking for Bernie. They'd had some arrangement to go for a walk, but Paige had received a text from her, something about a bonnet. He couldn't remember thinking about it since, but strangely, it had popped up in his dream last night. Paige had reminded him that Sam Flint was somewhere on the island and neither liked the idea of Bernie walking about on her own. They'd separated and gone off looking for her.

What was the significance of the word 'bonnet'? Why had it stuck in his brain all this time? The questions repeated over and over in his head all night, with no answers. Eventually, he found Paige's number and texted her to suggest a catch-up.

She called him just after 7:30 a.m.

'Jason, hi? Are you ok? It just seemed a strange time to receive a text from you. It worried me.'

'Oh hell, sorry!' Jason realised that his brief message, '*Can we talk*?', might appear rather urgent when received first thing in the morning. He explained what had been going through his head all night.

'Do you still have that message Bernie sent you? Could you forward it to me? If that's okay, I mean.'

A few minutes later, Paige sent him a screen grab of the last messages she'd had with Bernie.

08:05 Paige: Can't take any more of this. Fancy a brisk morning walk? (Video attachment)

08:07 Bernie: Yes! Can't see video. Phone battery not good. Let's meet at 10.

08:08 Paige: OK. C U Then x

09:12 Bernie: typically unscathed bonnet

09:30 Paige: ???

10:05 Paige: Where r u? x

Jason knew instantly what it meant. He pasted the three words, 'typically unscathed bonnet' into the What3Words app on his phone. It pinpointed a precise location. A location on Sannah. That was that then. He'd make that the destination of today's walk, but he'd have just ten more minutes in bed first. He closed his eyes and slept solidly for four hours.

It was another fine and fresh day on the island. He could hear gulls arguing over something down by the harbour, but his phone was directing Jason on another path; up the hill behind the hotel. After only a few hundred metres, he had a hunch where it was leading him. He passed the bothy, the viewpoint at the top of the hill, and the standing stone that Bernie had shown him on the first day — the punishment stone. He hurried on to the prison holes near the cliff edge, a place he'd not revisited since that first day. It wasn't a place relished the thought of walking alone. The app allowed him to zoom in on the exact location that Bernie had texted to Paige. The precise hole she wanted her to find. Why? Did she want to meet Paige there? He could think of easier places to meet. As he approached the edge of the hole, two crows flew out noisily. Angry at being disturbed.

He peered down. There was something purplish standing out from the black stone. He'd have to climb down there to find out what. As he descended, he wondered if Bernie had done the same that day. He remembered her dirty, wet clothes, the blood on the side of her face. The climbing today was relatively easy, but on a wet day it would be treacherous. He realised Bernie must have sent the location to Paige just in case she had an accident. That would be just like her. And no explanatory words, because her phone was running out of battery. It was going to give out any second.

The rock face was more difficult near the bottom of the pit. He had to concentrate on where he was putting his hands and feet, so he wasn't able to look around until he was standing on the prison hole floor. The shape he'd seen from the top turned out to be a torn purple hoodie. And the two crows he'd disturbed had been feasting on the disfigured corpse inside the hoodie. He felt his stomach heave, and he looked away. After a few seconds, he felt he could handle it. After all, this was the third dead body he'd encountered in the last month or so.

He examined the body. There were no recognisable features left, but he was in no doubt that these were the last remains of Sam Flint. He felt no shock or remorse. It almost worried him; he was so calm about it. But more than that, he was curious. How had Sam ended up here? How did it relate to Bernie? What had happened?

He looked around the hole. There were other bits of litter strewn around the floor of the hole, but against one wall were two lager cans set on either side of a plastic bag. It looked such a deliberate arrangement that it made him curious about what was inside the bag. He looked. The quaich! The wooden whisky cup. How did that get here?

Jason climbed out of the hole and sat by its edge in the sunshine, piecing together various stories to explain what he had found. Sam must have stolen the quaich from their room... how? ... when? And Bernie had followed him to the Prisoner's Holes, where he intended to hide it. Had they fought at the edge of the hole? Is that how Sam ended up at the bottom? It would explain why she looked so traumatised when Jason had met her later.

But hang on, Sam didn't know about the holes... but Bernie did. Did Sam follow Bernie out there, then? Carrying the quaich? Why would he do that? And why was she going there, anyway, when she was expecting to meet up with Paige later?

What if Sam hadn't stolen the quaich? What if Bernie had taken it? Intending to hide it from Jason. Oh, that struck a chord. He knew she didn't like the fact that he'd bought it for a song from Sandy. It had belonged to her uncle. It might have belonged to Sir Walter Scott. And if she was planning to break up with him, perhaps she had an idea to keep it as a parting gift.

Her walk to the holes would take her past the bothy where Sam had spent the night. Yes, he'd have seen her and followed her to the holes. No-one would ever know what he intended to do when he caught up with her. Jason went cold thinking about it.

But anyway, Bernie had returned, and Sam hadn't. She'd come back, traumatised and hypothermic.

He thought about what to do next. A big part of him wanted to just take the quaich back to the hotel and leave Sam to rot. As soon as they investigated this death, the police would work out that it was Sam Flint, who was presumably on the missing persons list by now, anyway. They'd talk to the locals, and someone, probably Sandy or Gracie, would remember that he'd shown up at the Sannah Hotel a few weeks ago, got into a drunken fight with Jason and been sent to spend the night in the bothy. Now, he might have wondered off, and fallen into the hole, possibly still drunk. But could Jason account for his whereabouts that night? Someone might wonder whether he'd left the hotel to finish the fight with Sam. His only alibi, Bernie, was dead. Did he really want to set himself up as a prime suspect in a murder case? However innocent he was?

He needed to be very careful about this. It was quite possible that no-one would discover that corpse for weeks, months or years even. Especially if someone were to fill the hole in a little, to cover the body. A few rocks, some shingle maybe. It wouldn't be too hard.

Immediately, he knew what he had to do. He phoned for Special Constable Evans to report the body he'd discovered. Jason Tranter knew what it was like attempting to evade the law and he wanted no more of it.

It only took Evans forty minutes to be on the scene. He'd borrowed a quad bike from a neighbour who was a crofter on the island, and he enjoyed the ride over the hill so much that he was grinning from ear to ear when he arrived.

'What's all this then, Mister Tranter? A body down the hole, is it?'

Jason nodded and gestured down the hole. Evans peered over and whistled.

'Bloody steep, innit?' he said. 'Still, if you say that's a body down there, I'm prepared to believe you. I'll need to get a team of lads over from the mainland. Do a proper job with ropes and whatnot. Get him, or her, out with no fuss. You didn't disturb the body, did you?'

'I didn't touch it. Him. You wouldn't want to. It's a bit of a mess. The crows have had a go, I'm afraid.'

Evans stepped back from the edge of the hole.

'Righty-ho. I'll need to tape the area off. These holes ought to be taped off permanently, if you ask me. Give us a hand, will you? Then I'll give you a lift back to the hotel and I'll take down your statement.'

SC Evans paused, and he lost his breezy joviality.

'I need to ask you one question, though, now,' he said. 'That bag you've got there — did you take that from the deceased?'

'This?' said Jason, holding up the white plastic bag containing the quaich. 'No. I brought this with me.'

'Aha, I see. I think I'll just look inside... if you don't mind?'

'No, of course, it's a wooden whisky cup. It may be extremely valuable, you see, so I carry it around with me.' He surprised himself by the ease with which he lied. He didn't want Evans to know about his theory that Bernie had hidden the quaich before she had an encounter with Sam. An encounter which ended with Sam dead at the bottom of a hole. It was just a theory, after all, and he hated the thought of incriminating Bernie.

'Ah yes. I remember now,' said Evans. 'You said that this cup had gone missing, when I was at the hotel, the day Miss Tenant had her accident. It turned up, then, did it?'

'Yes, I'd just mislaid it,' said Jason. He was already regretting his lie. If Evans remembered the cup, he'd also remember about Sam Flint. He wouldn't take long to join the dots between a valuable missing cup and Sam being found at the bottom of the hole. If forensics could ever find traces of this plastic bag down the hole, then... By trying to protect Bernie's reputation, Jason had just put himself into the firing line as the prime suspect for Sam's murder.

'Righty-ho,' said Evans, handing the bag back. 'Well, as I say, let's get back to the hotel and take your statement. Maybe we can get a cup of tea. I'm parched.'

The cup of tea seemed more important to Evans than the statement. Between sips, he told Jason that he'd need to give an account, in his own words, of the afternoon's events, describing how he came to be by the prisoner holes, what he found there and what action he took. But he didn't let Jason start until he'd drained his cup and had his hands free to take notes.

It gave Jason time to think about how much he would say. If he mentioned the 'typically unscathed bonnet' message, then it could lead to the conclusion that Bernie had something to do with Sam Flint's death. He didn't like the thought of that, but it might stop the finger of suspicion pointing at him. Also, if he didn't mention it, and somehow, later on, they questioned Paige Fellows and it emerged then, it would look very damning indeed. He told the day's entire story, including the details of the messages exchanged between Paige and Bernie, but omitting any mention of the wooden quaich.

At the end, SC Evans said, 'That's a bit of a coincidence, isn't it? Miss Tenant arranging to meet Miss Fellows at the exact spot where you find a body five weeks later.'

Jason said nothing. Gracie entered the room.

'Sorry to disturb, I'm just about to serve dinner. Chilli Con Carne. There's plenty... if you'd like to stay, Mr Evans?'

SC Evans looked at his watch. 'Goodness! Is that the time? Well, seeing as I am officially off duty now, I'll say yes, thank you very much! I think we can wrap this up. Thank you, Jason.'

It made a pleasant change to have an extra person round the table. Special Constable Evans rolled out his stories about crimes on the island, mostly just petty thefts, but also some more lurid tales of murder and fraud from his time as a regular officer in Wales. Wine flowed and Jason felt himself relax.

Sandy and Gracie cleared away the dishes and left the other two, making their way steadily down a bottle of whisky. Evans was interested in the plans to develop the hotel.

'Listen, son. You should definitely take Jack Tang up on his offer. He's a clever bloke, he is. I've seen his TV show. And that Miss Fellows he was with... she's a bit of alright, if you don't mind my saying. She was very cut up about Miss Tenant, wasn't she? Only natural, I suppose. She'd prepared that bath for her friend, hadn't she? Last person to see her alive...'

'It keeps going through my mind,' said Jason. 'I should have been the one to run that bath for her. I would have stayed with her, checked she was alright. I knew how slippy that bath was. Nearly came a cropper there myself.'

'Oh yeah?' said Evans and drained his glass. He poured another.

'First day we got here, Bernie ran a bath for me. Candles all around... everything. I fell asleep in the bath, the candles burned out, and I woke up and it was all pitch black. Proper scary, it was. I thought I was dead. But here was this thin beam of light —'

'Don't go towards the light, Jason!' Evans mocked gently.

'No, listen, I did. I hadn't a clue where I was. I went towards the light, thinking it must be coming from the door. It wasn't. I banged my head against the corner of the room. I had to feel my way around the walls to find the door.'

'So where was the light coming from then?'

'No clue, mate.'

'Ah well, what's happened has happened. Can't do anything about it now.' Evans stared wistfully into his wine glass.

Jason frowned. It was the first time he'd thought about that experience in the bathroom in weeks and it niggled him. The more he thought about it, the more he wanted to understand about that light.

'Come on, Rhodri. We're going to be detectives.'

He led the reluctant Special Constable up the stairs to the shared bathroom on the first floor.

'Come in,' he said, switching the light on his phone rather than switching on the room light, and closing the door. 'Over here, by the bath.' Then he switched off his phone light, and they were plunged into total darkness. No beam of light this time.

'As black as an undertaker's waistcoat,' pronounced Evans. 'Where was this light, then?'

Jason switched on the phone light again.

'I'm trying to remember,' he said. 'It must be from that corner.'

'Well, there's nothing there now.'

Jason inspected the corner. He couldn't see anything that could have shone or reflected a light. But then he saw a small, pencil-thin hole in the skirting board. 'Hang on. Look at this! Looks like it goes right through to the room next door.'

They walked round to that room. It was dark, with the curtains drawn against the light. Jason flicked the light switch, and they went back to the bathroom and closed the door. And there it was, light from the next-door room coming through that little hole, creating a narrow beam across the floor.

'That solves that minor puzzle,' said Evans. 'Well done, boy. Now I must be going back. Unless you fancy just one more for the road?'

'What's the hole for, though?' said Jason. He left Evans sitting on the edge of the bath and went back into the room next door. It was a neat, recently drilled hole, next to the electric socket. A nauseous feeling arose in him. He returned to the bathroom.

'Your theory... about how Bernie slipped in the bath and grabbed the light to steady her... There's something that's always bothered me.'

'Go on, then.'

'It's just that when Paige and I hauled Bernie's body out of the bath, I saw what looked like burn marks around her thighs and... um... her bottom. You must have seen them, too. Look, I'm no expert on the effects of electrocution, but surely if it happened how you said, any burn marks would have been around her hands, or her feet and calves. Those are the contact points if she was the electric path to earth between the light and the bath? Whereas if she'd been sitting in the bath...'

'Oh, steady on, Jason. The Procurator's report confirmed that the cause of death was electrocution. If it wasn't from the light, how else did the electricity...? Oh yes, I see what you're getting at. I suppose someone could have attached a wire between the bath and the socket next door.'

Evans inspected the bath. It was a freestanding tub with black enamelled cast-iron feet. He crouched down and ran his fingers over them and then lay flat on the floor to look at the underside of the bath.

'Pass me your torch,' he said, and Jason handed him his phone. 'Oh boy, oh boy! You'd better look at this. Scratch marks around the copper fitting where the waste pipe attaches to the bath. The sort of marks you'd see if someone had twisted a wire around it, and then later pulled the wire back through the hole from the room next door.'

Jason stared at him, wide eyed, as Evans rolled over and stood back up. 'So that's it then?'

Special Constable Evans chuckled. 'No, boy. I don't think so. Those scratch marks could have been made by a wire, but they could also have been made by a plumber, with his spanner, when he fitted the waste pipe.'

'But the hole in the corner...?'

'That'll be where someone's run a cable for an electric heater or something. There's no sockets in this room, see? And the burn marks on the lady's body? The Procurator agreed with me — it's very unpredictable where electrocution burn marks appear. It's like tracing a bolt of lightning, if you get my meaning. I'm sorry, Jason, lad. It's only understandable that you would look for wild theories about how your girlfriend died. It's probably one of those stages of grief. And I probably haven't helped tonight with all my tales of wickedness and murder over the dinner table. But Bernie's death was an accident. A senseless, random accident. I'm really sorry. I'd better go, and leave you to get some rest, man.'

Jason saw SC Evans down to the door, but then returned upstairs to the bathroom. All that Evans had said made sense; there really wasn't any reason to suspect foul play from the room next door. Especially when you considered who was the occupant of that room at the time: Mrs McCracken. She would hardly electrocute her own niece, would she?

Of course, she didn't know that Bernie was in the bath. In fact, hadn't there been a last-minute switch of bathrooms, with Paige running the bath for Bernie and Sarah running the bath for him? Mrs McCracken might have thought that the person in the bathroom next to her room would be Jason — her niece's treacherous boyfriend, and the only other person who knew about the body in her asparagus bed.

29

Sultan sat at his laptop in the study, or spare bedroom, of his home in Wall Heath. His head of department had told him to prepare material for online lessons for when the new term started. The school was closed except for the children of key workers and a few members of staff to look after them. He'd been an early adopter of Zoom, but the school was insisting on using Microsoft Teams, which looked more complicated. Still, he'd get the hang of it, and his class would get their maths lessons, whether they wanted them or not. He couldn't say the same for his 'private' pupils, the disadvantaged ones that could really benefit from his help. They didn't have laptops or even broadband, some of them. And who knew how long this lockdown would go on for? He wondered what would happen to these kids — what influences they would fall under, and it made him angry.

He wasn't sure who to direct his anger at, so some of it landed irrationally on Jason and Sarah. Sultan had always been passionate about both his day job and his voluntary work, but admittedly, they could be stressful. His friends and his social life provided the pressure valve that kept him sane. Jason and Sarah had destroyed that, and now the prospect of lockdown was a tough one.

An email dropped into his inbox. It was from Stuart. He'd not heard from him since he got back from Scotland. Sultan didn't know if he'd heard about what happened with Sarah and Jason. He read the email and smiled.

Subject: Help!
Remember me? I really need a big favour. Deepa's family is organising an online quiz. Could you join in, pleeeeze? I figure your general knowledge is even worse than mine, so you'll make me look intelligent by comparison. Ta! Deets below.

Robin Towers stood in her flat in Hambourne, next to a tower of packing crates. She was on the phone to her boss, Detective Inspector Wren.

'Hi Jenny. Bad news, I'm afraid. The move is on hold. The tenants further down the chain have got Covid, apparently, and no-one can budge. I've just found out. All my stuff's in boxes and it looks like I'm stuck in Hambourne for at least another couple of weeks.'

'Is this another one of your dodges, Towers? Has the millionaire Jason Tranter turned up again and you want another couple of weeks as Sarah Headly, to win him over?'

'Not funny, boss. No, there's no sign of Jason. I don't think I'll hear from him again. Believe me, I want out of this place so I can move on to my next assignment. Any news on that?'

'Desk work for you, Robin, for a while, anyway. In the meantime, you need to follow procedure and wind down the Sarah Headly cover neatly. Another two weeks won't be a problem. Luckily, Sharpie is in a good mood at the moment. She reckons the pandemic is going to be a quiet time for us. The threat seems to be shifting, anyway. There's more trouble these days from right-wing nutters. It'll be interesting to see how they react to being locked down for weeks on end. Some of them are already saying the virus is a hoax.'

Rebecca Leyden-Fuller's face popped into Robin's mind.

Jack Wren continued, 'Lots to look forward to. I'll send you some case files to look at. There's a company in Bilston, T F Scrap Metals. Looks like they're making regular payments to some individuals involved in a nationalist group. Might be worth investigating. Help you pass the time.'

The call ended, and Robin checked her phone — Sarah's phone, really — for messages. As usual, there were none. She looked at a dating app on the phone and thought about giving it a try. After all, she reckoned, if you've got a false identity, you might as well use it.

Terry Flint screwed up his eyes and sniffed the Mediterranean air. There was a whisper of a breeze coming from the west, but nothing he needed to pay any attention to as he teed off on the first hole of the 9-hole golf course on Isola Gallinara. He relaxed and took his shot.

'Nicely done, Terry,' said Mrs McCracken as she watched the ball fly down the fairway.

'That's a relief. I'm feeling the pressure, truth be told. If my new business partner is also going to be my golf partner, and she's a former Ladies Champion, well, I'd better be on my best game.'

'I was only runner-up. And your business experience is going to account for a lot more than my golfing prowess. And of course, your extensive range of contacts.'

'It's like I always say, "It's not what you know, it's who you can put the frighteners on that matters."'

'I can see we're going to get on splendidly, Terry Flint. Splendidly.'

Jason phoned Jack Tang.

'Okay, Jack. I'm in. I'll go fifty-fifty with you on the Sannah House project.'

'Great news! Welcome on board, my friend.'

'Just checking though — it's only my money you're after, isn't it? What I know about refitting hotels can be written on the back of a beer mat, and what with one thing and another, I think it's time for me to move on from here. I want to get away as soon as I can, really.'

'Jason, I hear you, bro. Not a problem. I've got people who can look after the entire project. I'm planning to just supervise remotely. So, you coming back to Birmingham?'

'No. Don't know where to go, to be honest. I just want to get away.'

'I know exactly what you mean. There's zero happening on the restaurant scene at the moment. Apart from "Tang's Take-outs. Let's do lockdown in luxury!" But that's already set up. I was thinking about getting over to the Caribbean, Barbados possibly. You up for it?'

'Er, there's a lockdown. Are there even flights...?'

'Chartered flights, yes, if you know who to ask. And fourteen day's quarantine when you get there. But believe me, bro, where I'm thinking of, quarantine will seem like a treat. Think about it.'

Jason thought about it. He wondered why Jack Tang was so keen on being his friend lately. They had little in common, except the ex-girlfriend thing. What a great connection that was. Jason found Jack amiable but slightly irritating. But he could cope with that. He'd been wondering how he would manage a great escape all by himself. Here was an opportunity handed to him on a plate. The universe must be looking out for him. About bloody time. And if there were divine forces at work, it was about bloody time that they sorted out this pandemic, too, come to think of it.

30

Perry's Bank on the Strand, like most of the City's financial institutions and offices, was closed. A sign on the door explained that in the current circumstances, they would conduct all business remotely and gave an email address and a phone number for enquiries. It was a superfluous note: Perry's wasn't the sort of bank that dealt with casual business from passers-by. No lights shone in the vast atrium behind the glass frontage, and the giant decorative waterfall that dominated the left-hand side of the hall had been switched off.

The building was silent; its meeting rooms and offices were empty, except for one third-floor office with the name 'Richards' on the door. Inside, a man sat on a swivel chair with his feet resting on the desk. It was Smethwick, and he was talking to the office's usual occupant on the phone.

'Yes, yes... as the proverbial grave. No, I don't mind popping in once a day. The walk into town is very pleasant, with all the quiet streets.'

'And you're sure you wouldn't rather be out here on Gallinara, Smethwick?'

Smethwick smiled to himself. He knew if he'd taken up the offer to join the members of Rara Avis on Isola Gallinara, he'd be spending each day organising entertainments for the guests: tennis tournaments, car races, and poker games. Here, he just needed to tour the building once a day, and then he could spend a couple of hours indulging in his new lockdown hobby: playing *Call of Duty* on an Xbox he'd hooked up to the TV in Richards' office.

'No, thank you, Mr Richards. It wouldn't sit right with me. I know the members of Rara Avis have got every right to enjoy the facilities, sir, but I can't help feeling that we should all be pulling together. I can't say that I've been adversely affected myself, but some people are having a very tough time indeed.'

'Laudable sentiments, Smethwick. But don't imagine that all our guests here are living a life of idle luxury. There are calls and meetings going on here every day. Relief funds are being organised. Research projects are being set up. I happen to know that work on vaccines for this virus is already underway in several countries. Things will get better again, Smethwick. Life will return to normal, I promise. Now, I must go. Lunch is calling... *Petto di pollo con funghi.* Cheerio, Smethwick.'

'That's wonderful news. Goodbye, sir,' said Smethwick. He scrunched up the greaseproof paper that had contained his ham and tomato sandwich into a ball and tossed it expertly into the wastepaper bin on the far side of the office.

The End

Did you enjoy this book?

I really hope you enjoyed this book, and that it didn't stir up terrible memories from the pandemic. Do you remember the 'R number'? The reproduction number? It was a representation of how many secondary infections resulted from a primary infection — in other words, if you caught Covid-19, how many people did you pass it on to? If the overall R-number was greater than one, the virus was spreading exponentially.

I think it would be really neat if this book had an R number greater than one. So please, if you did enjoy the book, please consider leaving a review, or a rating, or even just telling your friends about it. It may seem like a small action, but a few positive words can make all the difference when a prospective reader is weighing up whether to spend the time (and money) on reading my book.

After all, The Secret Millionaires' Club shouldn't be a secret, should it?

Jason Tranter will return

I can't leave Jason languishing in the doldrums. He needs to sort his life out. Or perhaps I need to sort it out for him. Work is underway on the third instalment of The Secret Millionaires' Club series. When will it be ready to read? I'm not sure, but I'll post progress updates on my website, authorfrost.com. There's other stuff there as well, so please, take a look.

Acknowledgements

Once again, I'd like to thank my early readers, David, Carol and Katherine, for their patient support and wise advice. I'd also like to thank everyone who has read the first book in the series, '*The Secret Millionaires' Club*'. The response from everyone has been wonderful and makes it all worthwhile.

About the author

Adrian Frost was born in Wolverhampton and can still just about do the accent, but now lives in Suffolk with his family and three imaginary cats.

Printed in Great Britain
by Amazon

44772976R00199